Rosalie Weller

CROMWELL & ELIZABETH - THE BEGINNING

Rosalie Weller

Cover design by Samuel A Weller

Copyright 2019 Samuel A Weller

Website: samwellerillustrations.com

Copyright © 2019 Rosalie Weller

All rights reserved.

ISBN: 9781689975704

Dedicated to Callum Marsh, my grandson, whose thirst for knowledge especially of history is an inspiration. Also to my other grandchildren Katie, Mila, Junior and Alfred.

Thanks to Diane Newton, my editor, for her help in getting this novel ready for publication, and special thanks to my husband, Sydney, for his support and encouragement.

CONTENTS

Prologue — page 1

Maid — page 5

Mistress — page 116

Mother — page 213

Major Historical Characters — page 308

Sources/Historical notes — page 319

About the author — page 322

Cromwell & Elizabeth – the Beginning   Rosalie Weller

Prologue

By the year 1617, when Robert Cromwell died, the Scottish King James had been on the English throne for fourteen years - time enough to acknowledge that his divine right to rule was less certain for his subjects than for himself. Scottish people were no less foreigners than the French, the Dutch or the hated Spanish. A promising start had soured. The uneasy truce between king and people was stretched by the favours he bestowed on his Scottish bodyguard and the officers of the bedchamber. The success of the union of the two kingdoms was far from a foregone conclusion.

Amongst some sections of the landed gentleman there was a feeling that although the new translation of the bible was very welcome it did not mitigate the fact, that there was a disappointing lack of reform in the, as yet, young Protestant church.

The bishops remained in post and there were still many vestiges of popery apparent during the compulsory worship services. Some godly "Puritan" members of the gentry could well understand a divine appointment as they themselves had been called by God for eternal salvation. Their lives evidenced that they were God's elect, as they were not shy to remind people.

However, life in the expanding towns was pleasant enough with the absence of plague and a good harvest. But, the threat of a war on the continent in which the King's daughter was implicated was somewhat unsettling. And although after the death of James' eldest son, the popular heir Henry, the King evoked some sympathy, the second in line, Charles, was proving an unpalatable heir apparent.

It was a time when the successful merchant could increase his standing in society by payment to the Crown. Trade was changing a country where farming and textiles had previously dominated. The most important decision to make would be your choice of marriage partner. That one decision would rule your life, and often your death. This was a discovery soon to be made by both monarch and people. However, there was still a new spirit of adventure pulsating throughout the land

Part I   Maid

Cromwell & Elizabeth – The Beginning

Chapter 1. A proposal

Elizabeth
Little Stambridge Hall. 24 April 1620

"But Madam, am I not too young?"

I feel a mounting panic in my breast. I have said the first thing that came into my head but I know it is ridiculous! I am of age. My mother is so skilled in the management of our household affairs that it is indeed not one of the objections which she expected. She pauses and looks directly at me with a hawkish eye, as if she can penetrate my inward soul.

"Elizabeth ... Elizabeth, age is less important than suitability. I was married at twenty-two just a little older than you are. Did you think this indulgence by your father would last forever?"

I ignore the sting of the last question as it is intentionally rhetorical. I try to digest the information relevant to the decision I must make. Why am I prevaricating? Am I still waiting for the proposal that I have been hoping for this past year? Neither father, nor mother are aware of my fondness for Master St John so they would not have approached him for a marriage proposal. It seems that he has made no offer to them! I ignore mother's obvious determination to make a quarrel. She continues as much to reassure herself, as to me.

"The Williams are a noble family with royal connections over generations, much respected in the county of Huntingdonshire. He is coming of age and the sudden death of his father means he has come into his estates rather sooner than expected. Your father and his political friends want to mould this young man to take a seat in the Palace of Westminster. His connections are not to be passed up without consideration. He comes from a long line of Earls."

Rosalie Weller

The fine earthy oak panels of the Great Hall seem to enclose me and I am suddenly filled with sadness at the realisation that I will have to leave this house. Will my husband provide me with such splendour? The bird-like chatter of my sisters at the other end of the Hall has suddenly become an irritation. My palms have moistened and my throat is parched. I must get out. I long to sit in the stillness of the rose garden and gather my thoughts.

Goodwife Appleby provides a welcome interruption as she waddles in to converse with my good lady mother about the victuals for the month. I seize the opportunity to escape with a quick curtsey and soon I am through the heavy entrance door and out into the courtyard.

The comforting sound of the horses' hooves fidgeting on the cobbled yard encourages my soul. The busy scene before me is a delight. I had quite forgotten that the furrier would be here today. Yes, our six horses are bridled but unsaddled and tied to the pole, as John attends to their hooves. The rasping of his file seems to calm them. Benjamin, our stable boy, holds the hoof of Blackie up as he uses a stick to pull out the stones and dirt between the horse's toes. I step closer.

"Hello, Arabella, you're my special girl." I whisper to my bay as I pass. As I stroke her golden mane, she nuzzles my arm in response.

I overhear my brother Richard talking to Benjamin.

"Yes indeed Benjamin. Felsted is a fine school and we learn all manner of things there. You know as the eldest son, I will be following my father in the leather trade but I still need to understand how this fine estate of ours, runs."

I am too far away now to hear Benjamin's reply. Strange that such a busy scene can calm and not fluster. I slow my pace and smile as caps are doffed on my passage to the far gate and across the bridge to the gardens. I hold back the tears which are demanding an entrance, until I am alone. I just need a moment to think.

Summer is still far away but spring is well advanced. The rose bushes are not yet blooming but primroses have sprouted below them, as if to encourage their awakening. I sit on my 'pondering' seat – the stump of a felled oak – and breathe in the fresh air. Little Stambridge Hall lies behind me. Across the moat, the Essex countryside calms my misgivings. The familiar bleating of the sheep awakens fresh questions in me. So much to think about. Wife? Will I survive childbearing? Will my husband converse with me, as does my father now – about all current topics, about trade, about reform in the church? How can I leave Little Stambridge Hall? My mind and heart are in a panic with the suddenness of what I now face!

I glance behind me. I can just see the imposing gatehouse. I know every inch of it with its tall tower and father's new coat of arms above the arch. Mother is so proud of those three leopards. I cannot begrudge her that. She has certainly been faithful in her duties to my father. I must return soon to face her irritation at my disappearance and hear further about this proposal. The scene stills me and my peace returns.

Dear father. He is so seldom here at Little Stambridge. Why does he not come home? I know he has a lot on his mind just now, what with all this controversy over the Book of Sports and the Lord's Sabbath. And it's all been made worse by these troubles with the farmers over the enclosure of land, but even so he should have come. He should have spoken to me himself about this proposed marriage.

Father has taught me to be an obedient daughter and obeying him is not onerous. He is a kind, godly man, always seeking goodness. Since I was a little girl, I have tried to copy his example. His business dealings are fair. He says God wants him to be successful in business so he can help others. He provides work for our sixteen servants. We must respect them and the work they do: each of us has a part to play in the society.

Am I ready to run my own household? I live a trouble free life – filled with learning, music and dancing, sometimes flirtatious. Father spoils us all. His trade has increased so that we three girls now have generous jointures. My brothers will follow him in the leather and fur trade; their future is assured.

Yes, I am ready to face my future - a new master! I quickly retrace my path - across the stone bridge and the courtyard. As I enter the Great Hall again, my lady mother is still by the fire, busy with Goodwife Appleby, and she has scarcely noticed my reappearance. I settle beside my sisters again, below the leaded window at the far end of the Great Hall. I stare at them. It is as if I have never seen them before. Alice, dear Alice, so kind and so loving. She is a quiet maid and in all she does, she shows great love to everyone whether they be servants or ladies. Frances, so pretty. Her thick dark hair is brushed up and back from her face but as a couple of curls escape they accentuate her gentle smile. A single string of pearls sits obediently, complimenting her slim, white neck. Oh, my sisters, I am soon to leave you.

I continue with my sewing not wishing mother to see that she has disturbed my thoughts. The conversation completed with the cook, she takes her place among us, continuing with her cloth. She glances at me but we all sit in silence, concentrating on the stitches. Sarah brings in the afternoon refreshment and I look through the window at the spring flowers outside – bluebells and bright yellow primroses blooming and I wonder what the summer will bring.

"I have your ale to refresh you," Sarah greets us, "And could I trouble Mistress Elizabeth to read the custard recipe from 'The Good Housewife's Jewell' for me?"

Cromwell & Elizabeth - The Beginning

Mother nods her assent and I get up to accompany Sarah to the kitchen where the book lays open at the 'custard' page. I do so love to read the recipes and encourage Sarah in her task.

Soon I go upstairs to my room to continue my studies. My little oak desk and chair, placed to one side, obediently conserve my notebook, a Latin grammar, my English bible and the household accounts which I am mastering. The big bed dominates the room; its feather pillows standing proud to attention. On the other side of the room, the washbasin and a pitcher of fresh water wait for use.

I persevere with the Latin grammar as a punishment for my ill temper. It seems such a long time until I hear the dust moving under the sure foot of a sturdy mount. My father has returned at last from his business. I know that I cannot speak to him immediately as I would wish, so I continue with my books, reading the Psalms for comfort. Father will not be disturbed on his immediate return. I wait for half an hour and then I descend the stairs. I control my agitation until my chance comes after our evening beverage.

"Father, what is this about? Marriage so soon?"

I can barely get my words out and my voice falters just slightly but father recognizes my hesitation immediately. We are out of earshot of the rest of the family so he answers with candour.

"Beth, my Beth, I am so sorry. It was remiss of me not to have discussed this matter with you but I have been somewhat distracted. I asked your mother to wait to tell you, but I see she has already done so."

Father pauses to glare at mother and then continues,

"Beth, it is not too late. We have not made the contract yet. We can rescind if you are desperately unhappy about it."

Rosalie Weller

I soften at his obvious discomfort. He is always so considerate about the desires of his daughters.

"No matter, sir. Perhaps it will be a good match."

I answer respectfully although my thoughts are quite to the contrary – nobility and titles in exchange for a merchant's prosperity.

"Father you have always been considerate and generous, more so than many fathers. You have seen that we girls are educated and well prepared to run our own households when the time comes. But that is not my fear. I value our conversations. That is what I will miss."

I am the eldest. I look at my sisters and my brothers. They are all so unaware of my inner turmoil.

"Elizabeth," the elongated form emphasises the seriousness of his tone and I am attentive once more.

"Regarding this young man. The prospects of his family have waned a little in the father's time – Robert was Joan Barrington's brother. You remember the Barringtons of Hatfield Broad Oak, don't you? Well, anyway, Robert was not as discerning as he could have been but the son, Oliver, is forthright and pious, schooled by Beard. It will be a godly match. I don't want to see you passed by. This is your chance, my dear."

"I know," I answer but not with a heavy heart. "This is what I want although it has come sooner than I imagined. I trust your judgement, father."

"Beth, you will still be able to continue your studies. Such a talent in Latin grammar will not be lost." Father laughs heartily and the conversation is ended.

Cromwell & Elizabeth - The Beginning

All of us are happy to have father with us again. I watch him as he converses with each child. I continue my reading until an appropriate time has elapsed to excuse myself and retire. I do not want to alarm father. As I ponder, I am filled once more with dread as the consequences of marriage begin to dawn on me. I will have to leave my home; this beautiful estate, which father has built for us. I love the meadows and orchards. I love walking along the rolling hills and in the woodlands picking bluebells.

I can fetch Arabella from Cony pasture for Daniel to saddle up for me. I know I will see the Gowers' shepherd bringing down the sheep on the tenanted land. This is the scene I have been a part of since I can remember. Now I will have to give it up and swap it for I don't know what.

Alice stirs in our bed as I re-enter the chamber. I try to be quiet but she is so perceptive she can sense my changing emotions in the darkness.

"Bessie what were you and Father discussing so earnestly? I know there is something brewing. Oh do tell!"

Stimulated by my sister's curiosity, I unexpectedly begin to weep. Alice, only a year my junior, draws me to her bosom. She has been more like a mother to me than a younger sister. Her warmth melts my natural reserve. We have shared so many joyous times together. As I look at her face, it dawns on me what father meant when he said he doesn't want me to be passed by. Alice has warmth, Frances has beauty. What do I have? Three sisters and we are all so different. What a strange family we are. Am I like mother? I hope not. She is very ordered but I hope I am kinder. Yes, in that I fancy I am more like father.

"Alice, I have no reason to weep. It is merely father's plans for me to marry. It has come more suddenly than I expected."

Rosalie Weller

"Oh," she squeals with delight, "Marry? Really Bessie?"

"Yes, I had hoped to remain a maid for a while longer. I wanted to do so much more with my studies, Alice, but now it is not to be."

"But surely you can still continue with your studies, Bessie? I sense there is something else worrying you, what is it, dear sister?" she says.

"I do care dearly for mother, Alice, but her one goal seems to be to marry me off. It seems any gentleman will do. I don't mean to be ungrateful but I just wish father had spoken to me first. We hardly seem to see him now. Nowhere near as often as we used to!"

"That's it. You have always been father's favourite. I swear you would marry him, Bessie, if you could. Won't it be wonderful for me to be an aunt? I will dote on a little Elizabeth or James." Alice cannot contain herself any longer as she reels off children's names.

Alice can only think of the advantages of marriage and none of its drawbacks. She is so delightfully naïve that I am forced to laugh at her enthusiasm. She does not think of never walking in this Essex countryside with free abandonment again, or the loss of time for reading. She can only think of dimpled children and servants to rule. I love her because we are so different. As we settle to sleep, I am comforted and look forward to my future with some hope.

Chapter 2. Husband

Oliver
'The Friars' Huntington 26 April 1620

Oliver was overwhelmed at the sudden upturn of his fortunes. The last three years had been difficult. The sudden death of his father had disrupted all of their lives but his marriage agreement would change everything. He looked at his mother and knew she, too, was pleased. Her wrinkled face and gloomy gown had shaded his once happy childhood home for too long.

He remembered that day clearly. It had started the same as any other day. They were sitting in the Cambridge halls for a study period. Henry had jibed,

"Oliver, that looks like a thorough analysis!"

Oliver was staring at a blank page. New verses by an Oxford man did not interest him at all. Quite unusually the dean appeared at the heavy dark wood door and said quite calmly as if he were announcing the evening meal,

"Cromwell, your father is seriously ill. You must return home immediately."

Then he was gone. The huge study hall was blank - no sound echoed in its cavernous space. Every face was turned towards him. The new verse by John Donne reverberated in every young head - 'death be not proud - one short sleep and we wake eternally.' Oliver was dazed but he managed to stride out of there with dignity.

"Sorry to hear it. Give our regards to your mother." An unfamiliar voice called after him.

Oliver packed his trunk quickly. Unfortunately, his mother had delayed sending word while recovery looked likely, but when the fever turned quite unexpectedly, the opportunity to see his father before his demise, was lost. The end had come too soon.

The large Huntington town house had absorbed the quiet, remorseless, sobbing. He had not. It oppressed his mind and highlighted his helplessness. His mind could not differentiate the cries. It was surely one of his grown-up sisters, Elizabeth, Catherine or Anna. Margaret, his married sister, was in her own house tending her infant. The loud wailing of the younger girls, Jane and Robina, knifed his soul, as he watched his mother stoically trying to comfort them. Death had made a loud entrance.

Very steadily the heavy air had cleared as Oliver busied himself with the matters of his father's estate. Having not yet reached his majority, he was ill-prepared. It was only swift action from Oliver St. John, his first cousin, which had prevented him from becoming a ward of the courts. St John had been a brilliant law student then, and a promising career lay ahead of him.

That was the first time Oliver had questioned his existence on this earth. Not why - that was easily answered from the catechism - for the glory of God. No, Oliver's question was how? How could he make his way in this world?

Life had not been easy. He was only two years old when his little sister, Joan, had died from fever. Her death had made his mother treasure him all the more dearly at the time. She never really got over the pain, and bore it still to this day. Although he couldn't remember the details clearly he did recall the sense of loss and grief in the house for weeks afterwards – a grey stillness in the air, an unapologetic foreboding – not dissimilar to the atmosphere that could be felt after the death of his father.

"Too much honey Robina, and you'll look like Buli - plump and round - and I'm sure I won't be able to tell the difference between you." Oliver had cajoled his sisters out of their melancholy.

Back in the present day, the fire crackled in the hearth, arousing him from his reverie. The pleasant aroma of broth began to pervade through every crack in the timbered side panels. He looked around the great hall of his abode - not as grand as many, but practical he thought.

His sisters, Elizabeth and Catherine, were sitting to one side of the huge fire. They busied themselves with fine embroidery for which they were renowned in the town. He watched his mother, before he spoke, as she prepared the home-grown vegetables to accompany the broth. Today was Anna's turn to help. She peeled the carrots noisily and carelessly, the skin falling to the floor.

"Well, mother, what do you think? Am I to be a married man this year?" Oliver's voice betrayed no foreboding and only contained the usual teasing tone.

"Yes, Oliver Williams, or have you decided to use your father's name again? Oliver Cromwell?" she replied, "This seems to be a suitable match. I am surprised by your Aunt Joan's intervention though, or should we say, interference. She scarcely bothered with us when your father was alive."

"Yes mother, I understand what you mean. But when I visited for the discussions last week, she was very hospitable. And it was good to see cousin Thomas again. You should have accompanied me... as for my name I find it a good jest to be called Williams as well as Cromwell. Williams stresses our Welsh blood."

He laughed as he looked at his mother but she betrayed no emotion and she did not reply. Oliver continued on a more serious note.

"Indeed every sentence that Aunt Joan pronounces includes a godly reference. It is as if she cannot proceed with the trivialities of life without some guidance from the Almighty."

At this his mother did respond. She said,

"Be that as it may, Oliver, she seems to have found you a suitable match."

"Yes, Sir James Bourchier is a wealthy merchant. He seems to be a man of strong principles and generous nature - a rare combination indeed. How is it mother, that we have not been introduced to his daughter before?"

"I really don't know," his mother replied, "I remember Oliver St John mentioning such a girl but it didn't seem to concern us then."

She hesitated, as Oliver's expression changed and she brought the conversation to an abrupt halt.

"I will say no more, Oliver. I will not spoil your opportunities." she said

As his mother left the Hall to attend to his younger sisters, Oliver went to his writing desk below the window to compose a letter.

It was not long before the deed had been accomplished. Oliver was relieved. His mother re-entered through the back door with his sister Margaret and her two young children in tow. He showed the letter to his mother, not so much for approval, but more for reassurance.

He had intended to ride over to see his cousin, Thomas Barrington soon but it had been a loose arrangement made over the card table. A detail, he did not wish either his mother or Aunt Joan to know. Still he would have to do something about his mounting debts. He would need Thomas' co-operation. Maybe a quiet word with Sir James would elicit a gift but he would make sure he was quite alone. Yes, the girl's father, Sir James, did seem to be a gentleman to be trusted – even if his money came from trade.

Oliver pushed the fears aside about his responsibilities and started to reflect on the advantages of marriage. A companion to share his life with might not be such an unpleasant course to take. Hopefully, she wouldn't be as pious as his aunt.

Breaking his train of thought, young Valentine seeing his uncle, ran to him crashing into his knees. Oliver responded by making the noise of a bear and grabbing the child's legs, hauling him upside down. The three year-old squealed with delight until his mother persuaded Oliver to right him, before she continued with her chores.

"Mother, why is it that you often find that ladies are more taken with religion than gentlemen?"

It was a question, which he had only formed after meeting his aunt again after so many years. Her husband, Sir Francis seemed a good fellow, as were his sons, but there was no doubt that his aunt was a very pious lady. Oliver was a little afraid of her.

"Well I cannot say." His mother replied, "Maybe because women go through the pains of childbirth and raising the children – there's many a hardship there, my boy.

At this young Valentine again interrupted by putting his finger on his nose and pulling a face, to which Oliver responded by chasing him around the huge table.

"Margaret, what do you think?"

The mother turned to her daughter who was remonstrating with another lively toddler. The little girl had decided that her brother would not be the only one to catch Oliver's attention. She clung to his legs screaming wildly. Catherine left her stitchery to catch hold of young Agnes and calm her down.

"Oliver, this is a sudden interest in the things of womankind," Margaret teased.

Before the women could continue the conversation, Oliver turned abruptly and left. He walked quickly to the postmaster's house, eager to trigger his destiny. Soon there, he greeted his friend William Kilbourne and arranged for his letter to be on its way.

Chapter 3. Courtship

Elizabeth
Little Stambridge Hall 3 May 1620

As I read my letter, I hear Frances giggling as she enters the walled rose garden. Her pretty brown ringlets gently pick up the slight breeze. She can see I am reading and just smiles as she seats herself next to me. I re-read my letter several times, resisting her curiosity. Newly delivered by the messenger, it is a little unexpected. Father and I only discussed the matter of marriage two weeks ago. Master Williams seems very frank and somewhat amusing. He writes in a clear, fine hand. The script is small and even but with just a slight lilt to the right.

My dear Mistress Bourchier (or may I call you Elizabeth)

I understand that you will entertain my suit with a view to marriage. Being a first cousin of Oliver St John, I have heard a little about you. It is strange that we have never really met. I do remember you visiting one of my aunts when you were about fifteen but I doubt you will remember me from then. You were very lively and engaged in a discussion about the prayer book with cousin Oliver. Even now I remember how red your cheeks were as you made your points, although I confess, I cannot remember what they were! I jest with you, dear Elizabeth. I admire a lively spirit.

I intend to visit Thomas Barrington, at Hatfield Broad Oak next week to do some hawking. It is within easy riding distance from Little Stambridge. Would you care to ride out with me so we can further our acquaintance? I would be happy if one of your sisters would like to accompany us. Should you not care to continue with our courtship after our first meeting, you will have made a friend without damage to your reputation.

Should I not hear to the contrary, expect me on Wednesday.

Rosalie Weller

I remain
A hopeful gentleman
Oliver

Yes, courting has commenced. I am excited and not quite sure how to proceed. Of course I will accept the invitation and Alice can accompany us. Mother and father will give their permission as it is they who have initiated this courtship. I know mother will want to let him know of her expectations, quite apart from the arrangements which father has negotiated.

I don't remember discussing the prayer book with Oliver St John and I don't remember Oliver Williams being present, but that is of no consequence. Master Williams acknowledges that I am a female with a questioning mind who wishes to explore and discuss current affairs, and not just a lady competent in music, embroidery and running a household.

I glance at my inquisitive sister and say,

"Frances, I am to be married. The young man has invited me to ride with him next week."

Frances makes no reply except a delighted squeal.

"Come on Frances, inside we go. I will write a reply." I say, "The messenger is waiting in the stables to take it."

Francis and I are skipping with excitement, as we re-enter the great hall. I see mother's household is running smoothly as usual. Rosie is heating water on the fire. Wednesdays means the washerwoman will be in from the village to help her.

Master Roberts has Christopher and Robert sitting on a bench quite near to the fire, reciting their lesson for today. The month of

May has arrived and it is still too cold for the schoolroom. I'm not sure whether this is for the boys' sake or to save the groaning bones of their elderly tutor.

I walk slowly to the writing desk at the end of the hall. It is conveniently situated under the newly glassed window. It gains the maximum light and now also excludes the draught. Alice is sitting at the virginals right at the end of the hall. What a merry tune she plays - only interrupted by an occasional howl from Bonnie, her dog, laying at her feet. She stops as I come across the room, looking intently at the paper in my hand.

"Yes," I say to her, "It is an invitation to ride out with Master Williams."

Alice is excited to accompany me as it brings distraction to an otherwise ordinary day. She too is anxious to meet Master Williams. I suspect she is looking for a suitor, should I not find him acceptable.

"You are far too earnest, for such a playful fellow," Alice says as she reads the letter. "Master William's love of jesting may be too much for your serious nature, Bessie."

Well we shall see about that! I suppose I am serious because I love to contemplate many issues not common for a lady. But I have also felt the stirrings of love within me – an emotion so strong that I almost regretted the intimacy. What could I have been thinking? I did not have a promise from Master St John, so I cannot say that was the reason. It was just that I assumed we had an understanding. Our companionship had so sweetly turned to romance. His kisses had awakened something new inside of me.

My heart was broken when he left for Lincoln's Inn so suddenly. A year long, I have been waiting to see if there was some mistake. I have been looking for a message or an invitation which has never arrived. Was it then just my girlish dreaming? Alice too had thought we would marry. Are all men so cruel and heartless?

I must put aside those feelings I had. Or maybe still have. I am embarking on a new journey now. Father has been careful to examine the heritage and background of this young man. This time there will be no mistake, no misunderstanding.

Mother re-enters from the kitchen areas, followed by Sarah. She is soon standing by the writing desk. Did she read the letter before me?

"My lady Mother, I have received a letter from this young man we have spoken about. It is an invitation to ride out with him next week as a beginning to our courtship. I presume this has your approval."

My mother just looks at me. She has seen the letter. Oh, she is so exasperating! My reply only needs to be short. Next week I shall meet him. I am so glad Alice shares my excitement. As I glance around it is clear that our household continues in its usual, ordered manner despite my inner turmoil.

Sarah cheerfully passes mother her leather gloves and smiles at me. Why on earth she agreed to come here and act as mother's maid defies reason. She is always so happy to do mother's bidding. I suppose being a niece rather than a daughter gives enough distance for friendship.

"I will be attending Frances, Lady Rich for dinner so do let Appleby know, Sarah." mother says and with that is gone.

"Sarah, why do you allow mother to talk to you so sharply?" I say.

"Elizabeth, don't upset yourself. I'm not distressed by what Aunt Frances says. To live in this beautiful house is wonderful. Who knows I may also find a good opportunity while I am here." She lowers her eyes deferentially not wanting to be accused of eavesdropping and continues, "I know my sister, Rachael, would come in my place without hesitation."

"Sarah you are so gracious. Of course we love having you here… Yes I am to meet a young man, next week. Maybe he will be my husband. Isn't it exciting? Have you heard from Wiltshire recently. Is all well there?"

Sarah reports that Mistress Brocket, mother's sister, has been unwell recently. I am as fond of her family as she is of ours. I look at Sarah. She shares the long pointed nose and thin lips of the Cranes. Yet with Sarah her face holds none of the strictness and shrewdness which I find in that other familiar face - mother!

Sarah busies herself with the duties she must complete - brushing out mother's furs.

Chapter 4. The Soothsayer

Oliver

Barrington Hall, Hatfield Broad Oak 10 May 1620

Chestnut stood patiently beside the tree stump, while Oliver hoisted himself up astride her. He wasn't looking forward to the fifty mile ride south to Barrington Hall that would take him down the Great North Road. It would be tiring and he could expect some muddy trails on the outskirts of the forest. Yet he was ready. He had donned his riding garments but kept his new breeches in his travelling bag, affixed to his saddle. He wanted to impress Mistress Bourchier. He had been warned by Aunt Joan that this merchant's family was a modern one. The girl was not to be coerced into marriage but won over by Oliver's noble charms. Oliver was not sure he had any. He was a plain-speaking person, not using flowery language to beguile, but relying on mutual respect and common interest to endear himself to people.

It was sunrise. Having six sisters had accustomed him to feminine ways but today he was glad to be without their silly chatter. Catherine was always worrying about new ribbons and whether she would ever marry, a topic recently revived by his own intentions. She directed these fears to her older sister, Elizabeth (known as Lizzie to prevent misunderstanding) and her younger sister, Anna on an almost daily basis.

He was closest to Margaret not only in age but in intellectual interests. It was convenient also that Margaret had married his friend at Cambridge, Val Walton, and lived with her young family in a small cottage near to the main house, just over the brook. Like Oliver, she had a persistently positive outlook on life and was always able to lighten the spirits in a sometimes sombre house. She looked after her two young children with enthusiasm, enjoying her mother's helpful advice and assistance with the youngsters.

As he rode across the Godmanchester bridge he thought about how his life was to change. A wife would not be a burden, but would enhance his social standing in the community. He had discussed with William how marriage not only changed a man's outlook on life, but it changed how others viewed him. The posting of his letter had been an opportune moment for an intimate conversation. William was very keen for Oliver to join him on the borough council and Oliver longed for the chance to stand in the longish line of Cromwells who had served as MPs. The borough council would be the first step.

There were few travellers going south but Oliver felt safe enough. Someone would always warn of any impassable stretches. An unusually dry April promised sure footing for Chestnut. Once over the bridge, it was an uneventful trudge. He stopped at 'The Old Bull' at Royston, not only to refresh himself, but also to let his palfrey have a well-earned rest.

The inn was a favourite with many travellers. It served as a posting house as well as accommodation. The large beamed house contained many comfortable rooms but it was the stables which were impressive. The landlord prided himself on the diligence of his stable lads. The horses for hire were trustworthy and well cared for. Oliver respected a man who cared for his animals.

He handed his mount to the ostler but hesitated as he was about to cross the threshold. Beside the doorway there was an old woman sitting on a milkmaid's stool. She was crouched over a basket of herbs, which indicated her living. Oliver had always been a little wary of these wise women since hearing about the sudden death of his grandfather's first wife. Joan Warren, Lady Joan Cromwell, had been killed by witchcraft. The Warboys Trial had been notorious in Huntington less than thirty years previously. That had been a strange event, not easily explained. He was not familiar with the ways and customs of these Essex folk either. But he had observed other travellers entering the inn before him without trouble. He stepped forward but as he was about to enter, the old woman caught the edge of his pantaloons and whispered,

"A great man, oh Lord Protector but much blood on your hands!"

He could scarcely believe his ears. Was she addressing him? What did she mean? Blood on his hands! Oliver was not a violent man. He stepped back in alarm and surveyed the old hag. She looked kindly enough as she busied herself with arranging her herbs in her basket. She was muttering but that was common with old women. Maybe he was mistaken. He paused, then made a second attempt to cross the threshold of the inn. The woman was reaching behind her and he thought that she was tidying her herbs. He was wrong. She suddenly turned around, stood up and breathed in his face,

"Lord Protector - there's blood, much blood."

The pungent garlic from her breath sullied the air around them. Her glare pierced him. She held out a small bunch of lavender. Then just as suddenly, she flopped back on her stool with a mild-mannered look on her face. He pulled himself roughly away and was still shaking as he entered the establishment. He greeted the other company inside politely. The ale was refreshing but those words reverberated in his head. He could not get rid of them. It was not unusual for old hags to try to intimidate gentlemen but it was usually when they were selling their wares. This old woman had not tried to sell him anything. She seemed as if she was giving him the lavender. She didn't ask for any money. Should he mention it to the landlord?

"I see Ol' Margrit's 'ere agin. What's she doing 'ere?"

Oliver was relieved when another new arrival broached the subject with the landlord.

"I really don't know," answered the innkeeper. "She hasn't been around these parts for months."

"Well, s'pose she means no 'arm. Just making a living selling her 'erbs," continued the old man.

"I heard she's been chased away by the committee and told not to return." The innkeeper replied.

The conversation about the old woman soon ceased as a new discussion on the late planting of spinach was discussed. Oliver was tempted to stay overnight at the inn but the old soothsayer had unnerved him and in any case he was eager to reach Barrington Hall.

Just one hour later after a dinner of hot potage and beans, he was leading Chestnut out of the stable and was again on his way. Oliver quickened his pace to calm his unsettled soul. The ride was tiresome but he did not encounter any soft ground and was soon entering the forests bordering the settled areas.

Thomas was expecting him and happy to be one of the brokers in his courtship. They had not had an appropriate moment to discuss the details of his involvement, so Oliver looked forward to a day of hawking when he was sure the matter would be settled. Thomas was a merry fellow, amused by his parents' religious strictness. On this first occasion, it was necessary for Oliver to ride to the Bourchiers, but later he would be able to invite Elizabeth to Barrington Hall as a guest where they would be able to conduct their courtship. Hatfield Broad Oak was conveniently positioned halfway between their two estates.

"Oliver you look quite exhausted. What a beautiful mare Chestnut is. Sure you don't want to sell her?"

Thomas laughed as he stopped to examine Chestnut. She was a superior animal. There were not many things which Oliver owned of which he was proud, but she was definitely one of them. She held her head straight and although finely honed she was sturdy and she had completed the day's ride with ease.

As Oliver dismounted, he glanced at Barrington Hall. Thomas was indeed very fortunate to inherit such a manor on his marriage. His mother and father had been obliging enough to move into the 'Priory', a smaller simpler dwelling at the back of the estate. This was undoubtedly one of the finest houses in the county, with its modern brick exterior looming large across the sky.

The impressive manor house stood in a large acreage of woods, fields, and orchards, the number of rooms too many to be counted. The courtyard bustled with activity as Oliver arrived. Besides the groom who had taken the horse after Thomas had examined her, a manservant carried his travelling bag inside while the gardener paused in his weeding and hoeing, to admire the visitor.

That evening the company was congenial and appeared very interested to hear Oliver's thoughts on marriage. Oliver didn't really know how to answer his aunt's probing about his ideas on Christian faith and the duties of a husband. He was delighted when Thomas suggested a diversion at the card table – for amusement only.

"Just to amuse ourselves, eh Oliver," Thomas pointed out, for the benefit of the godly company.

"Yes, deal me in," chirped William Meux, Winifred's husband.

Lady Joan Barrington excused herself to pray in the private chapel which she frequented often. Her chaplain was visiting for just a few days so it was an arrangement which suited them all. She took with her Thomas' wife, Frances and his sister, Winifred. Oliver was sure he and Elizabeth Bourchier would be one of the subjects of their prayers.

Rising early next day, Oliver, Thomas and Meux set off towards the wooded area in the south. Joan had been caged along with Thomas' birds on the last occasion they had hawked together. He was never happier than when he and his beloved peregrine worked together and there was duck to be put in the pot. He had named his hawk Joan for his dead sister, a constant reminder of his mortality.

Thomas was happy to accompany them although he explained his time for hawking had become more limited since taking over the management of Barrington Hall. Sir Francis was devoting more and more time to discussions at Westminster and so had passed on the household responsibilities to Thomas.

Oliver had wanted to discuss his debt problem with Thomas but a third party present prevented such a discussion. Although the matter was urgent and he wanted Thomas' advice, they seemed to talk about Thomas' problems rather than Oliver's. Strange, Oliver had never seen Thomas as a man with problems but it seemed that great responsibility brings great worries. More than ten years his senior, Thomas' concerns centred on his young children and their education. Never having attended Felstead, Oliver had no advice to give. He did, however, learn that several of Elizabeth's brothers were attending this very prestigious school. It seemed that they were all academically very clever. Sir William Meux led the conversation.

"No, Thomas, there is no doubt that your John will do well. That good influence will stay with a boy his whole life."

Thomas nodded glad the information he had been given had settled the matter in his mind. Oliver was slightly irritated that Meux had prevented any meaningful discussions with his old friend Thomas. Would his life be domesticated like Thomas'? Would family responsibilities invade his life so that he would have no time for gritty mature discussions? Was his life to be centred now on conversation about schools and tutors for his sons? He had been so full of anticipation at the prospect of a little hawking. His thoughts returned to the wise woman. Had she really prophesied, or was it his imagination? He shivered as he thought of the phrase, "blood on your hands". That had been another thing which he had wanted to share with Thomas. Damn you, Meux!

Three hours later, he remounted Chestnut to continue his journey to Little Stambridge Hall in Rochford to meet his turn of fortune, as that was how he had come to think of Elizabeth Bourchier. She was reputed to be quite plain but what did that matter! He had heard that she made lively company and had a very gentle heart. To Oliver this visit was a ritual, which had to be performed. He had no doubt that she would make a suitable wife.

Chapter 5. The First Meeting

Elizabeth
Little Stambridge Hall 11 May 1620

My first impression of Master Williams is favourable. He is taller than average, standing at least six feet. He wears the attire of a gentleman, of course, but not at all plain, as I would have expected. He looks very fashionable: his jerkin is black but sleeveless so that the apple-green of his doublet is revealed, complimenting the green breeches he is wearing. The colours suit him admirably as they highlight his unusual grey-green eyes which are his most alluring feature. They dance as he gesticulates to make a point in the discussion. I warm to him and wonder if this is how married love will feel.

I have asked Daniel to bring me the piebald palfrey, Heidi, instead of Arabella, wishing to amble at a slower pace than Master Williams' horse. This will ensure a more genial conversation. I know Alice will prefer the jennet and it will not worry her to ride a little slower behind us. I hear Arabella snort in the stable, wondering why she is not going out today. Heidi whinnies in response. These two are like sisters, always following each other when they are out to pasture.

"Thank you, Daniel," I greet him, as he assists me to mount. "Can you get someone to exercise Arabella today, I can hear her complaining."

It's not long before Alice and I are walking our mounts across the bridge. I glance behind me and see Master Williams is still addressing Daniel. I am a little surprised that he is taking the trouble to converse with someone who is, after all, only the groom. I wonder, has Master Williams mistaken him for one of my brothers?

"Master Oliver, you seem so affable in your conversation with the groom," I venture as he rides towards us.

"Excuse me, Mistress Elizabeth," he replies, "Daniel has heard of my falcon, Joan, and shared some information about the bait to use for the lure. My cousin, Thomas, who has been housing my Joan for me for a while now, has not kept up with the new ways. It was remiss of me to keep you waiting,"

So polite and sensitive to all around him. Alice nods to me as we quicken to a trot and I'm sure she is thinking the same. It is a beautiful day. The sun is warm and the ground is firm. We enjoy riding through the woods, conversing as we go, but suddenly Master Williams gallops south down a copse and disappears. I continue to amble steadily as Alice draws level beside me and we look at each other, perplexed.

"Has his horse spooked?" Alice enquires.

"I don't know," I reply, shaking my head. I cannot understand what has spurred this sudden movement.

It is not long before we see Master Williams riding back again towards us, carrying a bundle on his saddle. Yet with horror I realise that the bundle is in fact a small child! One leg looks strangely distorted, but the child, a young girl, makes no sound. Unconscious perhaps!

"What has occurred sir?" Alice and I cry simultaneously.

Breathless he replies, "The oxen have trampled this little mite. I heard a plaintive cry and rode down to find its cause. I've told the father I will take her to the physician. The bone must be set. She's passed out with the pain, poor little thing."

Alarmed by this interruption, I cannot speak. Alice is able to give directions to Dr Simcotts in the village, and Master Williams canters off with his small charge. I hate to see small children suffering but it is Master Williams' sudden flurry which has unsettled me.

"Alice," I urge my sister, "let's go to the place of this accident and see if we can discover any more information about what has happened. It looked like one of the Appleby children."

With that we gallop over the hill, and there we see Goodman Appleby with his hand clutched to his brow in an anguished condition.

"Good morning, Appleby." I begin, "What has happened here?"

"I was ploughing - I'm late for the spring sowing. My yung'un was just behind me, when all of a sudden like, the oxen stepped back instead of forrard, just as my Mattie stepped in the furrow. I can't understand it, nothing like this has ever happened 'afore."

Goodman Appleby is quite distressed and I am at a loss what to say to him except what he certainly already knows.

"Master Williams has ridden to the village to the physician. Surely she will live. Don't distress yourself. He will be back in no time."

With heavy hearts and a feeling of utter bewilderment, Alice and I ride back to Little Stambridge Hall and await Oliver's return. I am torn between anxiety for the child and disappointment that the ride has been curtailed. We cannot speak. We dismount and wait. I can only pace in the yard as Daniel unsaddles the horses. Alice hurries inside.

Just before the hour, I see Oliver riding towards the moat bridge at some speed. He slows as he goes under the gatehouse arch and returns to the stable yard. I can hear noises from the activity inside, in the kitchen area. The time which has elapsed has not delayed dinner at all, as we were expecting a long ride. We have a special guest and he must be refreshed. It is time for him to meet the rest of my family. But before we go into the main entrance to the Great Hall, he turns to me and addresses me in an informal manner.

"Elizabeth, I want to continue with this courtship. I find you both kind and interesting. I want my wife to be someone I can talk to. I have so needed that since my father died. Do you feel the same?"

I am a little startled by his forthrightness but I do not doubt his sincerity. How quickly he has made up his mind. But how flattering!

"Yes," I respond, "I was a little worried that you might find me plain, Oliver. But do you not need more time to ponder this important decision?"

"Plain, never my dear," he replies "Your mind is part of your beauty. I will never find that plain! As for time to ponder, we have a lifetime to find out if we have made the right decision. And even then we may never know! I am decided."

He makes no allusion to Matilda the injured farm child. My mother and my family are quite unaware of this interlude and I make up my mind not to refer to it until Master Williams does.

As we enter I look at Alice. She has quickly changed from her riding garments and is seated at the virginals. She looks at us both and I see disappointment on her face as she realises that Master Williams and I have found each other suitable and she will have to look elsewhere for a husband. The tune she plays is strangely wistful.

I find the next hour intriguing as I watch Oliver charm my mother and sisters. In father's absence, Richard and William have been asked to join us, the other brothers not being considered old enough for polite company. Oliver's forthright manner is somewhat beguiling because it is so unusual in a gentleman. Maybe it is the responsibility thrust upon him early by his father's sudden death. In any case he does not seem to be impressed by mother's hints and assertions of grandeur but she seems to be unaware of it as she addresses him,

"Do you have much occasion to frequent Hinchingbrooke?" she asks, "I hear good King James has been making that grand house a part of his progress."

Oliver hesitates for just a moment and I wonder if I am the only one to sense his discomfort as he answers,

"Lady Frances we do have that privilege, but not often and in any case we never know when my uncle, Sir Oliver, will be entertaining our monarch, his majesty."

"His grace," my mother corrects.

Oliver ignores this rude attention to detail. I suppose if you have grown up in an atmosphere where your uncle frequently entertains the king it will take a lot to impress you. I find myself liking my future husband more and more. Is it because he seems to have the measure of my pompous, snobbish mother and yet she is unaware of it? It will be amazing to be free from her! I wonder what life has in store for us.

"I do think it is important for families to be matched well, Oliver. What do you say?" mother turns to Oliver. Before he can reply, she continues, "Only yesterday I visited a poor girl who is distraught because her grandfather will not speak to her or visit her. A Catholic girl who has married a Protestant. It seems to be becoming more common in society today....."

Without warning, James bursts into the hall hardly able to contain himself,

"My lady mother," he gushes, "Have you not heard? We are entertaining a true gentleman. Elizabeth's friend has surely saved the life of Matilda Appleby. She was trampled by her father's oxen. The breath had gone out of her but he got her to the physician in time. She has a broken leg but she will survive! Such a quick action! Goodman Appleby is so beside himself with joy. He's in the yard telling Daniel at this moment."

All eyes turn to Oliver who is smiling broadly at my lady mother.

"Forgive the boy his interruption. It must seem very noble to one so young. I merely took the child to the physician's house. He was able to set the bone. He is the person to be commended."

Oliver is unable to discern my mother's momentary disgust at the information that he has picked up a farm child and believes she is open-mouthed because he has been declared a compassionate hero. But I know my mother. Alice gives me a warning stare not to alert Oliver to this undercurrent. We sisters understand each other so perfectly. As Sarah returns to replenish our ale, she ushers James towards the outer door and a confrontation is averted.

I find myself liking Master Williams more and more. He seems so unaffected by the manipulation and manoeuvring of people. He appears to be a simple honest gentleman. I just hope I will be as acceptable to his family as he is to mine!

Chapter 6. Huntington

Oliver
'The Friars' 11 May 1620

Finishing dinner, Oliver and Elizabeth were able to excuse themselves from the company. Oliver had made it quite clear to everyone, including Mistress Frances Bourchier, that he had decided Elizabeth would make a suitable wife. It was also apparent to Alice and Frances that the feeling was mutual.

Oliver allowed himself just one hour for general conversation with Elizabeth in the rose garden. Elizabeth was happy to explain how her father's trade was procured, and profit was made, dealing in leather and furs. Oliver's livelihood was based on the land and agriculture so he was glad to improve his knowledge.

"Elizabeth, my dear, I must ride back to the Barrington's before nightfall, then on to Huntington tomorrow," he said. "But I will send word soon for you to come to Huntington to meet my family."

Elizabeth wanted to confess to Oliver about her acquaintance with his first cousin but the moment had not presented itself. But then nothing had really happened, just a few innocent kisses exchanged. Did anything need to be said? She prided herself on her honesty and her conscience was deeply troubled by her own omission. But now that she had met Oliver Williams she was so eager to pursue the relationship, that she was able to quiet her conscience and overlook the gnawing voice in her heart.

As he looked back and waved goodbye, Oliver was content. This was more than a suitable match. How could such a warm-hearted creature have been nurtured in so cold an environment? Oliver decided that Elizabeth definitely took after her father!

He was soon once more entering Barrington Hall but was dismayed to find Thomas had been called away unexpectedly. He would have to postpone his enquiry about a loan yet again. For he had made up his mind that another loan, this time from Thomas, was necessary. Not being able to stomach either William Meux or his godly Aunt Joan he retired to his bed with the excuse that he must rise early to get back to Huntington without delay. His return journey was without incident as he decided not to rest at "The Old Bull". He had to pace Chestnut so that she could cope with the arduous journey but she did not let him down, and they approached Huntington before nightfall.

As Oliver rode into town, he was confronted by a cacophony of noise on the High Street - a squealing boar, the excited shrill cries of local children and Master Turner's deep booming voice trying to release the runaway creature from his cart wheel. Tired as he was, Oliver had resolved to involve himself more in local affairs. He therefore rode straight towards the disturbance, just outside St. John's church.

He quickly ascertained that the wheel had sustained serious damage and would soon be beyond repair. The boar's snout had engaged with one of the spokes and was firmly stuck. The poor animal could not come clear. In just a few seconds a large crowd had gathered.

Quickly dismounting, he said,

"Let's help you here, Master Turner I'll just pull his head out of the wheel."

"Much obliged, Master Cromwell."

The baker was grateful for Oliver's strength and bravery in engaging the boar.

"Is this Mistress Lacey's pig? I've heard he's quite a wayward animal!" Oliver said extracting the pig from the wheel.

The children laughed at the boar's discomfort but the problem was solved quickly. Oliver was just about to remount, when he spotted Thomas Beard, hurrying to speak to him. His old schoolmaster was always an enjoyable distraction from life's monotonies.

"Oliver, I would be much obliged if I could call in on you sometime this week. There's a question of a lectureship in Huntington to be decided and I'd like to enlist your support."

Oliver had not heard of any upcoming lectures in the area but he was flattered that the Reverend Beard should want his support. He began to feel satisfied in his growing importance in the town.

Beard continued, "And Oliver, I should like to go over with you the question of eternal calling and its consequences, if you would indulge me."

Oliver wasn't very keen on the topic, but hurriedly agreed to the meeting as he was eager now to return to his household. He greeted his mother soberly and was excited to tell her how the visit to the family of his future wife had gone. At last fortune was smiling on him. Recently, he had begun to feel that time was forever fixed on the most disastrous moments of his life. True it had not all been as a consequence of his own folly. Yes, he had been entirely to blame for his shocking gambling debts. He had been most unwise to get involved with those who could disregard them as inconsequential, when his debts took the very bread out of the mouths of his sisters. However, he could not have foreseen his father's untimely demise. Oliver did not waste time on pleasantries but straightway reported to his mother.

"Mother, the visit went splendidly. Mistress Bourchier is a most affable young lady. I think her mother and brothers and sisters were suitably impressed with me."

"Oh wonderful, Oliver. Do they live in a very grand house? I hear that merchants these days can afford glassed windows and lots of servants. Is it true, my son?"

"Yes," Oliver replied enthusiastically, "Their house is quite splendid."

He looked around their own shabby dwelling.

"But I know my Mistress Bourchier will not despise us when she comes to live here because she is so lacking in pretensions. A modest intelligent girl – most suitable."

"I am so delighted," his mother replied with unexpected zeal, "You will be a good husband, Oliver. Your sunny disposition far outweighs your lack of godliness. Surely she will find nothing to complain about in you."

Oliver was not sure he understood what she meant by a lack of godliness and his disposition had been far from sunny of late, but he let the remark pass because as she said this, Oliver became aware of something he had only sensed before but which had never been voiced. His mother had felt unworthy in her own marriage. Is that why she hadn't contacted her husband's relations when she had been in need? She had been quite alone. She had lost touch with her own family as well. It was as if that distance to Ely had just become too great for her to traverse.

There was something else. His mother seemed impressed with the wealth of the Bourchier family. He had thought she had been content with the simple life – without the jewels, extravagant gowns or servants they had at Hinchingbrooke. He had thought that her piety dictated her lack of desire to accumulate wealth. But perhaps that was not so.

"It was also an opportunity for me to renew my acquaintance with cousin Thomas. We seem to have more in common now. Did you know his son John is almost fifteen? It was cheery to be in their company and imagine that could be me in a few years' time – a family man with his children around him."

His mother's reply seemed guarded.

"Yes that is the way you must begin to think now, Oliver. The past is behind us and it will be good for me to be a grandma again." At this she laughed and the conversation was closed.

The courtship had advanced quickly but Oliver was a man who, once his mind was made up, did not hesitate in carrying through his responsibilities. He was truly a man. He had reached his majority last month. In a few months' time he would be married. The boyish foolishness of the past was behind him. Only one thing rankled in his mind. What was it that his cousin, Oliver St. John, had said about Elizabeth Bourchier last summer? He wished now he had been more attentive. He brushed aside that niggling doubt which he felt had been trying to surface. Elizabeth was quite unique in her family. She was unaffected by the new merchant-wealth of her father. She was not pretentious like her mother. No, she was a godly woman more precious than rubies –

"Charm is deceptive and beauty is fleeting; but a woman who fears the Lord is to be praised." These words went through his mind and echoed in his heart.

Chapter 7. Mother-in-law

Elizabeth
'The Friars', Huntington 19 May 1620

Only one week has passed but I find myself eager to meet Oliver Williams again today. No not just eager - excited. I find myself stuttering and unable to focus my thoughts on anything else. It is today that Alice and I will ride to Huntington. We will have to stop at Royston to rest our horses. A carriage is out of the question - our journey would take too long. I try to focus on what little John is saying,

"James pinched me, Bessie, tell him to stop!"

John lisps his complaint but James has already hurled himself out of the door into the kitchen. Why must boys fight all the time? James takes advantage of his younger brother because he knows John will always come running to me with his complaint. He doesn't do it to Robert or Christopher and certainly never to his older brothers. Oh, it is time to set off. I pat John's head and usher him back to Frances for comfort.

Whitsuntide is such a merry time but it seems so different when the boys are home from school. The house becomes noisy and there is scarce a place to go without boys banging and barging in the way. No wonder mother is always out visiting at this time of year.

Oliver, Oliver, my Oliver, not my brother Oliver - my husband, Oliver. The title Mistress Williams runs off the tongue so lightly. Alice tries to engage me in conversation as we ride but her efforts are wasted.

"Oh Bessie, you are quite changed this past week. I cannot get a sensible word out of you anymore," she exclaims.

"Alice, my heart is pounding at the thought of seeing Oliver again. He has quite captured me," I say.

We ride in a mutually agreed silence each with our own dreams and we are soon nearing Huntington. We slow our horses to a rhythmic trot as we enter the town. Here is the house! It was easily found because it is just as Oliver described it.

So this is soon to be my new home. The house is on the edge of town at the beginning of the High Street in Huntington. The gatehouse is unimpressive with no carving or crests or anything remotely heraldic – just an entrance arch. There is no groom to take our horses and I lead Arabella over to the gatepost myself, trying not to show any sense of alarm, or my growing disquiet. Alice follows me not saying anything, just looking around her. Oliver's house is so old-fashioned. Drab! I feel quite melancholy. Mother warned me not to be distracted by superficial furnishings as people in the town live differently from country folk, but she is so concerned about good breeding that she would forgive Oliver's family anything for the chance to have noble grandchildren.

As soon as we enter the house, the noise and bustle of activity envelop me so that I am no longer alarmed by the lack of grandeur nor fashionable decor but am delighted by the warmth I feel in this happy company.

There are five females of various ages. All from the same mould – slim tall girls with impish faces. I am so used to myself and my sisters being so different I had quite forgotten that trends and physical features can multiply themselves within a family. I can clearly see this here.

An older woman who was previously hidden by her daughters rises to her feet. Her rather plain, round wrinkled face with its sharp nose and a thin upper lip shows obvious alarm.

"Oliver, Oliver," she calls.

At once Master Williams appears, and greets me with a broad grin.

"Mistress Elizabeth," he soothes. His voice is mellow - a strange contrast to the flurry surrounding him. He calms his females back into their seats and the introductions take place. Each girl bobs a little curtsey and says,

"Delighted to make your acquaintance Mistress Bourchier."

The repetition of these greetings is making me quite giddy and I stumble back to the chair behind me which has suddenly appeared. They are treating me like royalty. Such deference – I cannot think why.

Lizzie, Catherine and Anna seem to be quite close in age. Lizzie seems slow in her movements, Catherine is fussing over her gown but it is Anna who catches my attention by her exuberant gestures and smiling face. She is beaming at me. I can sense that Mistress Cromwell is a little apprehensive although she says nothing. During the afternoon, her love for Oliver is so apparent that no indulgence seems too much trouble. The pastries are Oliver's favourites. The jam is specially made for him – he so loves blackberries. I feel almost that he is the guest. He is so treasured by his mother and his sisters and their love overflows to all who encounter them.

As we sit around Oliver, his sisters squawk with delight as he teases each one. I notice there seems to be only one young woman to assist with the household duties but I expect his sisters must have their household chores to do and Mistress Cromwell seems to be the cook. I comprehend this because it is she who rises to set the wooden table with a plethora of meats and fowl. Each sister seems to know her assigned task and the presentation of dinner is soon completed with little fuss.

Cromwell & Elizabeth - The Beginning

After we have eaten the meal, Oliver takes me for a stroll around the grounds. Alice is delighted to talk to Catherine and Anna about the latest fashions from Paris. The estate is not substantial at all but I remind myself that town people have different expectations from country people. Father always says that town life is a trade-off for social company instead of beautiful scenery, although I cannot understand why we cannot have both. Mother's stories of her childhood are full of social activity yet they lived on a huge country estate of a thousand acres – although it was in Wiltshire. The garden seems to be sufficient for the occupants' needs. The beds are neatly laid out but it is full of vegetables and herbs and there is no rose garden. I am a little taken by surprise and need to comment on it to Oliver.

"Does your mother not enjoy roses, Oliver?" I ask him.

"Certainly she does," he replies, "but the garden is taken up by usefulness since my father died and Elizabeth, you cannot eat roses." He laughs easily.

"I suppose not," I reply and I smile to hide my unease. This family seems to share some of the commonness of yeomanry and I do not see any signs of nobility at all.

I feel I need to address some issues which have arisen in my mind during this visit. How does he maintain his financial interests? Are they separate from his mother's? How will his sisters be supported when we marry? These are all relevant matters to my marriage and my future.

"Oliver," I begin, "You did start to explain... "

Just at that moment there is a shrill cry from one of Oliver's sisters and we both rush towards the house to see how serious the injury is. For sure, such a loud lament denotes at least a broken bone.

My intention to quiz Oliver about the obvious lack of tenanted land is forgotten. I am sure father will enquire into all these matters in any case. My place is to nurture appropriate relationships within this feminine brood.

We arrive at the back door just as the wailing child reaches it. It is Robina, the second youngest daughter. She has been examining the creatures in the garden. She holds her hand out to me with her upturned face still blotched from weeping. A fierce red mark extends across the palm of her hand and I can see a bee sting still in the wound. I take her onto my lap while Mistress Cromwell removes the sting and places dock leaves on the angry mark. She continues to wail and the other girls look on, glad that they are not also victims. Robina has the prettiest face even amidst her distress. Her grey-green eyes betray a softness of immaturity not unlike Oliver's. I am surprised that she has no fear of me. After all I am a complete stranger to her.

Just to be in Oliver's company makes me feel content and complete. How can it be that we have not yet known each other for a full month and I already feel like this? It's different from how I felt about Master St. John. Was that because those moments were stolen whereas these moments are part of my future?

This family is so strange. I am quite unused to it. All females. Our house, so dominated by the boys and their wrestling, their guffaws and their noises, overwhelms the feminine. This house embraces all its females. I find myself beginning to be woven into this new cloth and it warms me.

Chapter 8. Managing the household

Oliver
'The Friars', Huntington 20 May 1620

Joan Barrington had carried out all the negotiations with the Bourchiers so Oliver was not surprised when the formal invitation to dine at Barrington Hall arrived. Sir Francis had kept them well informed and this was the next step. The formal announcement of their engagement had to be made and his mother's lack of status as a widow had precluded notification being announced from their own house. However, he knew that although his mother shunned social company, she and his married sister, Margaret, would accompany him to this important event. Now that the couple was not only consenting but enthusiastic, there was no reason a date for the marriage could not be set.

Oliver was glad to have renewed his acquaintance with these relatives who looked after their interests – his and his mother's. He had little knowledge of law and when they had been threatened by the Court of Wards after his father's death, it had nearly resulted in severe melancholia. He had felt himself slipping into the depths of darkness – a place of sorrow and loneliness. But Oliver St. John had stepped in then and now in this most important event in his life, marriage, these others were helping him.

To old Elizabeth Cromwell, Oliver was her kindred spirit in a way her husband Robert had never been. She sensed a strength in Oliver which had not yet matured. Oliver had weaknesses of which she was only too aware but every day she prayed to God for her son that His strength would overcome her son's failings. Only God could do this. His mother often ruminated on these thoughts but never shared them with Oliver.

Elizabeth Cromwell had suffered all her married life from her husband's unwise choices; his continual selling off of the tenanted land had reduced their yearly income considerably. Robert had said he could not live as a gentleman should, without realising some assets but she came from Norfolk stock, the Stewards, where they thought differently. To the Stewards land was everything.

When she married Robert she had met his brother, the son of the Golden Knight – Sir Oliver. She had thought he was ostentatious and overbearing although she had never voiced her opinion, nor ever could. Now her son was being watched over by the sister of her dead husband, Joan Barrington. She was so unlike both her brothers. Joan was pious and godly to the extreme but Oliver needed a helping hand and this was the way to get it.

Elizabeth Cromwell, though, had one or two thoughts of her own on how Oliver could be helped. She would contact her brother and investigate what had happened to the lands her father had held. After all Thomas Steward was childless. Oliver's future should not be left entirely in Cromwell hands.

For his part, Oliver had always felt responsible for his mother beyond what normally would result from filial care. To others she appeared severe and disciplined but he remembered the nursery songs she would sing to him when he was young, not just on the odd occasion, but every single night. Her merry laughter seemed reserved just for him. He had always been special to her, and her attention and concern made this clear. It was more than being the only son. It was being the son who survived through childhood illness, through want, through the country's difficult times as well as personal misfortune.

Oliver hoped that more grandchildren would indeed bring comfort to his mother. Maybe it would even forge new relationships with her old family in Ely. Without the worry of finances, she could take more time for herself.

It was agreed that Mistress Cromwell, Margaret and Val would accompany him to the dinner party. There was some dispute as to whether Lizzie and Catherine should also go, as mixing in such company could better their marriage chances. This decision was left in abeyance. However, there was no question of Jane and Robina going. They were far too young.

"Mother, we must talk about the arrangements of the household after I am married." Oliver said.

He was not nervous about bringing this subject up with her because his mother was always ready to comply with his wishes, but it was necessary to iron out the details with her before Elizabeth questioned him on it, as he knew she would. He had already assessed his future bride as being a woman who did not leave anything to chance. She would certainly want to be clear on the details of their proposed marriage partnership. Oliver had always treasured, and been fascinated by, women but he was used to them doing what he wanted. Now he had met a woman who had a mind and thoughts of her own.

"Certainly, my son, what do you propose?"

Mistress Cromwell was always ready to drop her current task to converse with her son. She put down the embroidered cloth on which she was working and gave him her full attention.

"Elizabeth Bourchier is used to having servants to do her bidding although I think it is more important to her to be able to converse companionably in the household."

He cleared his throat knowing full well that he would have to explain carefully to his mother the matters which had already been conveyed to him by Elizabeth as non-negotiable. His mother replied unhesitatingly,

"Lizzie and Catherine will not make very good companions for her. Their silly heads are full of ribbons and gowns! Anna - no. She does seem to get on well with Margaret though. I shall talk to her. Margaret is younger in years than your Elizabeth but she is well informed on matters of common conversation. Oliver don't concern yourself. Women have a way of working these things out between them. Of course you must take the marriage bed. I shall sleep in the other chamber with Jane and Robina."

She waved off the grateful gesture which Oliver made.

"What other concerns have you?" his mother was determined to dismiss all possible problems before they could arise.

"Mother, the brewhouse... "

"We will keep that well-hidden, Oliver, do not concern yourself. It is obscured by the brook. She would take it for a shepherd's cottage. It is on the other side of the hedge to Margaret's cottage. She will have no need to go there." She smiled but it was through a visage of stubbornness. She continued,

"We must guard our income. We get precious little from the tenants..."

Oliver waited. He did not want his mother to know that those rents were fuelling his weakness for the cards. She hesitated just a moment while she mulled it over but she continued.

"and the tithes of the Rectory are less and less each year." Mistress Cromwell spoke softly as if she didn't want her younger daughters to hear although she need not have worried. Their laughter could be heard reverberating outside.

Oliver was satisfied and resolved not to mention these matters again. He had not specifically mentioned Elizabeth's concern about who would be mistress of the house but it was close enough for now. He kissed the top of his mother's head as he got up and said in a cheery tone,

"I'm just going to have a word with William, mother. He must be informed of the forthcoming nuptials, after all."

Mistress Elizabeth Cromwell took up her cloth again. Regardless of what had just been said, she knew who remained head of this household. The matriarch was satisfied. Thus that archetypal rivalry between a man's mother and wife would soon be replayed in the Cromwell household.

Chapter 9. The Announcement

Elizabeth
Barrington Hall 27 May 1620

I am wary. Today our families will meet again formally. Oliver and I have now met several times informally, riding out and walking. He is a competent horseman and a lively conversationalist and I find him to be very witty and interesting.

Lady Joan's private carriage has arrived to carry us to 'The Priory' at Hatfield Broad Oak. This is the first time I have been in one of these new contraptions although father says they are now commonplace in London and all the merchants use them to get around. When the four of us are seated, the coachman tickles the horses with his whip.

"Walk on," he commands and with a jolt the journey begins.

"I did not expect such a bumpy ride," mother immediately complains as she fusses over my two younger sisters. In the hustle and bustle of setting off mother has been much occupied, but now she turns her attention to me.

"Elizabeth, why are you in that gown? I ordered Sarah to bring you the red one. It is so much better with your pale complexion."

I do not need to respond. Mother continues her bantering without taking a breath. Her questions are rhetorical and I look out of the coach window at the fertile Essex countryside. Labourers till the ground and shepherds care for the sheep on the slopes as we pass. I have time to reflect. I have not met Lady Joan Barrington or her husband, Sir Francis. Of course they are Oliver's relations. As our country neighbours, father has had occasion to visit them many times but never on such a formal basis. The contract has been finalised and the wedding will take place in August. A jointure has been agreed and father is satisfied that I will be cared for. It is only the formal announcement which remains to be made.

I find Oliver Williams quite a cheerful but intense person. He is a thinker and shares his views readily with me even on the subjects of religion and politics. This is such a welcome relief. I wondered whether our relationship would be restricted to the management of the household and the nursery, as it is for many wives but it seems that Master Williams is more companionable. Father is pleased too.

We have but a short distance to travel but in this infernal carriage the journey takes two hours. Father and my brothers will have arrived on horseback a considerable time ago. For once I wish I were a boy. I can imagine the lively conversation they will have had as they canter across the fields. Perhaps they are discussing the rivalry between Jonson and Middleton, or the impending Mayflower voyage to the New World. How I would love to be with those brave souls now. I long to hear about the preparations the godly saints will be making right now. What will they take with them? What will they leave behind? Oh they have such important decisions to make. Maybe one day Oliver and I will join them.

We pass the forest and Barrington Hall comes into view. The Hall is occupied now by Sir Francis' son and it is a very grand building indeed. I know that "The Friars" where I shall live with Oliver is not so grand but it will be adequate and appropriate for our social standing. Mother is suitably impressed for it is her first visit, too. Although it is our first invitation it will surely not be our last. We are to be kin.

The footman opens the carriage door and we step out as graciously as we can, wearing our best gowns. I look at my mother's face and I see that she is ecstatic. My sisters are also impressed by the obvious standing of the Barringtons – our soon-to-be relatives. We are wealthy but these people have breeding. It is as if everything just happens. Everyone knows what he or she must do and they do it

– just like the footman. We are led into the bustling hallway where I glimpse Oliver out of the corner of my eye. I turn towards him with a polite greeting,

"Master Williams how good to see......"

Lady Joan cuts in abruptly and, dare I say, rather unkindly. "Surely you mean Master Cromwell, my dear."

I blush as I try to regain my composure at my apparent mistake. How has this happened? On all the previous occasions when we have met he has been Master Williams to me. Oliver, always gallante, whisks me aside out of earshot of the other mingling guests, now arriving.

"Why Mistress Elizabeth, I do believe we have confused you,"

His gentle teasing sends my heart fluttering and now I am angry with myself for succumbing to feminine weakness. All I can do is stammer.

"Um, um ..."

"Williams is the name of my Welsh ancestors and I suppose it is my legal name, but I only use it now for dealings in certain situations."

Situations! What situations! I am a little alarmed. Oliver sounds like a yeoman or even a common worker. I feel faint and the hallway goes dark.

As I open my eyes, mother is fanning me and holding a cup of ale in her hand and a scented handkerchief under my nose.

"Elizabeth," she says as if she is scolding me.

I am anxious to recover and continue the day without drawing attention to myself. I can't see Oliver anywhere. A young woman I recognise stands beside mother.

"Elizabeth, it's Margaret," she reminds me and as she does so, my mother hurries off to join her peers.

"I am so sorry... you have been... called away from the other guests, Margaret." I stammer, "I assure you I am quite well now. You do not need to stay with me."

She laughs encouragingly, "Oh but I do. Oliver has instructed me that I must not leave your side until he comes back. My own husband does not instruct me quite so commandingly as Oliver does."

"Your husband?"

I have forgotten that she is already married. She looks too young to be married and as she does not wear a ring I had forgotten this fact. When I visited "The Friars" I was so taken up with getting on with Mistress Cromwell, I did not make sense of all the relationships around me. I remember now that she was playing with a very young child whom I had assumed was another sibling but it must have been her own child.

"Valentine Walton" Margaret responds, "A boyhood friend of Oliver's. We have been married for four years and are blessed with two children, a boy of three, and a little girl." She is so free with her details that it inspires me to confide in her.

"What is it like? To be married I mean?"

"It is magnificent. Val is such a splendid father to the children and of course our mother is on hand to help me. Elizabeth you too shall be happy with Oliver. That is if you can get over his childish pranks. It is only mischief. Don't let it weigh heavily on your heart," she replies.

I assume she is talking about my confusion over their family name, but now another quandary, what did Oliver mean about certain situations? What situations would he use another name? That must have been a joke also? Surely?

Margaret leads me into the dining room where the other guests are already seated. I smile and greet everyone politely, sufficiently calmed. So I am to be Mistress Cromwell and not Mistress Williams. My mother in her haste to get me married off has been careless in her information and the mischievous Oliver has used this.

As the evening progresses I wonder if Oliver really does not find me dull. I am unable to converse in this company; I feel out of my depth. I cannot relax as I am used to do with my father and the merchants who visit us at Little Stambridge. But I watch Margaret, Val and Oliver conversing and my heart is warmed at the ease of their relationship. They are accustomed to each other's company and enjoy it. The seating arrangement is such that Oliver sits between his mother and his sister and opposite to me. His mother watches me with some suspicion. Why? This match was made between my father and Lady Joan Barrington. Mistress Elizabeth Cromwell has barely been consulted. I hope this does not bode ill for me. She is a widow and we will be brought into one household when Oliver and I are married. But maybe it is just my own imagining!

"Elizabeth Bourchier, you look more beautiful than ever," the voice behind me is enchanting.

I turn and I am face to face with Master St John. He indicates to the fellow on my right to move so that he can claim the seat next to me. I note the alarm on my hostess' face. I have not seen this man for nearly two years, since he went to Lincoln's Inn. I always thought we would marry although there has been no... serious... impropriety. Do stolen kisses count as impropriety? He made no move to claim my hand although we had spent many summers riding out together with my brother, Thomas. I have always counted him as a true friend.

We converse for no more than ten minutes yet it is just as it was before he left. I sense a tension come over the company and our hostess is staring at me in a rather hostile manner; I sense I have made another mistake. Why am I so hopeless at these grand occasions? Sir Francis strides into the room and with a barely perceptible nod from his wife, he catches St. John by the elbow and marches him to the other side of the dining table,

"May I introduce to you the Walton family," he says to him, graciously.

After the introductions I hear the conversation continue in a more amicable manner about Sir Francis' projected re-entry to Westminster later in the year. With St. John's attention diverted, I smile at my Oliver by way of apology. Perhaps I have been indiscrete again but it was such a short conversation and Master St. John has been a companion and friend since I was but a young girl.

Oliver smiles at me, "I think you must be feeling better Mistress Elizabeth. The colour has quite returned to your cheeks."

I smile back at him and tell myself I must leave behind any childish romantic notions, which linger with regard to St. John. We have known the St. Johns for many years but Master Cromwell and I are to be wed and I must behave appropriately. Sitting on my left, father pats my hand lovingly.

"Elizabeth we can call it off if you are not sure," father whispers in my ear.

"No father we will go ahead with it." I reply.

Not sure, not sure. Is anybody ever sure? Oliver Williams... I mean Cromwell... is a suitable match. I have prayed to the Lord for such a husband and I am satisfied with the Lord's choice. This other whim - it belongs to childhood. Master St. John is a friend, an old childhood friend. No marriage proposal was ever made. Tonight when the formal announcement is made, he will know for sure that I am to be Mistress Cromwell.

I have no time to talk to my Oliver now in an intimate way about the matters which have started to trouble me, but I am confident that he will have satisfactory answers. The conversation continues about hunting, hawking, and our King. I love the lively atmosphere. I begin to relax and join in the conversation, particularly with Margaret and Val. They are such a delightful couple, so obviously in love. They are totally devoted to each other.

I address Mistress Cromwell,

"Be assured, Mistress Cromwell, of my interest in the herb garden,"

That sounded so false and artificial. Mistress Cromwell does not answer me nor continue the conversation further but she does smile and I am reassured, even if just a little.

Chapter 10. Confrontation

Oliver
Barrington Hall 27 May 1620

After dinner, which was no mean fare with pigeon and venison included from the estate, the company gathered for amusements. This was limited to some singing of the psalms while Frances Barrington, Thomas' wife, played the virginals. The guests, mainly the godly people of the county, were entertained.

Sir Francis was eager to show his guests the many fine portraits of his ancestors in the long gallery so he encouraged them to move from the great hall up the great stair to view the pictures, before relaxing in the elaborate great chamber.

Lady Frances Bourchier, Elizabeth's mother, was eager to indulge him. Eustace de Barenton and Winifred Pole stared down at her from their immortalised images. Lady Frances noted the jewels they wore around their necks and on their arms. She noted the style of their clothes. She was careful to make sure a comparison of the fine ladies was made to her beautiful, youngest daughter, as yet unmarried. The young men were captivated by Frances' beauty and gathered around her as they moved along the gallery. One tour around was completed and then they returned to the stairs. Sir Francis graciously guided them across to the great chamber where the ladies would be able to sit in comfort and converse on huge leather chairs.

Elizabeth noticed the attention Frances was getting but her generous heart allowed her to rejoice for her sister. Unlike her mother, Elizabeth could only see the best in others and was not hampered by jealousy, envy or vanity.

The company numbered fifty without the servants, and included city merchants as well as various branches of the Cromwell family.

Rosalie Weller

All were overwhelmed to see the very expensive hangings depicting hunting scenes, as they at last entered the great chamber. The older gentlemen grouped together on one side of the chamber and their usual topic of politics did not take long to surface. Sir James, always eager to talk 'trade' only needed the word wool to be mentioned to set him off, but it was Sir Francis Barrington who led the conversation.

"So, Sir James, has your trade been affected by these problems with the cloth?" Sir Francis had no sense of occasion, considering that merchants were not really 'gentlemen' but tolerated because of their common unity in Christ.

"No, not yet, Francis. I don't export to Poland but I hear that it is the Polish mint that is the problem - debasing the silver coin that's at the heart of our economic crisis today!" James Bourchier replied.

"Is that so? Yes it makes sense. It is money which lies at the bottom of most of the problems we face today. What can be done about it?" Francis Barrington drew in the young lawyer, John Winthrop, hoping to get a legal aspect on the issues which England faced.

Eliciting no reply, he addressed him directly, "John what do you make of it? Is it the quality of our cloth or the corrupt mint at Bydgoszcz which is causing this economic crisis? And more to the point can we do anything about it legally?"

John Winthrop, an astute lawyer, was always careful when he voiced an opinion, aware of how often an opinion can turn round and bite you when you least expect it. He replied with deference.

"Well sir, the legal aspect concerns the contracts we make with the Baltic States. A corrupt coinage is the problem of their national government."

Cromwell & Elizabeth - The Beginning

Sir James now on a topic which interested him - trade - was keen for further discussion but was aware that the older men had begun to yawn.

"Francis, another factor to consider is that the Dutch cloth is more attractive to the market. It is cheaper and lighter - new draperies they are calling them. I expect my wife will be pestering me to get some for the wedding gown, eh? But England lags behind on all these new things. We've got to catch up with the 17th century instead of resting on our laurels from good Queen Bess' success of the past. Yes of course, we will all be affected by declining trade one way or another." Sir James said.

Francis Barrington had barely been listening. His eyes were keenly watching his son. Since Thomas had been a small child, his father knew he was often troubled by things other men took in their stride.

"It's this damn war! Wherever there is war, there is corruption. Some say this war is to keep us free from the Papists on the Continent but I think it is always about money." He said as Lady Joan called him to retire for the night. Lady Joan's piety did not allow her to enjoy any frivolity at a gathering so it was well known that she and her husband retired early.

Oliver and Thomas sat down to a few hands of trumps with the other gentlemen. Thomas had heard rumours that his younger cousin was under the spell of this game of chance but he wanted to observe for himself. Oliver was content. He did not converse but concentrated on the cards as they were dealt. Thomas noticed a change come over Oliver. His demeanour became rigid. His eyes were alert. His brow furrowed as he concentrated.

Thomas whispered that the younger gentlemen could withdraw to the billiard room for a game of billiards. A game of billiards for a small wager promised an exciting new venture. Not having a large manor house and its accompanying leisure rooms, this invitation awoke new excitement in Oliver. With the allure of further gaming, the young gentlemen remained patiently waiting until the mature company retired.

Oliver attentively bid the Bourchier family a good night, then he made his way to the great stairway and across the great hall again to the billiard room on the further side. He found his cousins Oliver St. John and Thomas Barrington in earnest conversation. When he approached them, he noticed that their conversation became guarded. Had they been discussing his fiancée? He was quite determined to pursue this matter of St. John's relationship with Elizabeth.

"So cousin, was it not my Elizabeth with whom you had a dalliance? I think it was two summers ago? I seem to remember you mentioning something about a young girl who could converse like a man? Certainly my Elizabeth would fit the description you gave. Although I must say I cannot remember the details of your relationship! As I recall you were somewhat disrespectful in your conversation about her," Oliver said.

The challenge had been issued. Oliver was not a man to shilly-shally. He was direct and to the point. Thomas Barrington shifted nervously from one foot to the other but Oliver did not notice. He was staring pointedly at his other cousin, determined to root out the truth. St John smiled a rare wide grin meant to disarm. He spoke slowly yet decisively.

Yes, he had wanted to marry Elizabeth but no-one had known about their closeness. When the opportunity arose ambition surpassed romantic inclinations. He had intended to come back and make his peace with Elizabeth but month quickly followed month without an opportunity to return. Now it was too late.

"No, Oliver, you must be mistaken." He lied, "I barely know your fiancée. I've only met her once or twice and you were there, don't you remember... when we were boys... " His confidence sapped Oliver's resolve as St. John continued,

"Life was easy then, wasn't it, Oliver? Tom says you two have done some hawking recently. Have you still got that magnificent Peregrine? To see her swoop is a sight indeed. She is so graceful and her accuracy is second to none.

Thomas Barrington stepped between the two men to reach behind them for two mugs of ale as he continued to play the billiards.

"Let's finish the evening as only gentlemen can," he said, handing both men a large pewter jug.

The mention of his beloved Peregrine diverted Oliver's attention and he proudly recounted the latest hunting adventure with Thomas, leaving out his disgust at William Meux's presence. The tension dissipated as the three cousins drank heartily while discussing the latest legal decisions in the land, which Oliver St. John was eager to share. He had the advantage over the other men with his superior knowledge and as he had helped both of them with legal matters, they were more than willing to listen. Oliver was not good at debating, questioning or pursuing an argument, particularly with his equals.

St. John's confidence and easy manner relaxed the tension. Any doubts Oliver had concerning his fiancée were pushed far below the surface of his thoughts, as he proudly spoke about his peregrine. He had enjoyed good ale, fine food and good company that day and felt far happier than he had ever been. The announcement of his forthcoming marriage to Elizabeth Bourchier had been made.

Chapter 11. Ambivalence

                Elizabeth
             Essex 28 May 1620

As I ride back through the woods and fields with my dear father, I am filled with a sense of loss. This is what I will miss! The crisp air is blowing through my hair. I always have such a feeling of independence when I am riding. I will have other responsibilities now. I am so glad brother Thomas swapped with me and wanted to ride back in the carriage – just to know what it was like, he said. It was no problem to loan riding garb from Lady Joan, although she couldn't understand why I wanted to ride and not go in that dreadful carriage. But she is such an example of what a godly woman should be. I shouldn't be cross with her. I think I may even grow quite fond of her.

We slow to a trot as we near "Little Stambridge".

"I do hope you will be happy with this Oliver, my dear," father says gently, "You look so thoughtful."

"There is no reason to think otherwise, father," I reply. "Oh father, I have such a story to tell you. While we were out riding last week, Oliver's quick reaction saved Maddie Appleby's life! Can you believe it?" I recount the incident to my father quite proudly. He isn't surprised at all. He says,

"Well, my dear, this young man certainly seems to be a man of action. Lady Joan told me how she had heard that Oliver had been of service to Master Turner, when a boar entangled itself in the wheel of a carriage in Huntington. The whole town was alive with news of it."

My heart is fuelled by love as I listen to my father's account. Oliver is so different from the other young men I know. He seems to be able to get straight to the point when we are discussing the issues of life. His language is not hampered by flowery nothings. He is decisive but he is also kind. One thing is certain. Life will never be tedious when I am married to Oliver Cromwell!

I want to talk to my father about my feelings for Master St. John but I do not think he will understand. He seems so impressed with my Oliver. I am too. The more I hear about his heroic actions, the more amazed I am. How can anyone understand my ambivalence? I hardly understand it myself. My lingering emotions for St John must go. I must push these feelings aside.

The sun begins to warm my face as our horses come to a walking pace alongside the fields. In some ways I will be happy to leave home. I have begun to feel stifled by mother's way of doing things. Everything provisioned for the house is to show the neighbours how grand we are. An item is never chosen for its usefulness. Soon I see the estate looming in the distance. Our lands are not enclosed as some have come to be of late. The view across the countryside stretches for miles. It is breathtaking. Yes this is what I will miss!

We are soon back at Little Stambridge Hall. As we clatter into the courtyard, Daniel is there ready to take the reins. I slip quickly from the saddle and go into the garden. My father follows me. The scent of lavender is comforting. It is a smell familiar since childhood. This is such a beautiful house and gardens; I will be loathe to leave them. My young brothers, Robert, John and Christopher, have heard us and are eager for company. But with one decisive gesture of the hand, father makes it clear they are not to interrupt. They must wait while we continue our conversation. Such obedient boys, they find the skittles to amuse themselves. They know they must be careful of the rose bushes, but there is plenty of grass for them to play on. Smiling and laughing they, too, are enjoying the estate on which we live.

"Beth, are you thinking about when you must leave Little Stambridge?"

"Why, yes, Father, I once thought it was so far off but now it is just a little step around the corner. It is nearly upon me, I'm afraid."

As father hugs me, I draw comfort from his presence. His shoulders are broad and his embrace is strong.

"It is always like this, but you are a strong, godly young woman. God will guide you in the right path. Huntington is not so very far away."

We stand awhile together, knowing our futures lie in different directions. I savour this precious time with my father. He begins to talk about his business again and I am happy to listen, just as I did when I was little. An hour passes as if it is just a few minutes.

We are startled by the sound of the carriage arriving. I hurry to greet Alice so we can talk about all that we have experienced at the Barringtons. Frances laughs with delight as she steps down from the carriage. Robert and John have come to greet her. She doesn't have to be told to mind her gown, she is always fastidious with her clothes. Is that why she always looks so pretty? No, she is fortunate to have a beautifully modelled face. Her nose is slender but not too long, her lips are just plump enough and her smile is so engaging.

Mother directs us, "Put away your gowns. You have one hour to rest before we take our afternoon refreshment."

Father stares adoringly at her quick transformation to the management of our household. Mother is so particular that the conventions of our lives are adhered to. We must take refreshment together because that is what modern ladies do. Alice and I are giggling even before we reach our room.

"Alice," I say, "I am really going to miss you. You have been such a good sister to me,"

"Yes," she replies cheerily, "But we will still be sisters, even when you are Mistress Cromwell. Oh Elizabeth, I like your Oliver more and more each time we meet him. He is so lively and full of fun!"

Her enthusiasm takes away any lingering thoughts of doubt about this marriage. But there is one thing I want to know from her. I had been obliged to attend the chapel prayers at the end of the evening and Alice had not. As I returned to the company, I overheard a remark about Oliver which troubled me.

"But tell me, what was it about the card table, Alice?" I ask, genuinely wanting an explanation. She replies with a wide grin on her face.

"Val Walton was teasing Oliver because he used to love playing cards and even bet on the games in Cambridge."

"Alice, I wish you hadn't told me that. It is hardly the pastime for a god-fearing gentleman."

"You're far too serious, Elizabeth. It was just boyishness – relaxation while they were studying. What about that pheasant dish on Lady Joan's table – wasn't it so tasty?" Alice remarks.

"I wanted to eat far more than is good for me. I was surprised there was no dancing though, and the music was quite plain, I thought." I reply to Alice.

"The lemon pudding was delicious. I think that chaplain fellow, what was his name? Ezekiel Rogers. He sounds so holy. He has quite an influence over Lady Joan. He doesn't permit dancing and the music must be only accompanying the psalms. Isn't it so grand Bessie, that Barrington Hall has its own chapel?"

Rosalie Weller

"Yes, I was obliged to say prayers with Lady Joan before she retired. It was so plain. I was quite taken aback. There were no pictures of the Virgin and not even a cross! Hark, Alice, mother is calling us. We must go down."

Alice still cannot contain herself. She says,

"When the engagement announcement was made everyone said what a handsome couple. Oh, Bessie I wish it was me!"

I do not reply. Yes, Alice, I too had glanced around the room. I had seen what others might not - the surprised look on Master St. John's face. Was that disappointment in those brown eyes?

Chapter 12. Friendship

Oliver
Huntington 1 June 1620

Both the Cromwell and the Bourchier households settled down to absorb and revel in their growing excitement at the forthcoming nuptials.

Oliver would be able to take his place in society as a gentleman with the support of Sir Francis. He would join his good friend, William Kilbourne, on the council and serve the people just as his father had done. Surely that was what gentlemen should do? He had known William from Master Beard's classroom. They had spent every moment together at education and play, discussing all Master Beard had instructed. They debated everything he put before them, eager to expand their minds and experience. Then as now, Oliver often found himself listening rather than talking.

William, four years his senior, could restrain Oliver's mischievous tendencies like no one else had been able to. Oliver took a walk to the Post House, where he knew he would find William. He walked slowly, mulling over the year past – the well-known path reviving the memories.

He passed St John's church on his left. Its imposing stature represented only contention with St. Mary's for him. The vicar of the latter church was prone to going back to Popish ways if gentlemen like him failed to be vigilant. On the contrary, Beard's lectures at St. John's were inspiring and basic to the Christian belief. Why could it not be just that simple in every church? Why did they need to indulge in all those excesses which still went on in churches today- the bishops, the incense, the elaborate rituals?

He spied the blacksmith working at his forge as he passed. Smithy doffed his cap as Oliver passed – acknowledgement that he was now one of the gentlemen in the town. Oliver smiled, self-satisfied that life at last was beginning to brighten. The square was empty of the usual sheep as the market was still one day away. Thankfully he could negotiate the cobbles with ease. "The George", owned by Sir Oliver, his uncle, bellowed raucous laughter as two drunken workmen were ejected. They scurried quickly past him, embarrassed by his witness of their inebriation.

He saw William leave his house just ahead of him.

"Will," he raised his voice to catch his friend's attention.

"Oliver," his friend turned round and greeted him, smiling. "I haven't seen you this month past, what have you been doing?"

"Are you on an errand? I had hoped we could talk for a while." Oliver replied.

"Yes, I'm afraid I'll be engaged for quite a while yet. Can I, perhaps, call on you and your good mother, this evening?"

The plan was struck and Oliver retraced his steps through the town. He had very much wished to share the news of his future, but he wanted to do it in private not on the public walkway. He was eager to get the last lingering doubt off his chest but he knew William was very busy getting the new postal service off the ground. What a change that would be! A definite route to take the post between towns instead of having to rely on infrequent messengers. Progress indeed! The world was opening up and becoming an exciting place, and he was part of it. If he got a place on the borough council the expenses received would improve his situation. He was soon re-entering his home.

"Mother, I am going to ride over to Hinchingbrooke House."

His mother only pursed her lips closer together. Oliver did not like gaining her displeasure but he continued,

"I would like to talk over with Sir Oliver his experiences at Westminster Palace. He understands the politics of this country, what with being ousted by Beavill. I know he intends to contest the seat next year. He understands both the intrigues of the court and the politics of men."

"Yes, Oliver and the last progress has almost cost him his house!"

Oliver knew this was true. The lavish gifts Sir Oliver had bestowed on King James were still the talk of the town and, indeed, the whole county. Costly but what a gain there had been in his reputation. Surprised by his mother's unusually cynical tone, Oliver quickly diverted any unpleasantness. He said,

"Mother, I was unable to talk to William this morning but he says he will call to visit this evening. I want to tell him about the engagement. Now it has been formally announced we can be quite open about it.

His mother's warm smile returned at the mention of William Kilbourne. She too admired him. He had bettered himself quite unusually. He had inherited a run-down hostelry, and had renovated the property and made it suitable for paying guests. He had also set up a system whereby the post could be delivered to various other cities and towns. He had gained the respect and esteem of the citizens of Huntington, not only through his clever skills in the renovation, but in his cheery character and his desire to help those less fortunate than himself, especially through his service as a burgher on the council. Oliver closed the door quickly to avoid any further discourse. Although the groom was in the stable, he saddled up his own horse. He was a practical man, preferring not to be served by others.

Hinchingbrooke House was barely an hour's ride away and he was greeted warmly. His uncle was delighted to see him and received his news warmly. Oliver was at ease with his uncle and did not hesitate to plunge into serious conversation without the preliminary pleasantries.

"Sir, I know the lack of estates hinders me from taking a county seat but what about representing the borough? Do you think that could be my way into government?"

"Oliver, far be it from me to be unkind, but to get on in government today you have to have favour at court and you just don't have the means to do that." His uncle paused and scratched his balding head thoughtfully. He continued,

"Hm, it's a good idea, though, to serve on the borough council with William. That will give you insight into the issues gentlemen should be concerned about."

"But it must be amazing to be involved in court affairs, Uncle, and what about Westminster Palace, participating in the discussions?" Oliver could not contain his enthusiasm any longer.

"No, Oliver, it is capricious at court, always sidestepping the intrigues of men. It is only because I held the favour of Queen Anne in the management of her legal requests which brought me an income. And I must say, she settled her accounts more speedily than Good King James does. Don't forget, Oliver, I built that favour up over the last thirty years, but now that she has passed on, that income is gone."

Sir Oliver's face became thoughtful once more.

"Yes, uncle," Oliver replied, "I never realised. Of course you have lost that income now."

"Well, it is part of life, but be ready, young man for the future," Sir Oliver encouraged, "Your fiancée's people, they are in trade. That is the future. See what can be done, there."

Their conversation was interrupted by Robert Ferrer, the estates manager, who urgently requested that Sir Oliver attend to another matter. Their discussion had been brief but it had allowed Oliver to share his good news with someone else in his locality.

In less than three hours Oliver was on his way back to Huntington anticipating a companionable evening. But on arrival home, he heard that William had sent a messenger to inform him that he would be unable to visit him that evening after all. Exhausted and disappointed again, Oliver retired for the night.

Chapter 13. An Invitation

Elizabeth
Little Stambridge Hall 1 June 1620

I cannot abide controversy. My lady mother is so overwhelmed by this latest event. I think she will drive us all to lunacy! All over a festival invitation!

"Elizabeth, how can we not accept?" she says, "It would be quite rude. You are to be a part of this noble family."

"Yes, madam," I have to agree with her, although I do not want to anger my fiancé.

She flounces out of the room to consult my father as to what will be done.

Sir Oliver and Lady Anna Cromwell sincerely request
The company of Sir James and Lady Frances Bourchier and
family
To the Ball at Hinchingbrooke House
Following the Whitsuntide Festivities
June 8-10 1620

"Oh Sarah, what is to be done?" I address my cousin who has been attending mother, waiting to see what her next duty is.

"Elizabeth, I cannot say, but if we are to go, may I invite my sister Rachael?" she asks hesitatingly.

I cannot find an answer to such impudence. Is our whole household insane?

Cromwell & Elizabeth - The Beginning

The invitation does indeed extend to the whole family including the servants who will be glad to enjoy the fair and the Morris dancing. It is to be specially put on for them. It will be quite difficult to move most of the household for those few days, but oh such fun and merriment. Our family has never known anything like this. It is beyond mother's wildest dreams and quite unexpected. Of course we know Oliver has noble relatives and I am sure that was behind her ambition in the joining of our two families but this has come less than two months after the announcement of our engagement – which was no business of Sir Oliver – or so says Lady Joan Barrington.

Sir Oliver has had no part in of any of the arrangements and my Oliver had wondered whether he would be upset by that. Apparently not! I do not know if Oliver is keen to go and now it seems that father is taking a similar attitude. Why must there be such intrigue and unpleasantness in families? I have been deliriously happy, as I have seen more and more of my betrothed and I don't want this to spoil everything.

At present, it is still quite chilly even though it is June. I put on my cloak and pull my hood over my head and walk out to the gardens where I can see my mother is rushing to challenge my father as he inspects his roses. I suspect that father's hesitation comes because of the influence of Joan Barrington but I am not clear about it - after all she is Sir Oliver's sister. I hear my mother's shrill voice and see her heated animated gesticulations. Poor father! James is trying to catch father's attention with his ball. Here also are the boys, Charles, John and Robert, playing tag. Frances' pretty head is hiding behind the shrubs. Is she waiting for young Christopher? Hide and seek is his favourite game. As I approach, mother enlists my support,

"Elizabeth come and tell your father what a fantastic opportunity this will be for your sisters to meet young men of the right standing."

"I know Alice would enjoy the opportunity," I begin but as I look up at my father's frowning face, I stop, "Um ... but that may not be the only consideration,"

"Elizabeth, I am concerned that you may be caught up by the ostentatiousness of such an occasion. You and your sisters have been protected from such worldliness but I do realise that not everyone has our godly standards and your new family is somewhat different. But at an event like this there is sure to be some uncouthness; there will be swearing and drunkenness during the servants' festivities which is not appropriate for young ladies to witness. I am sure many of the nobility will attend but is that sufficient reason to expose my children to such ungodliness?" he says.

Suddenly I seem to be the one who is driving this ambition, which clearly comes from my mother. I do not want to react because of this impossible situation she has put me in. This is all such new territory. I am the eldest and what happens with my marriage arrangements will set a pattern for all the children who follow. I agree with my father. He is right.

"Mother I do understand why father is hesitant but ..." I start but am interrupted by her.

"Yes but it is of utmost importance that your sisters meet suitable gentlemen. I could not abide a scandal such as has arisen in the Hatton family. We are all aghast that two sisters should generate such uproar." She rests her case.

Well I suppose it has been rather unfortunate that the step-sisters Frances Hatton and Frances Coke have been involved in these matters. But Frances Hatton could never have known that her grandfather would take such exception to Richard Rich. Who could have foreseen that Lady Hatton would kidnap her own daughter against her husband Sir Edward Coke's wishes – all over two competing suitors.

I am exasperated! Frances Hatton seems to be revived and dangled in front of us as a spectacle to be avoided at every opportunity. Yes, she has made a serious mistake but hardly one that Frances or Alice will make, I am sure.

These festivities will be the sort of occasion where we may feel uncomfortable because we are trying to lead a pious life, but I would like to meet this noble part of Oliver's family. I am young and surely God won't be cross with me for attending such a grand occasion once. Will He? Father is looking at me expecting an answer and I don't really know what the question is.

"What reason does Oliver give for his reluctance, Elizabeth?" he asks again with some impatience.

"We have not had occasion to discuss the matter, father. I only know what his sister Margaret has said to me about his relationship with Sir Oliver. She said that the family were not regular visitors at Hinchingbrooke. When I was speaking to mother, I did not mean that I had definite advice on the matter, father. I was merely thinking that a problem may arise"

"Well, Elizabeth, this is the result of that idle chatter!" he says.

How has mother now made this disagreement my fault? I am instructed by father to ride over to the Cromwells' without delay and find out exactly what the feelings of Oliver and his family are to this invitation. Alice is to accompany me to observe the proprieties.

The fair is less than a week away! I wish now I had not mentioned Oliver's anticipated reluctance to mother. As father has not given a final decision on the matter, mother is less affectionate than she could be towards me. It is not my fault. I am sometimes feeling that I am less a child of the family than a piece of property, which she can barter to pursue her ambitions.

Chapter 14. Intrigue

Oliver
Huntington 2 June 1620

The next evening, sooner than expected, William was able to keep his promise to visit Oliver and his mother. William's daughter had developed a worrying croup and he was needed to assist in the "steaming," to relieve the dangerous coughing and his toddler's distress. As the crisis was now under control, he was able once more to walk down the high street in Huntington to his friend's residence. It was Mistress Cromwell who warmly greeted him.

"I am so glad to hear Mary has come through the fever. William, you know our prayers are with you."

"Thank you gladly," he replied, "Bridgett has indeed been very anxious about little Mary's recovery. As I was too. As you know Bridgett helps a lot with the guests at the Fountain Inn so I needed to stay in our rooms with Mary and keep her calm. Praise be to the Lord, for today she was alert and almost entirely recovered."

William was helped out of his coat without a reply. Although it was June there was a chill in the air, which required this extra layer. Mistress Cromwell led him into the great hall, where Oliver was waiting to greet him. She discreetly rounded up her daughters to the other end of this large room, much to Anna and Catherine's disquiet. There was too little light to complete their embroidery so they were forced to converse with their mother. Oliver was glad to have the chairs by the fire.

"Ah William, there is so much to share with you. Come. Have a seat by the fire." Oliver drew his friend warmly towards him. Suddenly, he felt tired and realised that the past few weeks' nuptial arrangements had taken its toll on his peace of mind.

As they talked, Oliver was able to share his hopes and dreams of a companionable future with Elizabeth. William greeted the news with enthusiasm and recounted some of his own joys and burdens of domesticity. However, the conversation was soon dominated by the life of the borough. William confirmed the rumour that some of the burghers were petitioning for a new charter from the king.

"I don't understand why a new charter is necessary," Oliver enquired.

"Well really it isn't, though I am sure Master Walden and Master Bernard are trying to consolidate their power, somehow. I don't know the details of what they are asking, so I cannot say."

For Oliver it was the first time he was aware of the situation and the tensions, which existed in the town. He really did not understand the politics involved because the furtherance of his education at Cambridge had hindered his interest in local life. Since he had returned, he had been busy with the affairs of his late father, which were in a considerable mess. Robert Cromwell had sold considerably more land than he revealed to his wife. Most of the capital had been spent. What was it that Sir Oliver, his godfather, had said about the new charter? Oliver wished he could remember because that could possibly help his friend. But was there also something that Sir Oliver was holding back? Oliver's naivety in politics was a serious disadvantage.

Just an hour later, Oliver's voice softened to almost a whisper as he drew nearer to William in an abrupt change of subject.

"William, there is another matter I must gain your reassurance on."

His friend, surprised by the sudden change in manner, listened intently.

"William, the matter we dealt with for the king .... My Elizabeth, nor her family must ever know about it!"

"My dear Oliver, not a word will pass from my lips." William replied, "As I think upon it now, what young scoundrels we were." William laughed unashamedly so that the sudden rise in noise startled the children from their rhyming and singing. Oliver again cautioned his friend from speaking too loudly.

"Our trip to Heidelberg must remain a secret ... but I do think fondly now of the splendour of that court." he said.

Oliver thought back to the journey the two friends had made that time. The things they had seen seen and done as they witnessed the take-over of the fearless Hapsburg troops in the Palatinate. Oliver had seen and admired the military discipline of those men as they fought in hand to hand combat. The ordered nature of the battle inspired confidence but more than that, the soldiers were inspired by the cause. They believed in what they were fighting for. The military discipline of the Hapsburgs had captured Oliver's imagination. The dialogue lulled as the two of them engaged in their own quite different thoughts. For Oliver it was the row upon row of troops. His interest in soldiering had developed when he was a boy. It was quite unexplained and made him feel like a cuckoo in the nest.

At the time William had troubles of his own and was glad of the chance to escape to the Low Countries on their adventure. Their mission was simply the delivery of letters but it was the secrecy, which had been challenging. His interest in local politics had been revived by that journey. For the first time, he had seen how wealth and power could overrun the general hum of everyday life. It was his first chance to observe how the nobility lived, and at the court of Princess Elizabeth, he realised how much a man's position depended on the favour of the monarch. The opulence and extravagance of the court could not be equalled. Princess Elizabeth's silk dress was emblazoned with gold thread the like of which he had never seen. It shimmered as she walked. He had been glad that their mission was so short-lived and that Bohemia could now be left to itself.

But Sir Oliver's interest had been in political intrigue rather than the intensity of a battle. Sir Oliver, in wishing to advance his favour at court, had commissioned his nephew to take letters from King James to Princess Elizabeth. Oliver never knew the content of them but he assumed they were words of encouragement from father to daughter. It had been a welcome respite from his studies at the beginning of the year. It was a short adventure gladly undertaken with William on behalf of the King, and was, of course, accomplished in secret so that his mother had been completely unaware of it. William had met him in Cambridge and they had ridden on to Dover from there.

Oliver gave himself a mental shake and brought his thoughts back to the present moment. Once he had received his friend's reassurance Oliver became a lively host, and included his mother and sisters in the conversation and laughter. Two hours later William took his leave.

Chapter 15. Explanations

Elizabeth
Huntington 3 June 1620

Oliver sees us before we reach the top of the high street. As I slow Arabella to a walk, her hooves clattering along the cobbled street, my heart is racing in the knowledge that we will be able to spend some time together. He looks surprised as I dismount, but as our bodies and hands brush lightly against each other, he smiles.

"This is an unexpected pleasure, Elizabeth," Mistress Cromwell says, rising as we enter the house. Oliver's younger sisters giggle as they look from me to their brother. It is apparent that they had been called upon to look after their young nephew – Margaret's child. I suppose it must be quite amusing for them that their brother, who has been doted on by this otherwise all female family, will soon be marrying – and a girl from another county at that. I find their obvious affection for their brother endearing.

"Good day Mistress Cromwell," I reply, "My father has asked me to discuss an urgent matter with Oliver, if I have your leave?"

"Yes, go into the back chamber. Margaret is sitting there with little Agnes. You can converse with ease. Your sister can join us here while you discuss your business."

This is welcome news indeed. Margaret has already become my own confidante and I value her opinion. Oliver steers me into the back of the house hurriedly, disappointed that this visit is not merely for us to pursue our relationship.

He begins in his usual direct manner, "Whatever is the matter Elizabeth?" Oliver greets Margaret with a smile as we enter and then faces me.

"Oliver, I am so sorry to alarm you. It is merely a matter of facts that I must gather for my father to assist him in making his decision about the invitation we have received from Hinchingbrooke." I say.

"Ah, yes I can understand his concern. He does not have the full family history to ascertain how he should proceed." He replies and I can see that he is relieved that it is only a family matter which has resulted in this sudden appearance and not that my affections are waning.

"Elizabeth, why don't you take off your hood and cloak, and we shall have some ale as I explain the situation to you. You must surely stay this evening. It is too far to ride back to Little Stambridge in one day. You and Alice can bed with Catherine or Anna. That should be alright, eh Margaret?' He turns his face questioningly to his sister, who busy with her second child, just nods.

"Oh, thank you. It will be a pleasure to spend some time talking with you Oliver. We have little enough occasion to get to know each other." I respond with gratitude at his warmth.

As I start to talk, he puts his finger on my lips to quieten me and says,

"First the ale, Elizabeth and then the urgent matters." I acquiesce as he calls to Catherine to bring some ale.

There is something about the easy relationships within this house that makes me feel comfortable. I am not sure whether it is my mother or my sisters that makes our house feel so tense. I am always on edge there as if I have to live up to some insurmountable expectations and dreams. We are always worrying about our gowns, our hoods, our studies, and our music lessons. The boys constantly tease us about our marriage prospects. It seems that everyone else in the household stirs with this rhythm. I am the only one out of step with it. Dear father always assures me that it is good to discuss ideas, philosophy and poetry and I so enjoy talking to him. Mother has no interest in poetic verse! Only yesterday we looked at the poetry of Christopher Marlowe. Marlowe has an appreciation of nature but sometimes he just speaks about love,

> "Come live with me and be my love
> And we will all the pleasures prove."

As I reflect on the memory of what my father and I share, Oliver brings in the ale and I wonder if the dream of marriage will be as good in reality.

"Now my dear, you must reassure your father that it is because Sir Oliver is my godfather and I informed him of our engagement that this invitation has been extended to your family. Rather late I am afraid, because he did not know until yesterday. He is a kindly fellow although somewhat ungodly. But that is not the reason I hesitate. My mother is unhappy because she feels that Sir Oliver was less than gracious in his treatment of my father when he was alive. However, I believe it is a common problem of the elder and younger sons." I nod in agreement as Oliver explains,

"My Aunt Joan who you have already met is a very pious person, as is Sir Francis. They do not approve of the lavishness of Sir Oliver's house. Well, it is very showy, almost like the extravagance at the court of good King James, as I am sure you have heard. In fact His Majesty and a lot of nobles frequent Hinchingbrooke often as it is only a mile from the Great North Road and so it is very convenient when the King is on his progress around the country. Aunt Joan disapproves because she says that the King is merely playing to Sir Oliver's vanity in staying there. He never receives a penny towards his generous hospitality. Of course mother feels that Sir Oliver should rather have been more generous to his own brother than, dare I say, to his sovereign. There now you know why feelings run high."

We sit in silence for just a moment but he has not answered my unsaid question, I start hesitantly,

"Oliver, does this mean that we are not to accept the invitation? I know my mother is anxious to take my sisters to such a grand occasion yet I understand why my father hesitates. I am sure Lady Joan is influencing his reluctance."

Oliver now includes his sister in the conversation, "Well Margaret, how do you react? I know Val does not approve of our uncle, Sir Oliver."

Margaret is a practical person and for that reason perhaps, not a reasoned thinker. She replies,

"The invitation is extended in recognition of your intended marriage, Oliver. Yes, it will be frivolous and wasteful. Yes, Aunt Joan will disapprove. But what fun you shall have. Life is serious enough. You will find that out when you are married, Elizabeth. Then there will be no time for dancing and entertainments besides the moral consideration. Enjoy the invitation while it is given."

Oliver claps his hands in approval at his sister's advice, then turns to me.

"She is right, Elizabeth. Mother won't go and won't allow my sisters to attend but we shall go in respect of the fact that he is my godfather. Yes, it will be indeed be a most ungodly event but I hope that God shall forgive us. You must tell your father that I will be going although my mother and sisters will not attend. Feel free to explain why. Say that I would love you and your family to accompany me."

I am glad Oliver and his mother can disagree so amiably. Yes, I am excited to go to Hinchingbrooke House and join in the festivities. We now have less than a week to plan!

Chapter 16. More secrets

Oliver
Huntington 3 June 1620

Oliver had been delighted to receive Elizabeth and Alice on their unexpected visit. The lively laughter of his betrothed and the companionship she had found with his sister, Margaret, gave him great pleasure. He was sure Elizabeth would fit in well with his family, even though her family's wealth could have precluded it. She had high expectations in everyday living. He knew he would just not be able to afford to keep her in the style she was accustomed to. Elizabeth just assumed that she would be able to have all the gowns and hoods she wished. Strangely she thought she dressed modestly and indeed she did, but the sheer volume of clothes she owned was much beyond what his sisters had ever possessed. The amount of meat daily consumed at her family's table had never been enjoyed by the Cromwells. Elizabeth was not aware of this yet because Mistress Cromwell had chosen their meat days to coincide with her visits. Oliver had neither the heart nor the stomach to advise her otherwise.

As for Alice, each time they visited, she found plenty to discuss with Oliver's sister, Catherine, about embroidery stitches while his other sister, Anna had kept them all entertained with her noisy chatter. Anna had managed to interest the Bourchier sisters in her plays she enacted for her young nephew. Both sisters revelled in this mostly female household, so different from their own.

The finances were a matter which the couple had not yet discussed and Oliver was glad. Elizabeth was so naïve and without pretensions, it would indeed make his life easier, if reality were not poured on her too soon. She did not discern the politics around her, even though she prided herself on her intellectual ability. He was glad that she would be allowed to attend the ball at Hinchingbrooke as that would endear her to his uncle – a revered knight of the realm. It was important to Oliver that Elizabeth and her family felt as comfortable at Hinchingbrooke as they obviously had at Barrington Hall. After all they were all Oliver's relatives. Oliver had always managed to balance his allegiance to both Sir Oliver and Sir Francis. Up until now they had both seen him as just another young nephew but his father's death had triggered further interest in him from them. To Sir Oliver it was understandable that the announcement of Oliver's engagement had been made from the Barrington's manor. After all, that was where the connection to the Bourchiers was.

Oliver was ambitious to succeed where his father had failed. The family fortunes had taken a turn for the worse but he had made a secret appointment with Elizabeth's father and that conversation had gone better than expected. Now he was more confident that he would be able to meet his financial obligations. His dwindling fortune would be secured by Sir James as the jointure agreement which had been made between them was very neat on paper but would not actually cost him what it seemed to the curious eye. Sir James had merely laughed about the debts Oliver had incurred, joking about a young gentleman's financial mismanagement. Oliver's gambling habit had remained a secret as had his mother's brewhouse. It was regrettable that Oliver had been unable to be totally honest about the gravity of his financial situation but he could not bring himself to talk about his gambling to anyone. It was becoming a matter of shame for him. Why did he worry about it now when previously he had not given it a second thought? His intended marriage had caused deep contemplation. Things must change now. He would have to be strong in the fight against temptation. It must not happen again.

Oliver was also pleased that the service he and William had done for the King had been carried out in secret. He knew Sir James would not have approved. More likely it could have scuppered his matrimonial intentions. Yes, Oliver was pleased. He had grown to love Elizabeth Bourchier more than he cared to admit and there were matters which he was glad were to remain secret.

Rosalie Weller

As he mulled over this gambling problem, he realised that really it was Robert Ferrer who had drawn him into it when he had been at his lowest. His father had only just died and what had been a passing fancy at Cambridge had grown into something which he could not resist. The thrill of the win far outweighed the misery of defeat! He knew in his heart that it was wrong, that this was an addiction that he must overcome. But oh, that feeling, that excitement, the possibility that everything might change on one turn of the card!

He had come across Robert Ferrer at Hinchingbrooke House. He had emerged from the stables one day just as Oliver was riding in through the gate house to visit his godfather. The two had never met and civility never goes amiss. On that occasion, his uncle was not home, so when Robert had invited him to look at the new mare recently acquired, Oliver thought it only polite to turn in at the stables. But at the back of the stables, the lure of the table beckoned as the cards spread out in an obviously interrupted game.

"Good day to you," the pale faced scrawny occupant at the card table greeted him. "Have you got time for a hand?"

This was how the acquaintance had begun. It was done in all innocence. There was no discussion or premeditation. It had started as a pleasant hour to while away time as he waited for his uncle. The result had been regular visits where Oliver was unfortunate to inevitably end up in debt to the other two. Sometimes he thought he went back because he hoped the luck would turn and he would be able to recoup his losses. But in all honesty it was that he just couldn't resist the call of the cards. Now there were so many secrets to keep and Oliver was not good at secrets. In the course of just a couple of months, his life had changed from joy and laughter to serious problems. Was this what William had meant by the responsibilities of marriage? Life had become a drudgery.

Oliver was looking forward to the fair. He had hesitated at first when Elizabeth had mentioned her father's reservations, but

Margaret's light and hearty advice had swept away his doubts. It would be good for Elizabeth. She needed something to lighten her serious nature. It would be an opportunity for Oliver to be proud of his relatives and their opulence. He knew Lady Frances Bourchier would be delighted. He had taken the measure of her very quickly.

Chapter 17. Hinchingbrooke

Elizabeth
The Whitsuntide Fair 8 June 1620

It has been quite an effort to make all the arrangements for the household. When I returned from the Cromwell's to report back to father, his cross-examination forced me to think through some of my own beliefs. For that I am grateful to him.

If I want to honour our belief in the simplicity of faith, should I go to a place like Hinchingbrooke where appearances and finery are placed above godliness? I am sure Sir Oliver is a man to be respected. Indeed he has the reputation of a thoughtful politician – a man of integrity. I argued with father that surely supporting and enabling the servants in some leisure pursuits would please our Lord. The servants work very hard to serve us and they deserve to have a week's pleasure at Whitsuntide. But maybe I should have told the truth: for once in my life I desire to go to such an event!

Father does not agree with me but is allowing me to accompany Oliver, as our host is his godfather. Furthermore, mother is allowed to accompany my sisters but we have incurred Lady Joan's disapproval in our acceptance, even though it is an invitation from her own brother! Sometimes she seems too sober for any polite company.

Oliver did not put forward any matters of conscience to be considered and I find that quite odd. Rather his concern is that his mother should not be disrespected because of her dislike of her brother-in-law. When we asked Mistress Cromwell, she said that her own reservations were of a personal nature, to do with Sir Oliver's lack of help to her husband when he needed it. She declined to go into any further detail but she gave us her blessing to attend if we wished. She would not be attending, or allowing any of Oliver's sisters to attend. I had not realised until now that there seems to be some lack of unity in Oliver's wider family but I suppose that is true of all families. At least Oliver and I agree. I think it may be fun.

On Thursday and Friday the fair will be an exhibit of trade goods and wares, and fun and games for the servants to enjoy. On Saturday there will be the grand ball, almost as grand as any court affair. This will culminate with a thanksgiving service in the Hinchingbrooke private chapel on Sunday, which we will all attend.

Sarah, and her sister Rachael Brockett, are as excited as I am but Goodwife Appleby was reluctant to leave her recently injured child and wasn't so pleased to have to come to chaperone them. Her accommodation in this large house is not as grand as that in Little Stambridge Hall where she has her own room. The grooms have come to look after our horses. I understand they will be accommodated in the barn. As it is summer, I am sure that will be adequate.

As I ride into the grounds of Hinchingbrooke House with my brothers and father, I am astounded. The stalls are set out on the perimeter to display their wares to their best advantage and the people have already started to arrive. I am a little disturbed that there are charlatans selling miscellaneous cures, holy water and pilgrims' medallions. I thought we had got rid of such false trinkets years ago. There is a huge square preserved in front of the house for the Morris dancing and a new invention, the puppet house, is set up on the edge. Children are already seated on the grass before the stalls, excitedly laughing and pointing at the decoration around the little theatre, waiting for the puppets to begin. Such a merry scene.

Mother is to follow in the carriage with Frances and Alice. I will meet Oliver inside as soon as he arrives, if indeed he is not already here, so he can make the introductions. As we dismount our grooms are waiting to take our horses, as they travelled by cart yesterday. Daniel is grinning from ear to ear as he takes Arabella's reins. I can see he is enjoying this new scene tremendously.

"I'll take her Mistress Elizabeth. Master Oliver said to tell you he is waiting in the main hallway."

"Thank you, Daniel," I reply cheerily and call over my shoulder to my father, "Oliver is waiting inside for us, father."

As we enter the grand hallway, I can see my two brothers are overwhelmed by the opulence of this place. It is Sir Oliver's country seat but it is more like a palace. I too have never seen anything like it. The house is kept in constant readiness should Good King James visit. As he has not yet been welcomed at Hinchingbrooke this year, there is a possibility that he may arrive without warning.

There are at least twenty servants in attendance as we greet Sir Oliver. He barely returns our greeting before he is taking my father off to discuss merchants' business with him. After the introductions, Oliver and I are pleased to take a walk around the beautiful gardens.

It is like a dream come true. I feel very important in these surroundings. To think this is a relative of my fiancé. I feel quite dowdy in my plain gown and hood. Everyone seems to dress in silk and ruffs in such beautiful, expensive colours.

"I know that your father has an interest in rose-growing. I'm sure he would enjoy a stroll through these gardens, Elizabeth," Oliver remarks as we imbibe the heady perfumes in the rose garden.

"Yes I am sure you are right, Oliver," I reply, "but your uncle seems insistent in talking business to him. I did not expect so many merchants to be here, did you?"

"Yes, the charter is usually granted to St Ives but my uncle's close connection to His Majesty enabled him to divert this year's festival to be held at Hinchingbrooke. Sir Oliver is keen to extend his connections in the new monopolies."

Cromwell & Elizabeth - The Beginning

I am slightly irritated as I am sure such a fair will not advantage my father's business. The merchants have already established their links at Smithfield and he will not tolerate interference. I had thought the fair was to be merely entertainments and not trade. This will be a delicate matter and I don't want to distress either my father or Oliver, so I proceed with caution.

"Oliver, I don't think people can go backwards. The leather traders are using Smithfield now. I do not think they will go back to the market system for their trade."

Just at that moment I catch a glimpse of my father striding away from Sir Oliver and he looks slightly irritated. I am so glad when he joins us because I know the roses will distract his attention.

"Such beautiful blooms, Elizabeth, what do you think?" my father gasps at the beauty around him.

"Yes, father, walk with us a while." I reply.

The three of us enjoy the scene before us and I am glad a disagreement has not arisen. I am so enjoying this opportunity to be with Oliver and just absorb the atmosphere of the fair. As we re-enter the hallway of this huge mansion, I am again captured by its ornate design and the nobility of the columns. The music has already started in the ballroom and I can hear the rustle of the ladies' dresses as they begin the measures.

We enter the ballroom and the beautiful colours of the ladies' gowns take my breath away and I really feel quite dowdy but the feeling is soon forgotten as Oliver offers me his arm and, as I glimpse backwards, I see my father is smiling.

To dance is quite a new experience for me. Of course I have learnt the steps but we have never been to such an occasion for dancing before. Father does not really approve but has allowed our enjoyment to appease our new relatives. Oliver greets many of the young men as we pass on the dance floor. I suppose some of these will be his cousins but of course the opportunity to meet them all has not arisen. I am struck by their finery. I wonder will this be what my life will be like as Mistress Cromwell?

I see my mother and sisters sitting rather awkwardly to one side and I ask Oliver if we might join them. They seem very pleased to see us.

"Mother, are you quite well?" I ask, worried that she might want to retire early.

"Yes, Elizabeth, you young people must take the opportunity to enjoy the festivities. Oliver can you not find some partners for Frances and Alice?"

"Yes of course Mistress Bourchier," Oliver replies and glides off to fetch two of his cousins who are only too happy to oblige. They are introduced and they lead my sisters to join the dancing. I can see by their faces my two sisters are delighted.

I have never experienced such a night. The fun of dancing is matched only by the fact that Oliver is my partner. He has scarcely left my side the whole time. He is light of foot and very knowledgeable about the steps. We stay up well into the night, feasting and dancing and I am deliriously intoxicated with the atmosphere until my lady mother indicates it is time to retire.

We have barely laid our heads on our pillows, when we are disturbed by shrill screaming. I put my cloak over my shift and rush downstairs to see what has occurred. Goodwife Appleby is being carried into the hall and I can see blood streaming from a gash on the back of her head. She looks very still and pale. Sarah and Rachael are screaming hysterically, their dresses in disarray. It is really a shocking sight to see them. I rush to Sarah first,

"Sarah, what's happened?" I cry. It takes her a good few minutes before she can tell me,

"Oh Mistress Elizabeth we've been attacked. We were walking to our quarters. Rachael and I in front. We had had such an entertaining evening with the other servants of the house. Goodwife Appleby was behind us just a pace. Suddenly two men, sailors I think, foreign speaking, struck the Goodwife from behind. She fell to the ground. Before we realised it, they started to attack us. Oh the violation ... I can still smell the rum on his breath. Strong drink, not ale. He fumbled..."

At this Sarah begins to cry, tears streaming from her eyes. She is clearly distressed. Goodwife Appleby has already been settled in her quarters, insisting she wants to recover by herself. The doctor has been instructed to examine her wound and make suggestions about her recovery. Sir Oliver has reached us and taken command, directing the other visitors to return to their rooms. He ushers us into his study and pours some strong drink, which he hands to Sarah and Rachael.

I feel so wretched - as if this has happened to me. Tears are streaming down my face too, so that when my father enters, he does indeed think that I have been attacked. The local sheriff and the doctor are called and we are waiting on them to appear. Rachael is also distraught and I pat her hand to reassure her and calm her. To my surprise this does indeed have the required effect.

"Father, I am going upstairs with Rachael. She can speak to the sheriff tomorrow. I will not have her further distressed just now." I do not listen to anyone but support Rachael as she limps upstairs to the servants' rooms.

Sarah follows us and I observe father put his hand up to stop the sheriff but allows the doctor to follow us upstairs. Each of the women is examined in turn by the doctor as I prepare chamomile. At last he announces his verdict,

"Rest and cold cloths to be put on the swelling . There is some bruising but no extreme violation."

Oh, I am so relieved. Rachael's leg was swollen and bruised as she fell to the ground and Sarah's arm was severely wrenched when the sailor tried to embrace her. It was just so fortunate that Daniel, as he was taking the air, heard the commotion and shouted,
"Ere, what's going on?"

The sailors fled. No-one could recall in which direction. But how will we ever recover from this? How could I have been so vain? So easily influenced by finery, glitter and amusements? I blame myself for bringing us here!

Chapter 18. Aftermath

Oliver
Huntington 11 June 1620

As Oliver rode back to Huntington, he knew he would have to report on the fair in an honest manner. His mother was a discerning woman and would immediately know that something had occurred. It would not take long for the servants in the neighbourhood to bring the gossip back to the great houses of Huntington – Hinchingbrooke was after all just a stone's throw away. Certainly Elizabeth had received quite a shock and for that he was sad. She had lost her wonderful naivety, he thought. She blamed herself for the attack on her maids. Oliver could not understand why. No one could have known the foreign sailors would arrive like that; it was quite unheard of. They had not been located since, either. Probably they had jumped on the back of a cart and made their way to a port such as Harwich, before the alarm had been raised.

"Uncle Oliver has done all he can to catch the culprits, mother," Oliver insisted. "He has set men out on horseback to give chase, although they are not sure of the direction they were heading."

Mistress Cromwell did not reply. Her usually pleasant face was stern. She had no liking for her brother-in-law and this incident only fuelled her mounting disapproval.

"Oliver, you must remember the Bourchiers are a strict God-fearing family. You have jeopardised your union with this wealthy family by a foolish judgement to accept an invitation for fun."

Mistress Cromwell paused as she did not seem to have Oliver's attention. She continued, "Anyway I'm sure there was more to such a gathering than fun from Sir Oliver's point of view. He had another reason in mind, Oliver. Was it something to do with the merchants there? Were Walden and Bernard in attendance? Maybe it was something to do with them."

Mistress Cromwell was considering this matter with the unease she had felt previously. She knew Sir Oliver Cromwell far better than Oliver did.

"Mother, don't worry. Sir James doesn't hold me responsible for the raucous goings-on at a Whitsuntide fair. That is, after all what it was. The wedding is two months away and it will go ahead. Yes, indeed Elizabeth was quite distraught. She was sobbing so in the chapel on Sunday but she will settle and calm down. I will leave her alone for a couple of days and then ride over to Little Stambridge Hall and reassure her of my love. We have become very close in our recent outings. She is such a dear sweet maid! You will see, Mother, all will be well."

Suddenly, Oliver's demeanour slackened. His main concern had been explaining the misadventure from Elizabeth's point of view but it occurred to him that perhaps his mother was becoming aware of something which he had missed.

"But I do take your point about the merchants, mother," he said, "I don't know what transpired between Sir Oliver and Sir James but Sir James was certainly in a hurry to discontinue conversation with him."

Margaret had come into the Hall while they had been talking and overhearing the conversation, she voiced her opinion.

"Well if Walden and Bernard were there it means they hope to gain something, Oliver." She said.

"Yes but what could it be?" Mistress Cromwell asked.

"They want a new charter to be granted by King James; everybody in Huntington knows that. But who will recommend them? ..... Sir Oliver, of course." Margaret said.

Oliver looked thoughtful as he said, "What would Sir Oliver gain by conniving with Walden and Bernard?"

He paused for only a second, and then a look of understanding crossed his face. "The licence for 'The George'." He slapped his leg as it became clear to him.

"But surely Sir Oliver would have told you about such an agreement, if they was one, Oliver, wouldn't he? After all if they get a new charter all the business will be monopolised by them for the whole of their lifetime! No one else will have a chance." Margaret was quite weighed down by her own deduction.

"That's as maybe, Margaret, but the politics of this town are a secondary consideration to us now. Oliver's relationships with his new family are in jeopardy. You make too light of a serious assault, Oliver." His mother replied.

Margaret moved away from them and busied herself with the fresh rosemary which had been set aside on the table. She sniffed in the strong aroma. Rosemary seems to clear the head, she thought.

Oliver brought the conversation to a close quite decisively by his silence. Mistress Cromwell had heard a little catch in his breath as Oliver had described Elizabeth's reaction during the chapel service. She knew Oliver was putting a brave face on a potentially volatile situation. She also knew the damage had been done and there was nothing she could do to undo it. She would have to leave the matter in the hands of Almighty God.

The sisters who were silently sewing at the end of the hall felt the tension. They gazed at their mother, unused to this stillness. Anna and Catherine exchanged knowing glances. They had already overheard the servants' gossip in town. This had transported them from disappointment at not being allowed to attend the ball to relief and security that they had not endured such an outrageous attack.

The Cromwell females retired not sure what the future would bring. Not since Robert Cromwell's death, had such gloom hovered over the household. Oliver left the house, walking in the direction of the Post House. These ideas had to be shared with William, but by the time the sun had set, he had still not returned.

Chapter 19. Rebirth

Elizabeth
Little Stambridge Hall 2 June 1620

Mother has agreed that I can take my meals alone. Yes, our modern house affords me my own room now – Alice moved in with Frances more than a month ago to enable me to prepare for my wedding. Of that I am glad. I need time to be alone and to reflect on the events of the past few days. I am still prone to weeping at the least provocation – the beauty of a rose, the lilting call of the nightingale. Rachael has returned to Newton Tony, and Sarah does not want to talk about the incident, saying that these matters only provoke sorrow and she and her sister wish to continue their lives as best as is possible.

Yes, I blame myself. I had said that I wished the servants to have fun and rest for Whitsuntide but if I truly examine my motives, I know I was intrigued to be at this noble house, mixing with titled people, feeling that somehow their manners and customs would rub off on me. These are not noble values. They are the ambitions of a vain heart. I cannot discuss this with father, as I am ashamed to admit my failings. I have been much at prayer: I plead with the Lord Jesus for his forgiveness. How can I ever run a pious household if I am so easily tempted into these immature pleasures? Lady Joan was right. Her motives in her displeasure were not to stop our enjoyment but to keep us on a righteous path. I can see that now. She is so fortunate to have Reverend Ezekiel Rogers to guide her. I remember that she confided in me that the reverend had advised her that we should be careful in the friends we choose and the company we keep. He is so wise. I have been reflecting on my motivations in my quiet moments and I feel that God is listening to me,

"A humble heart He will in no ways cast out."

Rosalie Weller

The words of the bible bring comfort because I cannot go to mother for counsel. There is no one I can go to. The world seems to have just moved on. I know Sarah, Rachael and Goodwife Appleby do not blame me in any way; they have been so generous in their lack of apportioning blame. They say only that their assailants are responsible and that they had enjoyed themselves up to the point of the attack. No one else is 'brooding' as mother calls it. But in the past few days I have been changing. My heart is comforted by the words I read in the Bible and I feel a strange sort of peace, as if I am forgiven and all will be well. I wonder. Is this how Peter felt on the shore of Galilee as he met Jesus when our Lord cooked his breakfast? Yes, there seems to be some similarity. Peter denied Jesus and saw him crucified, but then Jesus returned to cook his breakfast. Peter couldn't believe his past was forgiven, his denial, his fear his anxiety – all gone. Just like mine.

In this last day, I have felt as if this burden has been lifted from my shoulders. I cannot explain it. I have heard of this happening before but never expected it to happen to me. It seems so strange that I cannot share these feelings. I shall fix my mind on the good I can do as Oliver's wife in Huntington. I have made a promise to myself and to Jesus that I will never again be swayed by a love of finery, appearances and titles. I have always condemned my mother for this sort of vanity and yet now I have found the same failing in myself. If there is something I can do to make amends, I am sure God will show me. Penances are for papists! I have not been able to discuss these new thoughts with anyone, not even my dearest Alice. Since I have found this peace I see the world in a new light. The primroses seem more vivid and vibrant – yellow as the sun. I take joy in simple pleasures; I delight in the laughter of the farm children.

I hear a movement outside my door and I know who it is.

"Father, father, come in," I call out.

"My dearest Beth," he says as he enters. "Dear child, are you over this melancholy yet?"

"Father, oh father, I cannot explain how a peace has come over my troubled soul. I have been going over the stories of Jesus, you used to tell me. And yes I have been much in prayer. I blamed myself because it was I who said we should go to the fair. I gave you the reason that the servants must enjoy time to rest. But that was not my true motive, father. Yes, I wanted the servants to enjoy it but it was more than that; I wanted to enjoy it, too. My troubled heart is taking solace. I realise now that no one is to blame for this unruly attack. But the Lord has shown me how vain and ungodly my heart is. I have been foolish and for that I have asked His forgiveness. But more amazing than that, I know I have received the forgiveness that I craved – I have received forgiveness from God!"

"My dear child, I have prayed for this day since your birth. God has turned this evil attack into a blessing from him. Praise be to God." Father replies.

He rests my head gently on his shoulder and just whispers, "Beth, my sweet girl," over and over again. I feel an overwhelming love which is so pure and so profound. My very being overflows with God's love? I fall asleep dreaming with a peace I have never felt before.

Chapter 20. Finances

Oliver
Huntington 23 July 1620

Oliver had left his house in a thoughtful mood. His reassurances to his mother had been less than truthful. Again William had been a comforting friend. William did not think it was likely that Elizabeth would renege on the agreement that had been reached, but it was possible. And if she did she would do so with all sympathy from society.

In the days that followed, Oliver continued his life much as before. He was less troubled by the recent events after he had briefly visited Little Stambridge Hall when he was reassured of Elizabeth's love for him. She was an honourable woman and she would not break her promise to him, particularly as she considered the unfortunate incident at the fair to be her fault. She did not assign any blame to Oliver at all – or to Sir Oliver. He was comforted by her sober reflections although he was a little alarmed that her sense of fun seemed to have diminished.

The wedding was now just one month away. He was not excited by the prospect of the ceremony, merely accepting as inevitable the fuss of his mother and his sisters made and their chatter about gowns, accommodation and fine food. Aunt Joan had been exceptionally generous in providing the groom's share of the finances for which he was grateful. True he had to endure several lectures on the duties of a husband but that was a small price to pay. Aunt Joan had heard about the unfortunate incident at the fair but she perceived both Oliver and Elizabeth as innocent victims at the hands of the debauched household of her flamboyant brother.

He was a little troubled that his mother would have to continue with the brewhouse to provide an additional income, but he hoped Elizabeth could come to terms with that when she eventually found out. He knew that such discovery was inevitable but he preferred to delay the eventual storm it would cause. Deceit did not come easily to Oliver but he knew this was necessary.

The small income from the tenanted land would barely cover the cost of food for them all. He hoped that an entry into civic duties would provide a small amount but he was reliant on the good nature of his fellow citizens of Huntington to provide gifts for the advice and services he provided. As this was on an ad hoc basis he could not really plan a financial future on it.

Oliver resolved once more that he must have another private conversation with Sir James. He could think of no other action to ease his mounting financial crisis. He did not want his fiancée to be involved in any arrangement he could come to with his father-in-law, so he decided the best course of action would be to meet with Sir James at his place of business, the merchant houses in London. This necessitated an early rising the following day.

The ride from Huntington to the City of London was arduous and took longer than he expected. He had hoped to call at Lincoln's Inn on his way. It would be pleasant to reacquaint himself with its present students but a shortage of time meant an immediate path to Leadenhall Market where he expected to find his future father-in-law.

He was surprised that Chestnut begun to show signs of distress at the commotion of the London streets but it had been over a year since his brief studies in the capital city ended. He dismounted and led the nervous horse through the unfamiliar streets. A sudden burst of rain had filled the track with puddles, which splashed uncomfortably on his hose. Rugamuffins constantly begged him for coins, which he did not have: half-starved boys weaved their way between the travellers. Oliver felt less desperate than he had ever felt as he looked at these despairing ones. He did at least have a roof over his head and food on the table. These poor lads had nothing.

Ahead he could see a cart with leather skins, newly tanned and was reassured that he must be nearing his destination. He followed as the cart made a right turn into Leadenhall Street. A huge warehouse opened before him with a cacophony of sound. Traders were calling out their wares to the casual visitor but it was mostly the apprentices inspecting the leather with their masters which attracted his attention. Each one wanted to get a good deal so they could carry on their shoe and boot trade.

Oliver glanced quickly at the traders, hoping to spot Sir James without delay. And there he was, talking intensely with one of the shoemakers and pointing at the leather skins on the stall. Then he passed his customer on to one of his assistants and engaged the next shoemaker. Oliver was impressed with how quickly Sir James was able to sift through the potential customers and assess their needs and redirect them. Yes, now he could see his old friend Richard and his brother, Thomas Bourchier, working alongside the assistants. Oliver stepped back as he didn't want to catch their attention. If they saw him, they would be sure to mention it to Elizabeth and he didn't want to be questioned about the purpose of this visit.

To his right was a structural column which he was able to slip behind and still observe the scene. The warehouse was full of both traders and buyers so that his presence could easily go undetected for a while, but he was clearly a gentleman and not a trader. As he pondered his situation an opportunity arose as a juggler entered the warehouse to entertain the weary traders. Sir James, seeing a short diversion in business strode towards the entrance of the warehouse, just near where Oliver was standing.

"Good day," he engaged Sir James, and merely smiled giving the older man the opportunity to continue the conversation.

Sir James, never being short of a word to say, was delighted although somewhat surprised to see Oliver.

"Oliver, how strange to see you here today."

"Yes, sir," Oliver hesitated, "I have come quite decidedly to talk to you, Sir James.'

There was no tension because of Sir James' easy manner and it took Oliver only a few seconds to explain the purpose of his visit, which did not seem unexpected. Sir James could not have been more attentive and understanding. Oliver did not need to give any further details about the reason for his financial needs. Sir James assumed quite wrongly that Oliver's problems had arisen again because of his late father's mismanagement. To Oliver's delight his future father-in-law considered the sum of money spoken of as a further gift and not a loan.

Sir James seemed ready to usher Oliver back into the warehouse, so delighted was he to meet him, but Oliver did not have any interest in the leather trade, He found the stench of the leather stung his nostrils and he shrunk back in disgust as he saw Elizabeth's two brothers handling the animal skins. When he had thought out the plan to visit Elizabeth's father at his place of work, he had not thought through the practicalities of what such trade meant. Now he was faced with its realities, he observed to himself that he could not get accustomed to it.

His business completed, Oliver was at a loss whether to ride home at once or to take accommodation for the night before curfew started. He looked at his tired palfrey and decided that he did not want to ride her hard, for surely that was what a speedy return would mean. The Playhouse was in the vicinity and could provide a relaxing diversion. For a fleeting moment Oliver considered that

Rosalie Weller

neither Elizabeth nor his mother would approve before he stepped on with a resolved purpose.

Chapter 21. Wedding day

Elizabeth
St Giles Church, Cripplegate, London 22 August 1620

Delighted and oh so happy! Oliver is quite matter-of-fact about the upcoming nuptials today but I know that he is pleased that this courtship can now reach its natural conclusion. We shall be like Jacob and Rachel, or Isaac and Rebecca – with a perfect love before God. I feel so blessed by the Lord now. He provides for my every need, just as he promises in His Word; he has provided this husband for me.

Father says that times have changed, but for the better. King James' Protestant upbringing has filtered through to almost every church in the land. This is a King who encourages the spiritual welfare of his people. The services are simpler than they used to be and it is such a blessing to be able to read the Bible for ourselves. I draw closer to the Lord, as I read my Bible, particularly about being a wife.

"Proverbs 31: Charm is deceptive and beauty is fleeting but a woman who fears the Lord is to be praised."

How I long to be this woman – Oliver says being godly is the quality which he wants above all else in his wife and he sees it in me. Can you believe it? It is here - my wedding day. My wedding day – how strange it is that a day is only special because of the event. August 22 was just any old day in years past and now it will always be special to me. The service is to be held at St. Giles's church just a step away, near father's London rooms in Tower Hill. We are to progress at 1.30 after the wedding breakfast. Then Oliver and I will ride to "The Friars" at Huntington. I know we stray a little from the usual custom but father says that there is no such thing as a typical wedding day any more.

Father has brought me a special blue silk gown with a matching hood following the French fashion and for once mother has not objected even though the sleeves lift up to reveal my wrists. My sisters have sat with me the whole morning, plaiting my hair. They have made a special garland with rosemary and flowers, which I place on my head under my hood.

Margaret has been so helpful. I've asked her so many questions to prepare myself for this marriage. I want to know what to expect and how to be a worthy wife and hopefully a good mother to the children we will have. I think I know how to run a good household already.

Mother's preparations for me have consisted of many lessons from the Proverbs, especially chapter 31. At the heart of it is wisdom but mother has such a gift for making all godliness seem dull. I'm sure it is not what the Lord intends but I am a dutiful daughter and listen without criticism.

'Come, sister, ... the procession is waiting."

My reverie is broken by Frances. As always, she looks so pretty. She, too, is wearing flowers in her hair, her curls are full. My heart flutters. The moment is here. We are such a happy band and as we pass, the people in the street clap and laugh at our happiness. I walk with my sisters and parents at the head of the procession and Oliver and his family walk behind us. They look so regal - all sisters and no brothers, like a queen with her courtiers. Also Mister Morley, a fellow merchant of father's, walks behind us with his family. They, too, will witness this sacred bond.

It takes us about twenty minutes to reach the church of St. Giles which is much larger than our village church. 1 am quite overwhelmed at its beauty with its high arches cascading into the carved ceiling.

The service follows the prayer book but father has been assured that we shall not have to kneel for the host and no psalms will be sung as is our custom.

"I, Elizabeth Bourchier, take thee Oliver Cromwell, alias Williams, to be my lawful husband .... to have and to hold from this day forth. And herewith I plight thee my troth." I say.

After Oliver has also said his promises, the reverend puts my hand on top of Oliver's and gives the blessing. I am sad that I will not have a ring. I would have loved a pretty band of gold but Oliver's Aunt Joan calls it a pagan custom.

Although we sing no psalms, Proverbs 31 and 1 Corinthians 13 are read by the Reverend Hunt. I see Oliver listening intently as if this is the first time he has heard these words. "Love is patient and is kind." I glance at him and know that this is the husband I have and I thank God.

When the service is finished we have a beaker of ale together to seal the agreement of our families. As we leave the church and my childhood behind, the sunshine breaks through the summer cloud and Oliver's little sisters, Jane and Robina, skip merrily and laugh.

We go back to father's townhouse and I change into my riding clothes in preparation for our journey. Indeed we have a good few hours of hard riding ahead of us. We shall be lucky to arrive before sunset. Tonight we shall be alone apart from the servants. Oliver's mother and sisters are to follow tomorrow. Father and mother and my sisters will of course return to Little Stambridge Hall. How strange it will be - I will not be accompanying them.

"Come Mistress Cromwell, we must ride," Oliver's greeting and the unfamiliarity of the address startles me for just a moment and I smile at my new husband. I was looking for Mistress Cromwell, and it is me! How absurd! My love for him must be obvious to everyone who beholds me.

Yes, I am now Mistress Cromwell and I have no regrets. I look around at my father's London rooms – many a girlhood memory of merchant furs and goods linger but they are shared with others. From today I will have new memories of life's journey, which I will share with Oliver.

I remember father proudly recounting transactions of sables for the royal family and how we laughed that royalty never pays. Father said that was a valuable lesson learned and since then he has avoided orders from the royal household. My new life as a gentleman farmer's wife will be so different from that of the daughter of a merchant but I am sure of one thing. This is God's path for me.

As we ride out Oliver says,

"I have just been speaking to your father. Sir James is bringing over Christopher Martin to entertain us with his plans to sail on the Mayflower in September. That should be interesting. What do you think?"

"When?" I ask.

"Next week sometime. They are due to sail so soon. It has to be next week. I'll invite John, Henry and a few others. It's sure to be of interest to them too. You can get some women from the village to help with the meal."

"Yes," I reply excitedly, "the Mayflower. Father has all the right connections, hasn't he?"

I laugh and we ride together towards Huntington and our new life.

Cromwell & Elizabeth - The Beginning

Part II. Mistress

Chapter 22. Wife and husband

Elizabeth
Huntington 23 August 1620

The sound of birds singing! Is it just my heart and my mood? No, it really is birds singing. How different this place is! I would have thought you could hear more birds in the country than the town. How mistaken I am. I have been married for just one day and I love Oliver more than I can say. I am sure I must look different to everyone. Surely all will notice my change from maid to mistress. I do feel so different as if I have grown up inside. I was very nervous but, to my surprise, so was Oliver. We were soon laughing at our own trepidation and sharing a very expensive bottle of wine sent from Hinchingbrooke. What a wonderful man Oliver is – strong and upright but so gentle in his caresses. The sweetness of our love remains in my body. I relive those caring moments followed by the more insistent drive to completion. I am sure that I will have a child this coming springtide. Of course there is no sign yet but I know it. I just know it will be a son. My world will be complete.

On reflection, this marriage has happened so quickly that I have barely drawn my breath to consider my changed circumstances. Just a few months ago I had been anxious and still under mother's charge and now here I am married to a respectable member of the gentry with my own household to command.

I hear the servants rise early as the sun comes up. For one day I am allowed to rise slowly as it is my first day as the mistress of the house. I laugh now at my worries that Oliver's mother would be ordering the household but Oliver has made it clear that I am the mistress and his mother will support me even though this has been her house since her own marriage. Many a young wife would be fearful in such a situation, worried that her mother-in-law would be meddling and bossy – as was my fear at first. But now I have got to know Mistress Cromwell a little, I am assured that she will help me to be a good wife to my Oliver – after all he is her Oliver as well. It is her love and her adoration of her son that reassures me. I love being married. The thought that there will always be another there to share my thoughts and desires, warms me. But I must get up now. She and her daughters will return soon.

I feel the warmth of Oliver's body as he lays beside me in this huge bed. Such a new affection! Oliver still sleeps and I rise softly so as not to disturb him.

Sarah is already in the kitchen starting the fire. Mother decided she could be with us for our first month of marriage. She seems to have recovered well from the incident at Hinchingbrooke and does not hold any complaint, for which I shall be always grateful. I blame myself for the whole incident. I was naïve and worldly, as father says, but now I have my full concentration on being a wholesome wife – godly.

We only need one fire for the cooking, as today is bright and the sunshine streams through the open shutters. Sarah has already fed the chickens and collected the eggs – a job I will normally do. I can see the shepherd has already started his journey to drive the sheep further up the hill. The landscape is unfamiliar to me. I am used to lusher fields and the more ordered towns of Essex but Huntington will do me just as well. Oliver's lands are well managed. The four tenanted farmers produce a good yield from the land and are able to pay a fair rent. Oliver has sowed part of the farm, too, with barley and peas - both yielding well. The sheep produce good quality wool for market and we are looking forward to increasing the flock. Oliver's new interest is in a beef herd, which he says he will buy soon. Father has been able to introduce some more contracts for the wool and in the future for the hides. I know Oliver was pleased about that. He has never had a good deal for his fleeces and skins.

I am used to keeping the books for father and in time I will take them over from Mistress Cromwell. I don't want to take away all her responsibilities too soon less she resent me. Our relationship has been quite courteous with both of us able to speak out clearly about what we expect from one another. I understand that is quite unique but it is because we both adore Oliver - our common unity.

Hark, I hear the hooves of the horses as Mistress Cromwell is arriving with her daughters and I hear Oliver rising from our marriage bed upstairs. Peter, Sarah's intended and now Oliver's manservant, is laying out Oliver's clothes but as he does so his low tones offer a friendly conversation with Oliver. This is such a merry household and I praise God I am part of it. I greet my mother-in-law, as she crosses the porch with Lizzie, Catherine and Anna in tow.

"Mistress Cromwell, I trust you had a good ride out and I see you have left Robina and Jane. Are they to follow in a carriage?"

"Yes Lady Joan offered her new one and it seemed too good an opportunity to pass up, so I agreed." She replied.

Lady Joan has also been very kind to me. She says I am the good wife the Lord promised Oliver since his birth. She was very fond of her brother Robert and has helped them all after his sudden death. I know they all had a sorrowful time when the estate had to be settled so shrewdly but our marriage seems to have been good closure to what could have been a legal wrangle – quite unnecessary.

As my sisters-in-law shake off the mud from their boots, I realise I am indeed pleased to see them. They all treat me respectfully in deference to their beloved brother. True, I have a great friend and confidante in Margaret who has her own household but I have got to know the younger girls a little and look forward to encouraging them in good matches as they grow into adulthood. Surely it will be a good practice for when I have my own daughters. How strange that already I have a closer bond with Oliver's sisters than with my own.

But Alice is going to be preparing for her own wedding soon. Just one day of marriage but it could as well be a lifetime. I am no longer part of the Bourchier household. How strange that I should feel so different in such a short space of time.

As these thoughts whirl through my brain I become aware of an awkwardness with which Mistress Cromwell and her daughters enter, not quite sure how they should address me now that I am the lady of the house. The tension is broken by Oliver's booming voice as he descends the stairway.

"Mother, how was your long ride back from Cripplegate? Pleasant I hope,"

Suddenly all we women are fussing around Oliver no longer tense about our new relationships, just eager to please him. I am glad. I don't mind being overlooked one bit. When Oliver is around we are a harmonious bunch! Oliver winks at me with mischief in his eyes.

"And we have a feast to plan for our special guests next week." Oliver reminds us.

Mistress Cromwell and the girls, used to Oliver's surprises, just giggle. I reflect upon this proposed visit from Master and Mistress Martin. Saints - they call themselves. They will be going on such an adventure!

Chapter 23. Master

Oliver
Huntington 23 August 1620

Oliver knew the world was at his feet. At least that is how he felt. The physical union with Elizabeth had surpassed his expectations. How could such a simple act of physical love bestow the loyalty and commitment which he had sensed from her? He was quite at a loss to explain it.

This must have been what William had meant. He and Oliver had discussed the bible's concept of one flesh; when a man and woman are joined physically it becomes a spiritual union too. They had also noted how perplexing women could be. Their moods seem to change dramatically. It was comforting to know that William's wife, Bridgett, behaved in a similar way to Elizabeth.

Oliver was surprised that Elizabeth had been so delighted at the forthcoming visit of the Mayflower adventurers. They had never really talked about it together although she must have discussed it with her father. He had wondered at one time if he might go himself but that had been pushed to the back of his mind while the marriage contract was being negotiated. Now Elizabeth had expressed some interest. Should he encourage it: should they go to the New World?

There was so much to consider. The whole of London had been abuzz with rumour, gossip and excitement, and there was increasing alarm at the growing number of deaths from the fever in the city. To some the New World seemed the only solution to a growing fear of persecution. Godly people were not able to obtain royal favour. They were being excluded in favour of papists. The former archdeacon of Huntington, William Laud, had criticised the services offered by Thomas Beard, saying they were too stern. Sir Francis Barrington had told Oliver that Laud was a dangerous superficial man – one whom the godly must be wary of.

The death of the heir apparent so suddenly had unsettled the people. Even after eight years, the people found it difficult to accept. His sickly brother offered just a shadow of the royal monarch that his late brother would have made. Years of preparation would not make this prince ready for kingship. Good King James himself seemed ever more sickly particularly after the death of his wife in the last year. However, the cessation of her indulgent court must be a good thing for the nation.

Oliver was hesitant to uproot himself from what he knew, yet there was something alluring about starting a new life. He had begun to feel a certain melancholy about his situation of late, but his nuptials had temporarily elevated his spirits. That reminded him of another problem he now faced. He would have to make another visit to London to finalise the loan from Sir James but how could he explain an absence from his new bride without arousing suspicion? How he hated secrets, but being a practical man, he acknowledged to himself they were often necessary evils. He could afford to wait a few days. His creditors had observed the niceties of society by celebrating his marriage with him and were waiting patiently. But Oliver knew that would not last.

He resolved to tell Elizabeth that he needed to advance his political ambitions and so he would have to renew acquaintances made at Lincoln's Inn the previous year. Yes, he had been disappointed to leave after only one year but even then his gambling had demanded all his available coins. He also needed to liaise with her father about the ensuing adventurers' visit. She could certainly occupy herself with the arrangements to be made for the special visitors and the guests from town who had been invited. Yes, he could do that anyway. Sir James was sure to invite him to stay at his comfortable house in Tower Hill. The Inns were just a short walk away and maybe, if he was lucky, he would be invited to attend a performance of one of Master Shakespeare's plays while he was there.

He had been so disappointed not to have been able to go on his last visit when an unexpected crisis had occurred. He put that to the back of his mind as he congratulated himself on putting his plan together. None of these ideas would seem suspicious for a newly married gentleman, to either Elizabeth or his mother.

Oliver felt he should be grateful to Lady Frances for the use of her manservant but he was quite unused to it. It seemed more trouble to instruct someone else on the preparation of your clothes than to do it yourself, but he supposed it was necessary for the females of the household. He resolved never to employ a manservant in his household himself. Lady Frances' interference in his household had been tolerated with due regard to his bride, but he would not endure it again!

As Oliver entered the kitchen and saw his new wife, he was overcome with joy and he knew at that moment that their life together would be fruitful and harmonious. He had never envisaged such happiness as he felt at that moment.

Elizabeth was already donning her cloak and it was obvious she was preparing to step out.

"Good morning, wife. Are you going into town?" he greeted her.

"Yes, I would like to see all the sights and sounds of my new home. Join me, Oliver, if you will." She replied.

"No, my darling, you know I must make preparations to meet your father. It's important for me to acquaint myself with the merchants in London. Perhaps I should go this very day. If I prepare my bag while you are out, I shall be able to leave when you return. Is that acceptable to you?"

To Oliver's delight, his wife offered no protest although she was surprised. As Elizabeth stepped out of the door, she could hear her mother-in-law teasing Oliver about his attire and his manservant.

"Mother, Peter is a fine fellow but he will have to be returned to Lady Frances. I am just not used to someone dressing me."

Oliver was hesitant to say too much as Sarah was hovering at the fire and it was not his wish to offend.

"Don't worry, Oliver. I have made arrangements for Peter to leave at the end of the month and Sarah will follow shortly afterwards."

Mistress Cromwell was careful to smile at Sarah as she said this; she too thought these servants were more than was required for her daughter-in-law to settle in. She wondered if they had been placed to report back to the Bourchiers on the comings and goings of the Cromwells. Her family had managed well enough without permanent servants. Mistress Cromwell preferred to take daily help from the town as they required it.

The garden was well maintained by Mistress Cromwell herself with only minimum input from Old Trenchard, who nevertheless insisted on a weekly visit to keep the hedges trimmed. He only required his daily meal and continued to garden for them out of respect for Master Robert.

While Elizabeth was taking her first visit into the town, Oliver began his preparations for his visit to London to see his father-in-law.

Chapter 24. New town

Elizabeth
Huntington 23 August 1620

This is my new home. As I step out of the front door, I want to examine every detail of this town. I am well aware that Oliver was born in this town and I'm sure he knows every shopkeeper, every master, every alehouse visitor that can be seen. But for me this is a new adventure. I am used to living in the country. To be sure Rochford has fewer buildings and is not as busy as this town. There is so much to explore here and so many new acquaintances to make. This county is not so pretty as my own – Essex. The land is flatter but you can see for miles without little hillocks to block the view.

There is the blacksmith working at his forge just a step from the house. A little way past the schoolhouse there is a delightful shop selling all sorts of silk and linen goods and materials: I can't wait to make some purchases. I nod to two ladies exiting that same shop and they acknowledge me as if they know who I am. Perhaps they do - our marriage was no secret but I'd forgotten that people in this town would be interested to see Master Cromwell's new wife just as much as they would be in our county. My dreaming means I do not see the elderly gentleman approaching me until he speaks.

"Good day Mistress Cromwell. May I introduce myself? Thomas Beard, schoolmaster."

Yes, Oliver has mentioned him as a pious and thoughtful man who has much influenced him. He dresses as a gentleman. I know he is not an ordinary schoolmaster but an admired and respected scholar. How pleasant to be greeted thus. I smile at him as he continues,

"I hope to call on you soon, Mistress Cromwell, if that is agreeable."

"It will be a pleasure, Master Beard," I reply feeling quite overwhelmed by my new status. As an unmarried lady, a gentleman would never have been so free in his greeting. I think I am going to enjoy being married.

"It would certainly be welcome if you could offer some guidance on the bible studies I want to instruct in the household," I continue.

He looks somewhat surprised, although not put out by my request.

"Yes, I should be delighted. I have some of the latest printings which could prove useful to you," he offers.

"And now I will be on my way, Mistress." He courteously returns his hat to his head and crosses back to the schoolyard.

Today is market day. We need no milk or cheese as Gertrude supplies all our needs. Maybe some poultry wouldn't go amiss, I muse. However, I do not have the liberty to purchase today. I still must make the arrangements with the shopkeepers and Mistress Cromwell.

But who is this leaving the premises within view? A rather stout gentlewoman shoos away the stray dog nipping at her ankles. Although she attempts to conceal her alarm, her agitation is clear to me. As I approach a young lad skilfully removes the animal with a curt nod to both of us.

"The new Mistress Cromwell, if I am not mistaken," she addresses me. Her peace is restored but I am at quite a loss. Her beautiful yellow silk gown betrays such an extravagance as I have not seen for a long time. Two younger women, whom I assume are her sisters, flutter beside her. They say nothing.

"Good day to you," I venture awaiting a proclamation of her identity.

"Yes, good day, I would be delighted if you would call on me one afternoon next week, Mistress Cromwell," she says and then after a painful silence, she continues,

"Mistress Walden of Walden Hall," and with her two chicks behind her, off she flounces.

I stand quite still to regain my composure. I know my cheeks have reddened at the excitement of such an unexpected invitation. I have not been in this town for a week and already I am sought after. I look at my dark dress and think of buying something to brighten me up as this may well be the first of many such invitations, but manage to resist the temptation. My previous encounter with my vanity still sparks in my imagination. I have married into a godly family. Fine silks and colourful ribbons are not important to them and will not be to me either. I am quite resolved.

I step a little further along the High Street for I am of a mind to call on William Kilbourne's wife, Bridgett, as I know it will please Oliver if I further her acquaintance. William has been Oliver's friend in the town since childhood. They share many interests in common. William is such a lively fellow and I wonder if his wife is like him at all. Ah here it is, "The Fountain Inn". I can see the lady of the house through the door of the establishment.

"Good day," I call out and am relieved that she hears me straightaway as I do not wish to raise my voice further.

At once a tidy, well-proportioned lady smiles a welcome.

"Good day, Mistress Cromwell, do come into our dwelling."

I am pleased by this welcome as I have come unannounced. How wonderful that she recognises me straightaway.

"Mistress Kilbourne, forgive the intrusion, but as I was walking through the High Street, I thought I would stop by to further my acquaintance with you. My Oliver is here so often talking business with Master Kilbourne."

"Yes, indeed," she replies.

As I survey the abode I am a little taken aback by the obvious bustle of the inn business. I had thought that William and Bridgett merely rented the rooms here but was not aware that they also transacted the business of the Inn. Bridgett, noticing my discomfort, explains the situation.

"Mistress Cromwell, William is responsible for the post boys here. As you know Good King James is often at Hinchingbrooke and messages must be purveyed to the town and, indeed, to London. William has been engaged to be responsible for the post. He has recently purchased a new string of horses so that his system can be the most efficient in the land, but of course we must maintain accommodation for the post boys when they are not in the saddle. We are still dwelling at the post house but must also maintain "The Fountain Inn". William is out at the moment so the tasks he usually does, have fallen to me."

I am grateful for the explanation and I am impressed by Bridgett's knowledge of her husband's business interests. The constant activity around her is handled with ease.

"You certainly have an enterprising husband, Bridgett. Such a novel idea. I won't keep you, I see that your attention must be elsewhere, but I will call on you next week, if I may."

Cromwell & Elizabeth - The Beginning

Mistress Kilbourne looks somewhat relieved that I have decided not to stay for refreshment. As I turn to leave, I see her usher an adorable little cherub back into the living space. I am wistful.

Oliver's mother has never mixed in the society of the town although I do not understand why. But it is no reason for me not to have company. Father has taught us to be careful whose company we seek; he does not want us to get into the habit of gossiping. Mother always laughs at his ideas. She says how can she pick out husbands for her other daughters if she does not attend the functions of society.

Where is the balance? Yes, I shall call on Mistress Walden and Bridgett Kilbourne but I shall not brighten up my gowns extravagantly, or buy new ones. My attire shall declare my devout faith.

I am almost at the end of the High Street now and it has been so pleasant to walk and greet all the townsfolk. I should be back before Oliver leaves if I quicken my pace. This is a fine town. The shops contain just about everything a lady could need.

Chapter 25. Degradation

Oliver

Huntington 23 August 1620

On the first day of his marriage, Oliver was pleased that Elizabeth had chosen to take a walk into the town. He had been able to deflect her wish for company by pointing out that his responsibilities lay in other directions. He was careful not to be too specific although he didn't like keeping secrets from her. But this was a necessity.

He closed the scullery door behind him and Buli bounded out from his usual corner at the side of the house. He was a Norfolk hunting dog – the runt of the litter from the Ely properties. But what a loving creature! His long floppy ears, one pure black and one mottled, gave him the appearance of a street urchin. His two black eyes were so soft and trusting. His white nose completed the colour mix adequately but it was his hunting skill which Oliver loved. He so perfectly complemented his falcon: bird and dog working together so perfectly to please him – their master. Buli looked to the sky for Joan and not seeing her began circling back to the house and then to Oliver, questioning.

Hurrying towards the brook at the boundary of the property, Oliver realised that his mother was right. There really was no reason to connect this outbuilding to the Cromwells. It could just as easily be part of the Garrett's property. He was able to slip behind the hedge, as was his usual custom, to the obscured building behind it. As he entered the brewhouse there was just one small lad there standing on the bench, stirring a huge wooden mash tun. The boy was glad to occupy himself thus and was careful to follow Oliver's instructions. Aaron Cooper was a discrete lad and not prone to gossip with others in the town. Ten years old, he was the oldest of the brood. His father was the local wheelwright and his mother served as midwife. He was glad to earn extra pennies for himself.

Cromwell & Elizabeth - The Beginning

Oliver checked the wooden casks and as he had assured his mother, all seven were still sealed and ready for sale. That would provide food for the whole month. The boy finishing his stirring, jumped down from the bench and picked up the broom. He was clearly working through a well-rehearsed routine.

"Aaron, lad, make sure to stir the brew again before you leave."

Oliver addressed the boy kindly but firmly. Aaron continued with his sweeping but nodded to his master in recognition of the command. The beautiful copper kettle for boiling the barley malt, glinted in the sunlight which was sneaking through the open door. The kettle was kept fastidiously clean and was an irreplaceable asset in this brewing business. His mother had carted it to Huntington from her family estate in Ely. It was the most beautiful, as well as the most practical, item she had ever owned and throughout their financial difficulties she had refused to give it up. Oliver was glad of that now, as brewing provided an indispensable income. He would, of course, discuss this business with Elizabeth, but in his own good time. Not yet, not yet.

Satisfied that all was in hand, Oliver called Buli and made his way back to the main house before Elizabeth reappeared. She was pleasantly distracted and full of her news about the people she had met in town.

Oliver had reconciled himself to the fact that another visit to London would be necessary to secure the promised gift. He was very pleased that Elizabeth had agreed because he had been careful to stress the necessity of the bonding of their two families. She had agreed that it was essential for her to spend time with her mother-in-law and Oliver's sisters, without Oliver being there as he was always the centre of attention with the female brood. She also had said she wanted Oliver to learn from her father about his trade.

Rosalie Weller

It could not have been easier. Elizabeth needed no persuasion, loathe as she was to part with Oliver so soon after they had married. Unaware of his previous visit to Leadenhall Market, Elizabeth gave him directions to reach her father's house in Tower Hill and she chatted brightly about his business and living arrangements. She seemed to know so much about her father's trade. Oliver would leave immediately and would stay in London for a few days. During this time, Elizabeth would make the arrangements for the visit by Master and Mistress Martin. What better way to start a clear understanding with her mother-in-law than by deciding the menu and provisions with her.

Oliver had intended to set out on that very day but when Elizabeth returned, he could not stir himself to leave her so soon. They agreed he should depart the next day. And so it was not but a day later when Oliver set out for Hinchingbrooke. He wanted to secure some letters of introduction from his uncle to a few gentlemen in London. He would then be able to give some positive account to his father-in-law to secure the loan he was desperate for.

In the distance a horse neighed not threateningly but playfully. Oliver had soon arrived at Hinchingbrooke. But he had not intended to meet either of the two men who now sat opposite him. He knew it was very wrong of him, he knew that this was the road to ruin but he just couldn't help himself. And so there he sat, despite all his good intentions, at the table of destruction.

Both men had the same Christian name, Robert, but they had different roles on the Hinchingbrooke estate. Captain Robert Ferrer was the master of the horse and this was the reason they were sitting at the table at the back of the stables, well hidden from view. Robert was relaxed in the game and looked eagerly as the dice settled on the table. He had already won a considerable amount from his companions and he was in no mood to end his lucky streak.

The bailiff, Rob Pepys, was in more haste. He did not expect to recover his losses today but he had other duties to discharge. Both had known Oliver for many years. Pepys despised Oliver. His master, son of the Great Knight, was a real gentleman and would never have sanctioned dice or cards on his property. This godson was another type altogether– called a gentleman, but a liar and a cheat.

Pepys picked up the dice, but then discarded them in favour of cards. His two companions' objections were quickly dismissed. Pepys shuffled slowly, aware of Oliver's need to recoup his losses and depart, no doubt to return seemingly innocently to his new bride. Another hour passed and Oliver's losses mounted. His mood became dark and he became agitated. He felt the weight of his own depravity. He stood up quite suddenly, startling his companions.

Captain Ferrer stood up too, keen to take leave on good terms. He held out his hand to Oliver, who merely scowled at him. Oliver reflected. If only his uncle had been there when he arrived, he would not have been lured to the table again. His mare neighed impatiently.

Oliver knew he could not now reach Tower Hill before nightfall and would be forced to stay at an inn along the route. Two hours' hard riding did not dissipate his angry mood, as he entered the courtyard of "The Bell" at Saffron Walden, without his letters of introduction.

He ordered a simple potage and retired to a dingy chamber to sleep before the lure of ale could ensnare him. Dice and cards were one temptation. Ale was another. He had cured himself of the desire for strong ale but he it seemed that nothing would cure him of the excitement of this other vice, gambling. Oliver slept fitfully, aware of the darkness of his degradation but unable to master it.

Chapter 26. A visitor

Elizabeth
Huntington 31 August 1620

We have had a magnificent first week. I have sorted out all the domestic issues, which are important. Oliver's sisters will continue with the chores they had before. I am to help with the dairy when Oliver gets the new herd and the hens. I have also offered to help Jane and Robina with their lessons. Oliver, like father, maintains that education is just as important for girls as for boys. Mistress Cromwell is to take more time to study the Bible especially as there are so many more study guides in English now. I am sure in that matter Reverend Thomas Beard will be of assistance. In the afternoons when we take our refreshment, we will be joined by Oliver who will guide us in a useful discussion about the Lord's word. I am truly happy that Mistress Cromwell has been so gracious about these new arrangements. There has only been one awkward moment.

"Mistress Cromwell I propose to ride over to Hinchingbrooke to secure a deer from the estate for our gathering. Shall I go today?"

The weather was quite fine but this suggestion met with a definite no. I will broach the subject again tomorrow.

Oliver is in London at present making new introductions. Father thinks this is absolutely necessary if Oliver is to realise his political ambitions to represent Huntington in Parliament. Of course he must make his interest known and familiarise himself with proceedings through sitting on the common council first. I think he has been discussing this with William already.

I am so glad Sarah is here to help with the preparations for our great feast, though I do not know quite how mother is managing without her. I think maybe her younger sister will have taken her place.

This is the first time that Oliver and I will host such a grand occasion together. I, of course, am used to discoursing with the merchants, but this is the first time I will be solely responsible for the victuals as well. I'm not sure Oliver feels so relaxed about it all but he says it will be good practice, as he becomes more involved with the affairs of the county. That is Sir Francis' advice.

Father will bring James and John, my brothers, with him as he feels they need to learn to participate in adult conversation. Of course Oliver's older sisters, Elizabeth and Catherine will attend as company for John and Henry. Mistress Cromwell is hesitating about Anna attending as she is so clumsy, and of course, she wants everything to be perfect. But the girl is old enough and must learn the correct way to behave. Oliver is more worried about her boisterousness, saying she will take over the conversation with frivolous matters if we are not careful.

I wonder if there will be a romance or two. Oliver says I must not get involved in silly matchmaking. It doesn't become a godly woman. He said this in a jesting tone so I'm not altogether sure whether he has another purpose in hosting this dinner than what it appears. I sometimes think I do not know Oliver at all.

We are all excited about meeting Master and Mistress Martin. Father knows them through the London merchants who he is involved with. They hail from Great Burstead, Billericay. Master Martin is a merchant by trade, and also a churchwarden. I wonder how they feel as they make their preparations. I understand they have already sold two pieces of land. Their children will not accompany them on this visit to us, as little Nathaniel is a sickly child and must recover his strength before they sail. They will stay with their grandmother.

Catherine is sitting patiently at her embroidery. A beautiful pattern is beginning to emerge.

"You have embroidered that cloth so beautifully, Catherine," I venture.

"Indeed Elizabeth. I learned from our sister Lizzie. She is sometimes slow of wit but her fingers are indeed nimble."

"Yes I have examined her work. It's splendid! I have noticed that her speech is sometimes slurred. Was it from birth?" I enquire.

"Mother says so. But with her deft fingers we are able to sell our skills to many of the ladies in the town." She lowers her voice and continues, "A word of warning, Elizabeth, mother does not like us to talk of Lizzie's condition."

Wanting to encourage Catherine, I answer,

"Well you both will be able to contribute to your keep with such a skill. You, too, could surely sell your paintings."

"Do you think so, Elizabeth," she replies "But I don't think it will be an economic necessity. I hope to be wed soon. Master Roger Whitestone has asked me already but I have waited until Oliver should marry you first."

I was not aware that Catherine had postponed her wedding. How patient and kind she is.

"Oh Catherine," I am suddenly overwhelmed with compassion for my sister-in-law. "I didn't know. We must start plans for your wedding at once."

Cromwell & Elizabeth - The Beginning

"Don't concern yourself, Elizabeth. It is in hand," Catherine replies and turns to me, her face shining with pride. Once more I am reminded that these three sisters have become so dear to me.

I can hear Mistress Cromwell talking to someone in the courtyard. I must see who it is: it sounds like a gentlewoman. As I cross the threshold I see the delightful Mistress Walden and she is dressed exquisitely in a fine gown of blue silk today. She is quite alone and as she sees me, she smiles merrily. My mother-in-law does not smile at all. Have I merited disfavour? In our first few days the relationship between us has been warm. I wonder if it is my visitor who has caused this sudden change.

"How delightful to see you again, Mistress Walden," I venture.

"Yes indeed, Mistress," she replies.

I am the mistress of the house now. I feel quite giddy with the responsibility but I must not show it to either my guest or my mother-in-law. That would be vanity.

"Do come inside and take some refreshment with us, Mistress Walden,"

As my guest steps across the threshold I am so glad Sarah is here. With just a smile, she knows she must bring something for us to drink. For once I am glad of a servant girl who is used to entertaining. I notice my mother-in-law making for the backdoor and I am quite certain she will not be joining us. Mistress Walden continues the conversation as we step through the door.

"I understand from Master Beard that you will be entertaining some adventurers next week. Lionel and I will of course be able to join you. Will they be arriving in time for dinner?"

I don't remember mentioning our guests to Master Beard. As Mistress Walden relays her intentions to me, I am trying to rack my brains to think if I have been untoward in my conversation. No, I don't think so. Her prattling becomes so irritating that indeed Mistress Cromwell might well have chosen the better path in the garden. I am relieved when after we have taken our refreshment she takes her leave and bustles out in much the same way as she appeared. I have accepted an invitation to dinner tomorrow, where I shall be able to meet other gentlewomen in the town.

It takes Mistress Cromwell no time at all to reappear and I wonder if she was waiting for my visitor to leave. But I am not left in doubt for long.

"Elizabeth," she starts scolding immediately, "Don't be taken in by Elizabeth Bowden. She is still full of airs and graces as was her mother. She is full of gossip and slandering!"

I am quite taken aback by the venom pouring forth from this usually silent woman. I am determined to find out more.

"Her name is Mistress Walden now, and she seems to be so very respectable. She was describing the development of her first son Lionel. She seems so friendly, Mistress." I reply.

"She has come here to see who you are. To see who Oliver has married. I think that at one time her parents had considered Oliver as a suitable husband for her. But they are local town's people. She ensnared Lionel Walden into marriage with her fine clothes and mischievous wiles. Don't be taken in. Have nothing to do with her, Elizabeth, I warn you. Nothing good can come from there."

"I understand that Master Walden is indeed quite the reformer in the town's affairs. Is that not so?" I challenge.

"Indeed, Elizabeth, but his reforming lines his own pockets. Elizabeth Bowden is not the gentlewoman she makes out to be. I'll say no more at the moment."

With that my mother-in-law hurries out to the garden once again, muttering about the rosemary and thyme which must be collected. I am somewhat baffled. It is quite unlike her to talk ill of our neighbours. Oliver has told me she has nothing to do with the ladies in the town. I had assumed it was her nature but maybe there is more to this than either of them have told me.

Nonetheless I shall find out more when I return this visit tomorrow and am introduced to the other gentlewomen of the town.

Chapter 27. Master Beard

1 September 1620

Oliver had not forgotten that in May he had promised to discuss matters of vital importance with Reverend Thomas Beard. He had intended to follow up on the question of the Huntington lectureship as soon as he had an opportunity. The other matter he knew would not be a theological discussion but one intended to challenge him personally. Oliver respected Master Beard. He was a fine scholar and a deeply religious man. But Oliver was just not ready to have such a conversation yet. He was burdened by his sins and he knew that deadened his spiritual life. He had been unable to pray or read his bible for months - a fact which he had hidden from both his mother and his wife. Another secret.

If Oliver had not forgotten, neither had Thomas Beard. He had ascertained from that short conversation in the street with Elizabeth what a modern but pious gentlewoman his old pupil had married and he was not a man to waste time. He had searched through the printings of bible notes which he had recently purchased in London and had found two which he knew would be suitable for Elizabeth's purpose. In spite of the considerable expense involved, he was ready to share them with her.

After a brief conversation with Trenchard as he approached the house, he knocked on the door. Mistress Cromwell greeted him warmly on his arrival and led him into the great hall. She instructed Sarah to inform her daughter-in-law of the visitor, unaware that they had met on the previous day. Before long Elizabeth joined them. She was obliged to sit on the hard chair as the two soft chairs were already occupied. Lizzie and Anna were sitting beneath the window at the other end of the hall, and Robina and Jane were outside with Margaret's children.

"You have wasted no time, Master Beard." Elizabeth said.

Cromwell & Elizabeth - The Beginning

Indeed he had not. He had intended to reacquaint Oliver with that frequent subject of his childhood - the tortures of eternal damnation. This was one of Reverend Beard's favourite subjects but not one easy to listen to. He had not had the opportunity to talk to Oliver previously and was disappointed once again at Oliver's absence. He hoped his wife would make an adequate substitute. He awaited his opportunity.

"Indeed, it is not often that I am so fortunate as to be invited to share from God's holy bible by a lady such as yourself - so it is indeed a privilege." Reverend Beard replied.

With this he handed Elizabeth two pamphlets printed on both sides. She could see that they were notes on the Psalms as the title indicated such. For the next half hour, Master Beard instructed Elizabeth on how to use the notes he shared. Mistress Cromwell made no comment as her poor literacy discounted any opinion, a fact of which Master Beard was aware but Elizabeth was not. In this matter of studying the bible Mistress Cromwell would be compliant with Oliver's wishes and take instruction from his wife.

Mistress Cromwell enjoyed visits from the learned schoolmaster. He oozed godliness. She could not understand why Elizabeth had now started questioning him about Elizabeth Bowden and what she did or didn't know about the intended visit of the Martins. Thomas Beard, though polite, was as confused as Mistress Cromwell herself but endeavoured to answer Elizabeth's probing with as best a civility as he could muster. It was with regret that Master Beard felt he should decline refreshment, offered by Mistress Cromwell, because Elizabeth had made it clear that she was on her way out.

For Mistress Cromwell it had been a very confusing day, alleviated only by the welcome interruption of the arrival of Margaret and her toddlers. Earlier Elizabeth had wanted to discuss the menu for the forthcoming visit by the adventurers and implied that she was ready to go to the butcher and put in an order for pheasants and partridge and ride to Hinchingbrooke to fetch venison. Mistress Cromwell was well aware of their true financial situation and knew that this would be out of the question. So far she had avoided a detailed discussion but she knew the questions would come. She didn't have the answers. She knew what the situation was although she did not understand quite why it had come to this.

She had asked Oliver to speak to his new bride about their situation but he obviously hadn't done so yet. This put Mistress Cromwell in an awkward situation. She had agreed to allow Elizabeth the mastery of the household, yet in reality what did that mean? All the vegetables and herbs came from their garden as did the eggs and the occasional chicken that found its way into the pot. The partridge and pheasant came from Barrington Hall when Oliver went to hawk there and it was a rare treat to get venison from Hinchingbrooke. There wasn't a lot of mastery to be had there.

Did Elizabeth want to take over the hoeing in the garden from Trenchard? Mistress Cromwell smiled to herself at that thought. As for the servants - well Sarah was Elizabeth's kin anyway. Yes, Elizabeth could have the mastery of the household whatever that meant!

Master Beard went away without having introduced his most pressing topic and vowed he must return. He was sure that had he managed to broach the topic, he would have got a far better response from Elizabeth than from Oliver on the subject of the eternal damnation of the soul.

Chapter 28. In town

Elizabeth
Huntington 1 September 1620

I am glad of Master Beard's spontaneous visit. I had not expected that he would appear so soon after we had met. Of course, I am delighted with his instruction but it has made me slightly late for my dinner engagement.

It is not really necessary to ride out to visit Mistress Walden as Walden House lies only a short walk at the North end of Huntington. However, on this occasion I shall put on my riding dress because I want the visit to appear less formal than perhaps it might otherwise do.

Arabella walks slowly along the cobbles until I approach the huge manor house. Immediately a groom takes the bridle from my hand as I dismount. This is more like the wealth I have been accustomed to at home so I feel quite at ease here. My lack of familiarity is merely of personage, not of custom.

I am announced as I complete the ascent of the stone steps and enter the immense waiting hall. Mistress Walden is at my side immediately to escort me into the great hall and introduce me to the other four gentlewomen gathered around a beautiful walnut table where dinner is ready to be served.

"I am so sorry if I am late." I say, "But Reverend Beard decided to visit without warning."

"Not at all," my hostess replies graciously.

"Delighted to meet you," coos a plump pretty-eyed matron.

"Mistress Paulina Pepys has recently married Sir Sidney Montague, and has only just moved into Brampton," explains my hostess.

"I understand your husband is acquainted with my nephew Robert, bailiff on the Hinchingbrooke estate." Paulina states.

I cannot think that Oliver would know any of the hired men on Sir Oliver's estate more than just a nod of the head. I don't know what to say so I move on. I know of both the Pepys and Montague families although I have never met either of these branches before. This female gives me a huge wink as if we share some secret jest. I find this to be totally inappropriate but I cannot fault the friendliness with which it is given.

The next visitor is more aloof and cold as she is introduced.

"Elizabeth Tallakerne, married to the barrister Robert Bernard," Mistress Walden continues.

I know, too, of the barrister Robert Bernard. He has recently been the talk of the town because of his interest in the renewed cases of witches reported in the area. Witchcraft is a subject which Oliver refuses to discuss. It holds a strange mystery for me as it was a subject on which my father has also forbade discussion. I have no personal experience of such a matter although I have of course seen the wise women selling their herbs. This has never troubled me and I can see no reason why anyone else should be troubled by it either.

"Delighted," intones a stunning beauty from behind an exquisite fan. Mistress Elizabeth Hatton, the wife of the recently shamed Sir Edward Coke. Not only was her husband dismissed from the Kings's service but she and her husband disagreed about a suitor for their daughter and a whole debacle ensued. The couple's disagreements have become common knowledge even to the extent that she refuses to use her husband's name.

"How the mighty have fallen," I reflect inwardly, but say, "I believe we are acquainted with your cousin, Frances. My mother visited her last year in Essex."

The company goes silent. The Hatton women do not like to be reminded of their misfortunes. But it is only a very brief pause for soon I am ushered into a seat and we commence dinner. These are surely the influential wives of Huntington. I am so happy!

"He is such a bright boy – barely the year and already he walks sturdily on his feet."

I know Mistress Walden is speaking of her first child and I listen with interest. That could soon be me. I hope so! I wonder about her arrangements.

"Do you employ a wet nurse?" I timidly enquire.

"Of course, Mistress Cromwell," she laughs as she answers, "otherwise I should be severely restricted in the town's affairs, then what would Lionel say?"

I listen attentively, only too aware that I am the youngest of this wifely group and the least experienced. I am glad that I can make a purposeful exit as soon as dinner is finished.

"Do excuse me, Mistress Walden. My sisters and Mistress Cromwell are waiting for me to instruct them on the bible. Yes, we are to start this very day. I was going to delay but Master Beard so graciously visited this morning with the precise instructions and a command that I am to start immediately."

Mistress Walden cannot contain her surprise,
"Well, Mistress, what a thoroughly modern woman you are! Instruction and in your home, too."

Rosalie Weller

I hear a little murmur behind me as I leave. I don't mind a bit.

I am soon back in "The Friars" where Mistress Cromwell is waiting to begin. Elizabeth, Catherine and Anna take their seats on the bench. None of them are able to read fluently as the family considered it only appropriate that Oliver should receive any education. However, since my abiding in this home, Anna has began to learn her letters but she is the only one interested in being educated. Our progress is slow as Mistress Cromwell does not encourage us in this venture but is only present to please Oliver. I am looking forward to the day when Anna will be able to take a turn in reading the good Lord's word. But today, I alone, can read. Catherine is yawning.

"Are you tired, Catherine?" I say gently, "Today we read from the gospel of Luke and from the psalms. And Master Beard has kindly loaned us some bible study notes which will help us to reflect on what we read."

"When do we read from the Psalms?" Lizzie asks in her slow drawl. "I so love the Psalms."

"After our reading from Luke. Remember Luke wrote the account which tells us what the Lord Jesus said and did. Today's reading is about the words of Jesus as he told the story of the Prodigal Son."

I am so pleased to be able to read to my new family. They seem to enjoy it too. Catherine soon forgets her tiredness and joins in the discussion we have about the elder brother who did not rejoice when his brother came home. None of us can understand his attitude at all. No, no one here would have been jealous!

Chapter 29. London

Oliver
Tower Hill 25 August 1620

Oliver rose early next day. The stench of stale ale still invaded his senses. As he approached London, the carts and wagons increased. Geese being driven ahead of him impeded his speed but caused him to smile to himself. What a grand opportunity for people to sell their wares in this great city! The noise from the increased volume of travellers, far from depressing him, actually exhilarated him.

He intended to visit Sir James before the merchant travelled to the market. It was always good to speak to a man before the troubles of the day crowded in on him. It would also mean Oliver would have time later to visit some of his old friends, as well as make new acquaintances.

Just as he reached Sir James' townhouse, he saw a hackney approaching from the other direction. Just in time, he said to himself.

"Wait up Sir James," he hailed him and was greeted by an enthusiastic laugh from his father-in-law.

"Good heavens, Oliver, what are you doing here?" replied Sir James, "Come inside, the hackney can wait."

And with that, he held up his hand to the driver. Oliver handed the reins of his horse to a waiting servant to be taken to the stable for a much needed rest, while he followed Sir James back inside. After a few hasty pleasantries, Oliver forthrightly declared the reason for his visit. Gravely, Sir James nodded his head,

"I am so sorry, Oliver. Alice is to be married soon and the Crown has imposed new licences on furs and skins so I won't be able to oblige with that loan at the moment. But I am sure it is not so desperate, eh?"

Oliver, his heart sinking tried to sound hearty.

"Don't worry, sir. No not so desperate,"

Hoping to salvage something fruitful from this London visit, Oliver then discussed an introduction to merchants who were known to his father-in-law, who could be used to further his political ambitions. Fishbourne was one such mercer whose acquaintance Oliver wished to make and he was known to Sir James. An introduction was hastily written and Oliver continued on his way, leaving his relative to pursue his business.

It had been an unwelcome shock for Oliver, but he had managed to cover his consternation and been very cautious in his reaction from this news from Sir James. He did not wish Elizabeth to be alerted to their financial difficulties by her father. He was sure he could resolve this situation without her ever finding out. He was deeply disappointed but he did know the leather merchants were protesting about the new customs imposed by Good King James on their trade, so it was no great surprise to him. He was still optimistic that much could be achieved on this day. With the letter safely in his pocket he set out to visit Richard Fishbourne.

Fishbourne was delighted to make his acquaintance. He was now a successful London merchant but, unlike Sir James, did not frequent his hometown as much as he would wish. He rarely had the opportunity to reminisce. He eagerly clasped his hands together and threw his head back in laughter as Oliver recounted the local gossip, and listened carefully to the more serious affairs of Huntington. Oliver was invited to stay to eat dinner with his new acquaintance, which pleased him very much. The table boasted a plump goose and sweetmeats which Oliver could not resist.

They discussed the matter of the lectureship at Huntington at some length and Oliver was satisfied that it would be to the benefit of his old tutor. As he took his leave, his spirits were uplifted and he looked forward to renewing acquaintances at Lincoln's Inn, before hopefully a visit to a play by Master Shakespeare. Lincoln's Inn had not changed at all since he had left. Oliver was still impressed by its lofty grandeur.

"This is a welcome relief to our studies in law," young Holborne greeted Oliver.

"Yes," replied Oliver "Is Master Pym in the courts today?"

"Indeed he is. Although we don't see him so often now that he takes his seat in Westminster. Go over to Middle Temple, Oliver. I'm sure you'll find him there."

"Thank you. Will you be going to see the actors this evening?"

"Yes, will you join us? Five at the lodgings. I'll tell the fellows to expect you."

This brief encounter brought a smile to Oliver's face as he fondly remembered his own time at Lincoln's Inn. His study had been brief and informal but it had awakened a sense of danger and duty in him. He had seen how the law could ravish unfortunates and bring them to ruin.

The distance between the Inns was short and he was soon in the Middle Temple. He recognised the sturdy figure of John Pym from behind immediately. There was no mistaking that short muscular frame even when bedecked by the traditional barrister's gown.

"Good day to you Master Pym," Oliver greeted the older man with the respect becoming his success and his birth.

"Why Oliver, what brings you here today?" Pym replied with enthusiasm.

It took Oliver only a few minutes to explain his need for introductions to the influential and powerful people trading in London. Oliver knew it would take more than this first meeting to get to know these people who would be willing to guide him, but Pym's redeeming quality – his nurturing spirit, would be used to its full advantage. They discussed the current affairs of the state. Acknowledging Oliver as a like-minded godly person, Pym was openly critical of the Crown.

"What sticks in the craw, Oliver, is this insistence by Good King James that he is appointed by God to rule on his own. So Parliament must bow to his every whim, good idea, or cost that he chooses." Pym backed up his hardline attitude by an accompanying fist thumping down on the table.

Oliver was surprised at the vehemence his advisor displayed. He had not thought through the importance some people placed on the relationship between God and the ruling elite. He had always accepted that there was an order to the world. But he had been on the wrong end of the ruling classes. Born the son of the younger son of a gentleman, fineness of birth had brought no advantage to himself or his mother. He knew he would have to make his own advantage if he were to succeed in his life. If he could make the right connections, he could take his place in the House of Westminster, a much needed step towards being able to support his wife, his mother and his sisters properly.

Pym was looking at Oliver intently. He expected a response.

"But can Good King James ignore Parliament, Master Pym?"

The question went unanswered as the lively presence of the Rich family intruded. Oliver knew the two older men slightly - Henry

Rich, first Earl of Holland, and his brother, Robert Rich, newly appointed third Earl of Warwick. It was the young boy who was with them who drew Oliver's interest. His striking appearance - dark eyes and even darker curly black hair contrasted sharply with the sandy brown hair of the two adults.

His confidence, as he bowed slightly to Oliver, was astounding.

"Good day to you - Nathaniel Rich," he introduced himself to Oliver.

"Don't mind him; he's a young pup, so sure of himself," bellowed his father, "Oliver, we knew your father, Robert, so well. Sad to hear of his sudden demise."

The conversation became more intense as the three men chewed over small details of the latest scandal – there had been no Parliament sitting for six years. While the older men talked, Oliver made polite conversation with the charming well-informed boy who seemed to know more about what was going on in the Royal Court than any of the adults! After a modicum of time had passed Oliver saw his chance to exit and with a gallante farewell, he made his way to Staples Inn in Chancery Lane.

Oliver was reassured by the introductions he had made. Now he was looking forward to an evening of fun. It was but a short walk and he enjoyed the vibrant bubble of London. Even this late in the afternoon, the traders were plying their wares to anyone who would listen. The prices were reduced on perishable goods as, at this time, any price was better than rotting fruit and fish. He offered a shilling for a halibut as the fishmonger was about to close his doors. Delighted at this chance of a bargain and a useful contribution to put in the pot, Oliver soon reached the fellows.

Within the hour a bawdy bunch of law students were making their way across London Bridge towards Blackfriars for an impromptu rendering of "The Winter's Tale" to be performed by The King's Men. Since his death Master Shakespeare's work had become ever more popular. Oliver knew Elizabeth would probably not approve of this visit but better to beg forgiveness than to ask permission, he thought.

"We're in luck," said Holborne, "The players are doing "The Winter's Tale after all. There was some talk about them doing Webster's "Duchess of Malfi" but I've heard that has been postponed until next year."

Lively chatter followed all to the celebration of their good fortune on this evening. Oliver marvelled at the superb Playhouse – twice the entrance fee of "The Globe" but you could be sure only to rub shoulders with gentlefolk.

The company of his good friends reassured Oliver and lifted his spirits. Blackfriars Playhouse was an impressive building, built for the popular entertainment. The buzz of anticipation oozed around him. The audience was excited. This play was a common theme which all could enjoy – jealousy and misunderstanding - and Master Shakespeare was a master of words that would entertain all who came to see the play. As Camillo and Archidamus made their entry onto the stage a hush ensued and Oliver felt privileged to be part of it.

Chapter 30. Entertaining

Elizabeth
'The Friars', Huntington 2 September 1620

Henry Downhall arrived last evening and he says he is quite determined to continue the debate he started with Oliver these three years past at Cambridge. Unfinished business he calls it. John Hampden is riding over with father. We are really honoured that he is joining us. He is becoming quite the statesman in Westminster. And to think he is a first cousin to Oliver.

I hear Margaret's children laughing as her family cross the stile from the field. The children always accompany her when she visits and Mistress Cromwell invariably tends them so Margaret can converse with me. They live so near to us so we see them often. Suddenly it's all happening. Father's group canter in and the grooms stand by waiting at the same time that Lizzie comes out of the front door to greet her sister and the children.

I greet my father and I see Anna is welcoming Alice and John Hamilton. I feel quite proud that I am now my own mistress. I'm surprised to see that my mother is not with the party and I look questioningly to father to understand why, although I cannot say that I am sorry.

"Mother is quite indisposed today. She won't be joining us and sends her apology to you and Oliver, my dear. Ahum... she has been so busy with the arrangements for Alice's wedding, she has tired herself out. So sorry." My father, always the peacemaker, apologises and we both know this is a weak excuse.

Can it be that now I am no longer a burden to be married off, she is not concerned about me? No matter. Ah there is Alice with her fiancé, conversing now with Catherine. They are probably discussing weddings as both are to be married soon. I look around the party and see a slight young woman who must be Mistress Mary Martin dismount. The ride over has taken its toll on her; I do not think she is used to riding so far. Indeed she does look very out of place.

"Mistress Martin, do come and sit. I'm sure you must be quite exhausted after your journey," I say and she responds in a friendly wave of her hand as she follows me into our house. The sound of another horse and carriage startles me as I am not expecting any other guests. I look back to the courtyard and see a very expensive carriage arriving and who is that emerging?

"Good Heavens," I exclaim.

I have quite forgotten that we could expect Mistress Walden and I haven't warned Oliver. Well, with Henry arriving last night and Oliver staying in London longer than I expected is it any wonder?

The fine carriage draws up and stops in the courtyard. Trenchard is not quite sure how to respond but he scuttles to the carriage door, hoe still in hand. I notice a look of disgust as Mistress Elizabeth Walden emerges wearing the finest silk I have ever seen. It is a magnificent yellow, as bright as the sun and suits her complexion splendidly. Torn between politeness to Mistress Martin and panic to receive our unexpected guest, I whisk Mistress Martin into my mother-in-law's hands and rush back out the door.

"Mistress Walden," I stammer, "I had no confirmation that you would be joining us today."

"My dear," she lies, "I made myself very clear when you visited, but a couple of days ago."

I catch Oliver's horror-stricken face out of the corner of my eye and wonder what on earth is the matter with him? Fortunately Sarah has observed the whole event and has quickly laid a further two places.

Oliver sensing my discomfort, comes to my side and says,

"Will Master Walden be joining you?"

"No," she replies rather tartly, "He is busy with the affairs of the town today. I bought my sister with me."

The hall table is already laid for dinner, which Sarah indicates, can be served quite soon.

"But Downhall, my good friend, it is God who calls us to salvation," I can hear Oliver good-naturedly arguing with his friend and know that this is the start and not the end of the theological discussion. I am quite relieved he has regained his usual good-humoured composure.

"Oliver," I remind him, "we have other guests to include in your discussion. Please wait until we are all seated." I smile at him and Henry, as if they are two naughty children and they respond amicably.

Oliver takes his place at the head of the table, with father on his right. Master Martin is put just a little further down the table on father's right, in respect of his great adventure. The rest of us sit in our regular places with Oliver's sisters and my brothers taking places further down the table.

Sir Francis Barrington has also turned up with Thomas. I am surprised that Lady Joan and her daughter-in-law, Frances have not accompanied them, as I was sure they would be interested to hear Master Martin speak about his new adventure.

The lamb has been slaughtered early this year and I am glad, as there won't be many other occasions like this one. In the end it was my mother-in-law who arranged our table. She said there are more important things to concern myself with, and she was right. What a privilege for us to hear first-hand about the plans Master and Mistress Martin are making to join others on a journey to the New World.

"Mistress Martin, are you excited or apprehensive to go on this great adventure?" I ask her, to set the conversation going, so we can all gain some insight into this interesting life of hers.

"Well, Mistress Cromwell, I must follow my husband to be sure. My Nathaniel is none too well at the moment and certainly there isn't anything to keep us here. Maybe the different climate will do him good!"

'I understand there was an incident at the church recently which helped you make your decision. Whatever happened?"

Mary Martin turned to look me full in the face, her eyes welling with tears.

"These times are very confusing, Mistress Cromwell," she continued, "My Christopher has been reading his Bible for himself and it doesn't say anything about kneeling to take the Host. So when we went to take the host, Christopher said to me, don't kneel Mary and I didn't."

"Oh how very brave," I respond, "Then what happened?"

"The minister passed by us, not offering to us. He just went on to the butcher and his wife. It was as if we didn't exist. It is popery to be kneeling, isn't it Mistress Cromwell? Christopher says the communion is just to say we remember what Jesus did on the cross. It's nothing more than that, is it?"

Mary Martin seems unsure and in need of encouragement. Our church in Little Stambridge has been reformed for quite some years now and I am surprised that these simple folk have been so affected and discouraged in their faith.

"Mistress Martin, you did the right thing. Our communion in Little Stambridge and, of course, Reverend Beard at St. John's here in Huntington have followed the new ways for quite a number of years now. I am surprised that you are hemmed in by this popery."

On my other side, Margaret taps me gently and Mistress Martin starts to converse with Mistress Cromwell on her other side.

"Oh Elizabeth, how exciting this is to have these adventurers to converse with. Mistress Martin seems so ordinary and yet she is going to the New World with her husband and children, moving far away. I cannot imagine what I would do if Valentine wanted to go with them. What about you? Would you go, Elizabeth?"

The thought had indeed crossed my mind when father had told me about the Merchants' scheme to fund the pilgrims and others to go to the New World. In fact father was rather keen that Oliver and I should consider a new life. His interest of course was from the merchant's point of view. He would have us there to make contracts for the furs and other commodities the New World would offer. They say that the beaver fur is such good quality. How I love father, always the businessman!

But there would be other things to consider. How would we fare if we were to leave England – our home. True there would be no persecution, nor popish ways. We could pursue our faith unhindered. I could continue with my studies. Oliver could farm new land with far more acreage than we have here – an opportunity he hasn't really had since his father has squandered all the family money. I heard last week that Hinchingbrooke is also to be sold. Even Sir Oliver's fortune has declined. These nobles may be good at entertaining royalty but they have no head for business! Maybe the New World would give Oliver and me a new start!

Rosalie Weller

Times are so uncertain. It was only three weeks ago that I was musing about what it would be like to live at Hinchingbrooke and be visited by Good King James, but soon it is to be gone from the family altogether.

'Do not store up treasures on earth.' St. Matthew tells us and how true that seems to be. I have learnt my lesson from the fair.

Chapter 31. Adventurers

Oliver
'The Friars' Huntington 2 September 1620

Oliver was not sure what the wife of the person he most despised in the town of Huntington was doing at his dinner table. Since he had returned he had barely had time to check with Elizabeth about the arrangements for the food which would be served, let alone which guests had confirmed their invitations His mother had mentioned that there had been some difficulties with the provisioning while he had been away, but he would be able to smooth that over. His two day visit to London had stretched to four days. It was clear from the conversation that Mistress Walden had introduced herself to Elizabeth when they had met in the town. It seemed like a coincidence to naïve Elizabeth but Oliver knew it was contrived. Lionel Walden was using his wife to find out Oliver's business.

Oliver manoeuvred the seating arrangements at the dining table so that Mistress Walden and her sister sat on either side of Henry Downhall. He was loathe to do his good friend such a disservice but Henry was well able to cope with such a misfortune. He and Henry would have plenty of opportunity to debate during this stay. Elizabeth too was relieved to see that Oliver guided the two unexpected guests to the far end of the table, well out of harm's way.

Before dinner, Oliver had made sure the seat on his left was vacant and invited Thomas Barrington to sit there. During the second course, he seized the opportunity to ask about the much-needed loan.

"I really am sorry Oliver, we have needed so much money for Frances' medicine," Thomas' anxious face contorted with discomfort. "Why don't you approach Sir James?" he continued.

Oliver was immediately sorry he had approached his cousin and friend. He could see Thomas was disquieted and as he scrutinised his face, he could see there was something amiss. He did not want to reveal that he had already approached Sir James and been unsuccessful, so he attempted to make light of the matter.

"Thomas," he said, "You seem out of sorts. Is there something troubling you? Don't worry about a loan. I'll settle some other way."

Thomas groaned. It was a sort of despair deep from within. Oliver had sometimes felt like that himself but to see it acted out in another human being was more than he could bear. He turned his attention to the other side of the table, ashamed to not have offered some solace. He did not want to hear another man's troubles. He was relieved when he noticed his mother, sitting on Thomas' other side, engaging him in conversation about her garden.

He directed his attention to the guest of honour, Master Martin, who fortunately was not engaged in conversation with anyone at the time. To outward appearances Oliver seemed the perfect host, engaging with his guests in turn. Inwardly his despair was eating his soul. How had it come to this!

Oliver knew he was being selfish. He had just ignored the distress of a much loved cousin and friend because he was more interested in his own business – the business of borrowing money to pay off his shameful gambling debts. That matter had occupied his whole being since returning from London. His thoughts, his motivations, his actions – all had been engaged in his depravity. He could not conjure interests in the Martins or their proposed trip. He could not enjoy the feast his wife and mother had prepared for fear of the cost of it all. Yes he was the perfect host, taking his place in Huntington society with his new wife but his innards were twisting horrifically and he could not do a thing about it.

"Oliver, I hear you visited Lincoln's Inn this week. Did you see John Pym?" Henry called out to him from almost the other end of the table. Most of the guests were engaged in their own conversations and were able to ignore this rudeness, but Oliver noted that Elizabeth looked up at him when she heard this. Something else he would have to explain.

"Yes," Oliver called back to Henry, "We must discuss Pym's ideas later. We don't want to bore the other guests with our private interests. We must take this opportunity before us, to find out every little detail about this adventure."

The other men nodded to Oliver in agreement and the conversation reverted to the long trip on a sailing ship. Both Master and Mistress Martin had spent considerable time contemplating the ardours of their forthcoming journey, so as to prepare themselves. They knew they would probably suffer lack of provisions and disease aboard the ship.

"I hear the colony of Virginia is beginning to thrive since De le Warr's group arrived," Elizabeth questioned Mistress Martin.

"Oh yes, Mistress Elizabeth, and to think it was nearly all up as the last remaining strangers sailed out of the bay just ten years ago. It is God's will that they turned back with the arrival of De le Warr's' group and the colony survives, and by God's will, we will join them."

It had been easy for Elizabeth to increase her knowledge of the new Colonists, as her father's connections to the Merchant Adventurers provided her with all the information she required. To the company, she was the charming, educated hostess. She was enjoying her new position and status. As she conversed with her guests, Oliver too was impressed and more than a little ashamed of his own preoccupations.

Oliver was glad that John Hamilton had been able to attend with Alice. He could see that her presence with her intended husband gave Elizabeth much joy. John, the son of a fellow merchant of Sir James, seemed a very kind and devoted person. Alice was being well rewarded for her patience during Oliver and Elizabeth's courtship. Her loyalty to her sister deserved recognition.

Chapter 32. Quarrelling

Elizabeth
'The Friars', Huntington 2 September 1620

Our guests have retired for the evening. It has all been such a thrill. We are fortunate that one of the ships is kept in port for repairs so their departure has been delayed, otherwise they would not have had time to visit.

As I reflect, I think that Mistress Martin is definitely a very brave woman. At heart she is a simple woman who does what her husband tells her. She really doesn't have particularly strong convictions but when she married Master Martin she had to change parishes. Her first husband lived in a different village where the reformed ways had already taken a hold. When she married Mister Martin his church was still tainted with its papist ceremonies instead of simple religion. She and her older son just carried on worshipping as she had been taught. It seems strange to me that Master Martin had agreed to become a churchwarden if the minister was practicing the sacraments so against his conscience.

As Sarah and I clear the table and pack the left-over dishes into the pantry, Oliver walks towards me.

"I'm not sure I like Master Martin as much as I like his wife, Oliver. What about you?" I say.

"Why ever not?" Oliver replies rather surprised, "It's not like you to condemn a man without knowing your whole way around the story."

As I consider his reproof, I realise why it is that Master Martin has not lived up to my expectations and I reply,

"He's so brash and glib!"

Rosalie Weller

"Well," Oliver responds thoughtfully, "If you are going on such an adventure, you would need to be quite brash wouldn't you?"

I leave Sarah to finish and walk towards the stairs with Oliver. Yes I suppose that is true. I do not utter this thought but I turn to my husband to find out the outcome of his visit to London. Mistress Cromwell is still hovering at the other end of the great hall, helping Sarah to get the house back together again before they retire for the evening.

"So husband, we have not yet had time to converse about your trip to London. Was it a successful outcome?"

"Yes. I followed up on the business introductions your father gave me and I was able to visit old acquaintances at Lincoln's Inn and I managed to see Master Shakespeare's play – The Winter's Tale."

I am quite taken aback – The Winter's Tale? I realise that Master Shakespeare is popular to all, and known for his wit and comedy but this play has a disturbing themes – jealousy and suspected adultery!

"Oliver," I respond with caution, "Is adultery a suitable theme for entertainment?"

My husband does not respond but turns on his heels and ascends to our bedchamber, the door bangs with a resounding thud. Mistress Cromwell who has heard this exchange from the other end of the great hall, replies with a shake of her head,

"Oliver will not be reprimanded for his moral conduct, mistress. Particularly on the night when he had to speak civilly to the wife of his only enemy in this town."

Cromwell & Elizabeth - The Beginning

I am utterly desperate. Two reproofs from the Cromwells. I become aware suddenly that these people, and this county, are not my kin. Yes we get on well; we tolerate and acquiesce to each other. With kin there is an unspoken bond which forms as you grow up together; a bond which forgives easily. We take it for granted but nonetheless it is there. Maybe we only notice it when we don't have it anymore.

I am unable to answer as a teardrop settles in my eye. I am confused. Was Master Walden not a friend of Oliver's as Mistress Walden has led me to believe? I have offended my husband twice. But maybe Mistress Cromwell is not correct. Oliver did not seem upset before I mentioned the theatre. I am sure I can put this right.

As for Mistress Cromwell, this is the first time I have been scolded by her. It has come as a shock. I will ignore her for the time being. I must sort this out with Oliver first. I ascend the stairs slowly and can hear he is blustering around the chamber.

"I am not one of your sisters to be teased and coerced, Oliver! I want an answer. Do you think it is a wholesome and godly act to attend a play about adultery? Laughing at this act which destroys love, destroys trust and can never be put right." I surprise myself with my ferocity.

Oliver replies, "No I do not. No, it isn't godly but it was merely an occasion to reacquaint myself with some of the fellows I met when I was at Lincoln's Inn. I did not finish what was started there, neither with learning nor friendship. Come on Elizabeth, you are making a fuss about nothing."

I am horrified.

I say, "A fuss about nothing! Nothing! I have set my mind to being a pious wife ... to be an example to your sisters in this household, and I get no encouragement at all, not from you, not from your mother. Maybe from Anna and Margaret and that is about it. I have given up my beautiful home, my own family, what I know and love to be part of your household. I have to listen while you boast about watching a play about adultery. My sister Alice and her fiancé - everyone heard your recommendation."

"Ah," he replies but with a smile this time, "So now you are anxious about what others think?"

I am exasperated. "No, I am anxious for your eternal soul - this worldliness damages you little by little… "

I am weeping and desperate for Oliver to understand my concern.

"You concentrate on being the good wife. I will attend to my own soul." Oliver says menacingly.

Chapter 33. A morning ride

Oliver
'The Friars', Huntington 2 September 1620

Although Oliver was furious with Elizabeth for raising her voice, particularly within the earshot of his guests, she had hit a sore wound - his eternal soul. Yes he was angry; not at her but at himself. His anger soon subsided as he strode around the barn.

Although he had left Elizabeth abruptly, the conversation about the New World had awakened a desire in Oliver. He had not realised how favourably Elizabeth viewed such a drastic change. He resolved to speak further to Hampden about this great adventure. They would be too late to join this sailing, but surely there would be others.

He was disgusted with his own behaviour towards his old friend Thomas Barrington and couldn't let that pass. His conscience would not allow him to say nothing – no words of comfort, so it was a great relief to see Thomas propped up against the edge of the barn. At least he could put this right. He approached cautiously. The man stood with his head bowed and Oliver thought he had never seen his friend in such a distressed state. Oliver knew that the responsibilities passed onto him from his father weighed heavily on him and that Frances' ill-health was a matter of concern.

"If I can do anything to alleviate your distress Thomas, please let me know," he said kindly.

Thomas bitterly retorted, "No, Oliver, you know nothing about having to follow in the footsteps of such a masterful leader, where every decision is scrutinised and compared. I cannot carry this load. I cannot live up to my father's expectations. He is such a great man – member of parliament, justice of the peace, a leader in the county. I cannot speak in public. I do not have his gifts or flair. I cannot even make a decision about the education of my sons without help."

Oliver felt unable to continue with this conversation. The noise of the bolt on the back door startled them and Oliver saw Sir Francis striding towards them and was happy to allow him to direct his own son. Quietly and earnestly, Sir Francis quietened his son. He too was concerned about the state of Thomas' mind.

Thomas' distress caused deep reflection on the part of Oliver. He knew he was close to the edge of disaster himself. His gambling debts were mounting and his creditors were demanding payment. But more importantly, Oliver still had not disclosed his true financial state to his wife and that lay heavily on his heart. It was only a matter of weeks that they had been married, but Oliver was already worried about their relationship. Elizabeth had lost her sparkle and seemed to be fretting. She was no longer interested in accompanying him to visit William or other friends in the town and she certainly wasn't interested in his work in the borough.

However, he had come into his own of late. The business of administering the Poor Law interested him. He enjoyed talking to the common people and did not think himself so far removed from them. The reality was somewhat different. He, although not titled himself, was related to the wealthy gentry of the county. It could be said he was on the fringes. That is how he felt. He knew he was lacking in the godliness he saw in others. He could ably converse, even argue, but he lacked Cousin John's oratory skill, or Sir Francis' purity.

So it was, the following morning Oliver insisted his new wife should go on a ride with him. He thought she might enjoy a canter over to Hinchingbrooke. There was always activity going on there with frequent house visitors and was sure to be pleasant. Elizabeth was not happy to be ordered to ride but she held her tongue to keep the peace in the household. She donned her riding dress and insisted that her young sister-in-law Jane should accompany them, together with Alice. Her sister's presence always had a moderating effect bringing calmness to every situation.

Cromwell & Elizabeth - The Beginning

They set off away from the High Street towards the rambling estates of Hinchingbrooke. Oliver rode silently beside his wife not wishing further reproof from her. Elizabeth soon relaxed in the pleasant breeze as the air began to warm on this beautiful autumn morning. They cantered comfortably through the woods and onto the meadows surrounding the big estate. Jane and Alice rode just slightly behind them.

In the distance Elizabeth caught sight of another family group walking their horses on the boundary of Hinchingbrooke. As they got nearer, it was obvious why the group was walking. Two very young boys were in the centre, their horses on lead reins. Elizabeth loved to watch young children begin their relationship with horses. After all a good horse was prized by all. The boys seemed so natural in the saddle although they couldn't have been older than four or five years old. She was so overcome by the beauty of it that she could maintain her silence no longer. She voiced her opinion to her husband.

"Look Oliver, those youngsters are just getting used to their horses. I remember my first time on Arabella. Do you know the family?"

It was apparent from their apparel that these gentry were wealthy. The three older men were brothers – the Montagues. The young children Oliver did not recognise, but they were their sons. Oliver recognised the man three years his junior, the son of Henry Montague, the Earl of Manchester, Edward. He had had occasion to ride over to Kimbolton after his father's death where he had encountered Edward. He had found him to be a serious fellow with airs and graces far beyond his station. His affectations did not ring true with Oliver. This fellow was fortunate to be born into a wealthy and powerful family. Oliver could not see any merit in him at all. However, he did not wish to upset Elizabeth further in view of the tense words they had the previous evening.

Oliver greeted the riders, "Good day to you sirs, Is my uncle at home?"

Edward replied, "Indeed he is. But I fear he will be busy with my father organising the King's Progress this year. We are merely accompanying the children on a short ride for their amusement."

The words were in no way offensive but there was something in Edward's tone, hardly perceptible, which implied that Sir Oliver would not find time for Oliver and his new wife today.

Elizabeth could not contain herself, "Is the progress this year to include Hinchingbrooke?"

The eldest gentleman, whom Oliver recognised as Sir Sidney Montague, reined his horse to a standstill and pulled up alongside Elizabeth.

"I don't think we have been introduced my dear," he said. "Although I understand you have met my wife, Paulina."

Oliver, aware of his omission, immediately introduced his wife to the company and Sir Sidney gestured to his brother to reply to Elizabeth's question.

Sir Henry Montague acquiesced,

"At this present time, we have not confirmed a visit to Hinchingbrooke. Good King James has suggested he might like to visit Bletsoe, Castle Ashby and Kirby Hall this year, my dear. We are merely discussing the possibilities at the moment."

It was clear to Oliver that their presence could be an embarrassment to his uncle. He did not know why this rich and powerful family were visiting at present. If the King was not including Hinchingbrooke in his progress, what were they doing here? He did not want to know. He had enough cares of his own. He turned to Elizabeth resolutely,

"Well gentlemen, please excuse us. We were merely taking the air. Greet my godfather for us, if you please."

With that Oliver turned his reins back in the direction of Huntington. He heard a frustrated sigh from Elizabeth but he decided to ignore it because just ahead of him he could see swirls of grey smoke billowing from the direction of the town.

Not wishing to alarm his wife, Oliver rode a little faster without saying anything.

"Oliver, what is that? It looks like fire!" Elizabeth too had spotted the swirling smoke. Oliver and Elizabeth galloped home, wanting to alert everyone of the imminent danger. The ride had established a truce - for the present.

Chapter 34. Fire

Elizabeth
Huntington 3 September 1620

Shouting and screaming. The town crier is ringing his bell sounding the alarm. Something serious is happening. I have been quick to dismount and I rush past the front door, unaware that the others have gone to the back door. I see billows of grey smoke ahead of me, catching the wind and blowing past me. I walk quickly but cautiously, as do my neighbours, as they appear at their gateways.

Is it "The George" or further down the street? I cannot tell and I creep closer to ascertain. As I draw nearer what has been merely a sound suddenly becomes an uncomfortable smell and taste, as the sooty mess engulfs my lungs. I can see what it is now. The bakery is on fire. Mistress Eversham is shouting desperately from the first floor to those below. She wants them to catch the children. There is Mistress Blake with her servants carrying a huge sheet. Oh, this is dreadful! Perhaps the babies can be saved! The first, a little girl is screaming her head off but she lands safely, praise be to God.

But the next little one, a boy, is there any hope for him? His little body is already limp, probably overcome by the smoke. This is too awful to watch but what else can I do? There's a line of hands from the fire to the brook passing leather buckets. Everyone is out and helping to quench this blaze. What must I do?

I see Oliver directing farm labourers to throw the water on the base of the blaze. Only one half of the house is burning. Perhaps the other half can be saved. The quick action by the townspeople seems to be dampening the flames. Oliver sees me.

"Go back to the house," he calls "It's almost out. Put cloths up at the windows."

Yes, I must protect our family and guests. The windows here have no glass yet! Of course I must put the cloths up. As I glance around I realise that quite suddenly the wind has changed direction. The smoke is billowing away from our dwelling – a little to the west.

As I reach the front of the house, I can hear Mistress Cromwell and the sisters at the back. They must have gone to the brook to help with the buckets. Their faces are blackened. They look weary.

"Don't mind us, Elizabeth." Anna says. She must have noted the concern from my face.

"The danger is over for the bakery but it does look as if the fields of barley behind are ablaze." Catherine says.

As they go into the house, I wonder if there is something further I can do to help. I know, I'll go down to the brook and collect our buckets. Generally they are held in common but it does not go amiss to have a few in the house.

The smoke still lurks overhead and I see two buckets straight away on the grass beside the brook. As I pick them up, I see something I haven't seen before. That barn-like building seems to be in use. The pungent smell also indicates what its use is – a brewhouse. I'm curious.

As I step inside the huge door, a young lad is stirring the contents of a huge barrel. He is startled by the suddenness of my appearance and almost falls off his stool. He takes off his cap as a mark of respect and his demeanour suggests that he knows me, but I have never encountered this boy before.

"I did not mean to disturb you," I say "I was just collecting the buckets after the fire." The boy does not need an explanation.

As I turn to go the boy says to me, "Please tell Master Cromwell, I have to go home early because of the fire."

"Master Cromwell," I ask, "What has it got to do with Master Cromwell, boy? Do you mean Master Garret?"

The boy is embarrassed at my question and only hangs his head. We stand in silence for what seems an age and then it dawns on me.

"Does the brewhouse belong to the Cromwells?" I ask, afraid to hear the answer. The answer though is not spoken. The boy merely nods his head. How can this be? Oliver had made a jest about a brewhouse on that day we had dinner at Barrington Hall. Had it not been a joke after all? How could he not have told me? I am betrayed. Not only by Oliver, but by his sisters and his mother. No one has ever spoken about this. What other secrets have they kept? What else is there that I do not know? Tears sting my eyes as I run back to the house, the edge of my gown touching the mud on the grass.

I find out the truth from Catherine. Their business has been conducted discretely because failure to obtain one of the new government licences has meant that sales must be carried out without the clientele being able to drink their brew on the premises. The wives of the tradesmen bring their jugs and their accounts are tallied and credited monthly. The customers always use the back entrance from the path to the brook side as it is quicker from town.

If it had not been for the fire and my desire to help, I would not have discovered this secret – yet.

Chapter 35. The brewhouse

Oliver
'The Friars' Huntington 3 September 1620

When Oliver returned to "The Friars" he knew something was wrong before Elizabeth spoke. Her eyes were red and swollen. Her face was sullen.

"How could you keep such a secret?" Elizabeth wailed, "All of you and no-one said a word.

Mistress Cromwell walked purposefully from the embroidery window to the huge table where Elizabeth sat.

"She has discovered the brewhouse, Oliver," Mistress Cromwell explained.

"They only did what I told them, Elizabeth." Oliver paused. "Do not lay any blame on my family!"

Elizabeth ran upstairs to the bedchamber still wailing loudly. Mistress Cromwell nodded to Oliver raising her eyes to the chamber to indicate a suggested course of action. He went upstairs reluctantly, weighing each tread carefully to slow his ascent.

The Cromwell females were frozen by this sudden breakdown of marital bliss amongst them. Their usual girlish chatter had turned to an apprehensive silence. Even Jane the youngest knew the situation was serious.

Mistress Cromwell spoke first, addressing Robina she said,

"Take Buli outside and gather some field flowers."

"Shall we get some for Elizabeth." Jane lisped innocently. Their mother just nodded.

"Anna, go and fetch Margaret," she instructed, unwilling to intervene in her son's marriage herself.

Anna relieved to escape the tension bolted out of the backdoor, leaving Catherine and Lizzie at their sewing, their heads bowed. Mistress Cromwell continued her instructions.

"Catherine, Lizzie, set the table for dinner. It will be a light repast today - bread and potage on the stove. Yes and see if there is a little cheese for Oliver."

If there was one blessing in all of this, it was that Sir James and the other Bourchier guests had already gone on their way taking Sarah with them. It would not have been good for them to witness this disagreement, thought Mistress Cromwell. She mopped up the crumbs from the floor just as she mopped up her son's mistakes - a little dab here and there until everything was as good as new. Harsh voices could still be heard from the upper floor.

Mistress Cromwell knew her son had not handled the question of the brewhouse wisely. She had warned Oliver that Elizabeth Bourchier would not take kindly to secrets. He did not know women as well as he thought he did. The necessity of the brewhouse was without question and it had only been a matter of time before Elizabeth had found out. In fact, Mistress Cromwell was surprised it had not come out before. Elizabeth's frequent visits to the gentlewomen of the town would not have precluded an intimacy which would lead to a revelation from one of them. But that had not happened.

Margaret and Anna entered through the back door.

"So mother what must I do?" Margaret asked.

"Well, Oliver is up in the chamber. Go up and tell him that we are waiting to eat our dinner. You talk to Elizabeth, calm her down. She has been a spoilt young woman, used to getting her own way. What's done is done. But Margaret, the brewhouse - don't back down on that. I will not give it up, until I am ready! Perhaps Mistress Bourchier does not understand that it is my house she is living in and not Oliver's!"

Margaret grimaced at her mother's uncompromising tone but also knew she was the right one to talk to Elizabeth. After all she knew what compromises have to be made in marriage. As she went up the stairs, Oliver was just closing the door of the chamber and coming down.

"It's no good, Margaret. She says she won't speak to anyone. Leave her be. She'll soon get fed up with her own company."

Margaret obeyed and they both descended, Margaret to her own cottage and Oliver ready to enjoy a simple supper. After the initial shock, the sisters were chatting again, albeit a little subdued.

Before they could sit down Henry Downhall suddenly appeared through the front door, totally unaware of the skirmish he had narrowly missed.

"A bracing walk, must have covered ten miles, Godmanchester way. I could see the smoke billowing above the houses, but couldn't do anything myself, too far away. Is everything under control now?" Henry asked.

"Just in time for supper, Henry. Elizabeth is a little indisposed and will not be joining us but we have the pleasure of the company of my delightful sisters," He winked at Catherine and Anna as he said it.

Oliver continued, "So Godmanchester. Yes we rode the other way to Hinchingbrooke, then we spotted the smoke. It's all just about out now, although I hear there was some fear of it spreading to the fields. We will see!"

The reappearance of Henry had brought some sense of normality to the table. The sisters chatted amongst themselves and to their guest. Oliver so enjoyed Henry's company that he was able to forget the disharmony in the house. In any case he did not view the presence of the brewhouse as seriously as did Elizabeth. The sounds of distress had ceased from the upper chamber and from the company's minds.

When the simple meal was completed, Margaret returned and once again climbed the stairs to the bedchamber in an effort to comfort and explain to her friend.

Chapter 36. Betrayal

Elizabeth
Huntington 3 September 1620

I cannot believe I have been betrayed so heartlessly by my husband. I wanted to help after the fire: help them by collecting up the buckets. Oh it is just too terrible, too humiliating. Running a brewhouse. I cannot imagine anything so godless in all of my life. Making money from others' debauchery and lack of will – for to be sure this ale will not be our usual refreshment. This liquid will be a strong brew otherwise why would the townsfolk pay for it? How can it be that I did not go down to the brook before? No, it is not my job to find out what is going on. It is up to my husband to inform me.

I trusted him. I thought there were no secrets between us. Who is this man? It is as if I don't know him. Why did Mistress Cromwell not inform me? Why did my new sisters not let me know? We are studying the good Lord's Holy Word together and reflecting on how as believers we must be honest, pure and sanctified. How does this breach of trust fit in with that?

I know Oliver is standing behind me but I cannot turn and face him. I cannot look into his face. I am too distraught.

"Elizabeth," Oliver quietly whispers my name. He seems to be quite calm. He has no understanding of what he has done to me. Or how great a betrayal this is!

"No. I cannot speak about this now," I gasp between my sobs. "Leave me alone for now."

I hear the latch on the chamber door lifted, released than caught up from the other side. Muffled voices from the stairs, then quiet. At least Oliver has the good sense to leave me to think. When does a wife stand her ground and say to a husband no more? Oliver and the

Cromwell household have been running this business for years. They must have been. Does the whole town of Huntington know about it? Has everyone been laughing behind my back?

Only last week I discussed with Mistress Walden, Paulina and Elizabeth Hatton about the evils of strong drink. None of them agreed on my god-fearing stand that we must avoid strong drink at all costs. None of them support the new licenses brought in by Good King James. I do. But they did not tell me either about the brewhouse on the estate. Mistress Walden would surely know even if the others are newcomers. They must judge me a hypocrite.

I am so glad father and my sisters have returned to Little Stambridge Hall. I could not bear it if they knew of my shame. I am wretched indeed. How can I deal with it? This abomination, this brewhouse must be closed. We do not need this income and if it has been a family tradition then I will start a new family tradition of godliness and purity. There is a knock on the door and Margaret appears.

"Elizabeth, I am so sorry you have had this upset," she begins.

Her face betrays her response as I begin to question.

"Why did you not tell me?" I say, "Oh, I suppose because Oliver told you not to!"

"Elizabeth the brewhouse has been part of this family for... "

I do not give her time to finish.

"Margaret how long and how firmly your family has been caught in this trade does not interest me. That my husband seems to be so drawn into it does. I worry for his eternal soul and this trade just keeps him ensnared in the devil's toils. So Margaret, this has to be stopped immediately."

For the first time I have said your family and not our family. I have drawn a line. She puts her hand up to protest but I ignore it.

"This brewhouse must be closed, Margaret." I warn her.

"But Elizabeth, you do not understand. The brewhouse belongs to my mother, not Oliver, as does this house. Oliver owns half the estate but the rest is mothers. Oh yes it will be inherited by Oliver eventually but it was all part of mother's jointure. The ownership cannot be taken from her."

I feel the colour draining from my face, life drawing out of me. I thought the house and the lands had belonged to Robert Cromwell and had passed to Oliver on his death. That is what I was led to believe. My knees are wobbly. I must sit down. I say,

"Go Margaret, please leave me alone."

"Elizabeth, you are ill, white, let me stay awhile with you to comfort you." She says.

"No, go... please"

The truth of the matter sinks into my heart. Oliver owns nothing. He is dependent on his mother. I am dependent on Oliver. I sit at my desk and open my bible at the gospel of Matthew.

'Do not worry about what you wear.
Do not worry about what you eat.'

Once this was a pretty saying. Now it is a saying I must live by. Margaret's words have wounded me severely. I do not blame Oliver really. He is as much in this trap as his sisters. We, Oliver and I, will stay here until we have an opportunity to leave. Maybe it will be to the New World, maybe another town. I do not know. But I do know

Rosalie Weller

my life will be one of godliness and piety, regardless of those around me.

Chapter 37. Death of a child

Oliver
Huntington 25 October 1620

The Cromwell household took a while to settle. Indeed it never returned to the happy-go-lucky carefree haven it had been when Elizabeth descended as a new bride. But an uneasy truce had been reached.

Mistress Cromwell continued to supplement her income with the brewing but each of her customers was informed of the need for discretion so the business became the unspoken secret of the community, much to the amusement of many.

Oliver, in his first official capacity as a local councillor, was asked to witness the indenture of the two members for Huntingdon – his cousin Henry St John and Sir Miles Sandys. It was only a signature but Oliver felt a sense of destiny, that on a day not too far in the future it would be his turn to be nominated to serve the town.

As Elizabeth had realised, Oliver never fully understood the magnitude of his indiscretion, nor the deep wound he had inflicted on his deeply religious wife. But he continued to grow in influence and status in the town in his own right and not just as the grandson of the Great Knight. Elizabeth continued with her bible studies for the family and was delighted by Anna's progress as she, too, began to read.

Elizabeth still had a great love for her husband but she had lost her naivety. She knew he did not share her desire for piety. She continued to develop her friendship with Bridgett Kilbourne which was of mutual benefit to them both. Her relationships with the other gentlewomen of the town remained courteous and tolerant with an infrequency which could just be discerned as polite. From these meetings Elizabeth gauged what was, and was not, acceptable to the town of Huntington. She did not try to compete with Elizabeth Walden and her costly extravagance in gowns, nor with Paulina Pepys and her expensive taste in furniture. She had some sympathy with Elizabeth Hatton, understanding her loss of standing in society after her husband's disgrace. Afterall Sir Edward did follow through on a point of principle. The law is the law and not for kings to interfere with.

But Elizabeth pursued her own path. Despite Oliver's failings she resolved to pray for him each day. Her prayers contained an earnestness as she feared for his very salvation. She loved him in this life, and couldn't bear the thought of him being cast into the fires of hell in the next. Elizabeth knew that she could not command her mother-in-law's love and no longer wanted to. It was used up solely on Oliver. She realised that Mistress Cromwell was indeed the matriarch of the house and there was nothing she could do about it. She did not share these thoughts with Oliver; she kept them to herself.

But another tragedy occurred in which Elizabeth needed the support of this substitute family, regardless of how flawed it was. It was only two weeks later that the fragile peace was again shattered by a knocking on the door. There stood William Kilbourne pale and trembling.

"Could Elizabeth come, please," he hesitated, "It's Mary! Bridgett needs someone with her. I am no comfort. Is it possible for Elizabeth to come and stay just for a while?"

"Yes, of course, "Oliver reassured his friend, "She'll come immediately. Anna go upstairs and fetch Elizabeth."

Oliver had no doubt Elizabeth would go; the tension of the Cromwell household needed a brief respite. When someone else's tragedy intrudes on your own it becomes a healer. Three days and nights, Elizabeth laboured with Bridgett to bring down Mary's fever. The little mite struggled for breath, her forehead clammy and her throat and tongue strawberry red and burning. Her little body was covered with a bright red rash. The doctor was called but he could do nothing and sadly, despite all their efforts, Mary passed on to the next world. The same happened in many households in Huntington that year. Some children recovered with no ill effects, and some, like little Mary, died. Who was taken and who was spared was an arbitrary decision which none could fathom. The ways of the Lord are strange, indeed, thought a distraught Elizabeth.

As Elizabeth watched Bridgett grieving, she was able to see something of what her mother-in-law had also suffered. For the first time she glimpsed into Mistress Cromwell's soul. When you lose a child there is nothing which can replace it. Your stomach empties and cannot be sated. Your very bones begin to press on your heart which tightens and struggles to comprehend what has happened. She offered words of comfort which could not abate the pain. At the funeral of the little girl, Elizabeth stood opposite her friend and as the body was lowered into the grave, Bridgett's twisted expression said what no words could convey. A mother should not have to bury a child. It is a mother's nature to create and nurture, and she cannot come to terms with destruction and death.

Elizabeth stayed in Bridget's house a further two days but could offer no consolation. She cared for the other children and a girl came in daily from the town to help with the business and the cooking. William was able to accept the death of his daughter more stoically. Several families had also lost children from this fever. As is always the case, it struck then passed on to the next town.

This was a dreadful tragedy to strike the town, but life moves on regardless and not long after this the townsfolk's thoughts started to turn towards preparations for the Christmas celebrations. The talk was of holly and ivy being woven into wreaths and of the yule logs to be searched out to decorate the houses. The fathers began to whittle wood into toys and the mothers sewed new clothes for the children. Animals were slaughtered to save the foodstuff. The temperature began to drop and more wood was needed for the fires. Young Valentine, Margaret's son, was anticipating a joyful time. The twelve days were celebrated with singing and lighting special candles. Dancing bears were brought in to the town to delight children and adults alike.

Mistress Cromwell did not allow her family to participate in all the merrymaking. For once Elizabeth agreed with her. Most of the traditions had pagan origins. But the celebrations were enjoyed by the rest of the townsfolk.

Chapter 38. News of a baby

Elizabeth
'The Friars', Huntington 30 March 1621

It has been such a cold winter and Huntington seems such a long way from Little Stambridge Hall. I miss Alice. Oh how I took her for granted – such a sweet sister! I am so unhappy. Life as a gentleman farmer's wife is just not the same as that of a merchant's daughter. I thought I would be one of the gentry but I can see now that I fooled myself. We do not mix in the right circles. Oliver and I seem to be growing apart and his mood seems to be less jolly than it was.

The arrival of spring has made me feel I need to make sure I occupy myself appropriately. As Mistress Cromwell enters from the backdoor I say,

"Mistress Cromwell, can I look at the household accounts? I really do think it is time I relieved you of this duty."

It is as if I had attacked her with a sword. She does not move. She does not shout. She does not smile. I cannot gauge her reaction at all. Is she angry? Why is she so shocked? Oliver says he has spoken to her about me managing the household and I think it is time for me to take on all the responsibility.

At last she responds,

"No that is not possible."

I immediately reply, like a petulant child,

"But why not? I need to take some responsibility myself. I know this house belongs to you but the running of the household must surely be a joint venture! I cannot see my way clear to new gowns and maybe books for our study lessons unless I know how much we have to spend."

She does not reply but puts her rosemary stems on the table and returns to the herb garden.

I am not a young girl to be ignored like this. I feel like just another daughter in this female household. I'm not sure what to do now. It is late in the day – too late to take Arabella out for a ride in the forests. No I must confront the issues now. Mistress Cromwell and my sisters-in-law are mostly obliging but somehow it all gets under my skin. I don't mean to behave like a spoilt daughter but when I go to collect the eggs, Robina or Jane have been before me. I call the sheep and they don't respond. I can't milk the cow or the goats with any success. But I will be mistress of this house. Today I will tell them. I mean to have my way. Oliver is away discussing politics with Sir Francis Barrington in Essex and I will get this matter sorted out before he gets back.

I ascend the stairs to the bedchamber I am quite sure Catherine and Anna are well aware of what is happening. I can hear them whispering together. However, I mean to calm myself and then I will rehearse my speech. I reach for my bible. Yes, I will review the reading passage we have looked at. Psalm 1 – I am so glad we have begun our study of the Psalms. They are such a blessing. I read aloud the passage. Yes we are blessed when we follow the Lord's righteous ways. I pause. I wait what seems hours but is probably only minutes.

I descend the stairs, quietly rehearsing my speech before I reach the hall. I think I shall conduct our daily reading before I tell them what is troubling me. Mistress Cromwell is now seated by the fire amusing Margaret's youngest. I do not acknowledge the pleasant smile which greets me, and take a deep breath. I will wait until after our reading.

I walk to the table with my bible, and it is only a few seconds before Catherine, Anna and Lizzie prepare to join me. This bible reading has become a regular daily occurrence. I am pleased and I know, too, that Oliver is glad that I have introduced this new element to the family. Old Mistress Cromwell does not seem particularly pleased but she does not really encourage the education of girls and I am not going to let it unsettle me.

"Have you practiced your letters today?" I ask Anna.

She giggles as she glances at her mother and says defiantly, "Yes of course Elizabeth. I am quite determined I shall read too!"

I am delighted. Of the three sisters, it is only Anna who has felt encouraged to try to read. Catherine does not have the interest and would rather improve her stitching in any time we have. She also is so quiet it is difficult to tell whether she would have sufficient determination. Lizzie, poor Lizzie, I must admit I have no hope for her to learn to read for herself. I know it is possible she has suffered at her birth because now I can discern there is something lacking in her general understanding. Her slowness of speech is not detectable in general company but on close conversation, it is clearly heard.

So my only hope lies in Anna's progress. Anna, I have discovered, is also gifted in her musical ability; she is very talented in her playing on the virginals. She also organises little plays for Margaret's children and is so delighted to act with the children for her mother's amusement. Anna adds sparkle to our company although sometimes I find her just a little boisterous. Today our reading and discussion is soon finished.

"Make I speak to you quite frankly, Mistress Cromwell?" I begin. The girls have left the table.

"Well you look as if you are determined to do so. What is it, Elizabeth?" she replies cheerily.

I start to recite my carefully rehearsed speech but instead a tirade bursts forth from my mouth and quite to my surprise Mistress Cromwell bursts out laughing. I am quite taken aback and cannot imagine how this outcome has occurred. As I stutter tearfully, Margaret enters the room, pulling young Valentine behind her.

"Why Mother, whatever is the matter?" she asks looking from her mother to me.

"Elizabeth has just had an outburst. Her emotions are so heightened she is quite flushed. Tell her sweet Margaret, what is happening to her."

Margaret smiles at me. I am still utterly bewildered.

"Elizabeth, dear Elizabeth, you must be with child. Have you had nausea especially in the morning time? What about your natural course. Is it present?"

"I... I... " I am lost for words. How can these two know this when I am not sure myself? Can it be? Heightened emotions? Yes I have had feelings of sickness. And my courses have not been regular, but although I did expect these physical changes in my body, I did not expect the change in my sensibilities. To be sure it is not like me to be at odds with the women of the Cromwell household. I really have nothing to complain about. It's just that the physical changes had not shown themselves quite as I imagined.

I am filled with remorse and sorrow for my outburst, and my inner anger. I see now it was ill deserved.

"Can it be?" I ask them.

Margaret clasps my hand. "Yes Elizabeth. I so want cousins for Valentine. We noticed the thickening around your waist but didn't say anything until you told us yourself."

"We didn't want to be forward, my dear," says Mistress Cromwell.

Now it makes sense. My irritability with the Cromwell women was out of all proportion. I'm filled with joy and laugh at myself. How could I have been so silly? I know the symptoms alright but didn't relate them to myself. I can't wait to tell Oliver. Suddenly I feel the need of these womenfolk. These are my kinswomen now.

"You must ride over to see your mother," Mistress Cromwell says gently, "See if she wants to come over when your time gets near."

No I don't want her to come, I think and I answer quickly,

"No she will be too busy with the younger children. Oliver can inform Sir Francis and father next time he rides over to Essex. Mother will know soon enough. We'll manage." I smile. She and Margaret smile back.

Chapter 39. Local politics

Oliver
'Barrington Hall', Hatfield Broad Oak, 30 March 1621

When Oliver and Val Walton arrived at The Priory, Hatfield Broad Oak most of the invited gentlemen had already arrived. As they strode into the great hall, Oliver nodded to Hampden, Pym and cousin Thomas. This made a break in their discussion unnecessary and Sir Francis continued his discourse on the reconvened Parliament.

"If indeed he has accepted bribes, then he must be punished." Sir Francis Barrington's fine sense of justice imposed its will on the company. No one dissented or protested or even put up an argument in Sir Francis Bacon's defence. The case was still under investigation. Some thought it prudent not to offer any opinion particularly against this Lord Chancellor of England.

Oliver sensed the sombre mood of the company. He did not altogether agree. It was so difficult to discern the difference between genuine affection for one's friends and a little favour extended and bribery per se. He and Val had debated this very point as they rode over from Huntington.

Oliver was surprised to note that the Montagues were also present on this occasion. The regular gathering had never included them. Why were they here today? Sir Sidney Montague and his brother, Lord Edward, were contemporaries of Sir Francis and, of course, his late father. As wealthy landowners they too were concerned about the developments in the country but their concern was more in Huntington, not in Essex.

The conversation quickly moved on to a more threatening subject. A certain Mistress Hooker had been accused locally of practising the old arts. Was it the Throckmorton era all over again? Oliver had not yet been born when his ancestor, Lady Susan Cromwell, second wife to Sir Henry, had been bewitched by Alice Samuel but he had often been warned to stay away from spinsters in the town, especially any hailing from Warboys. It was a subject which intrigued Oliver. How close the ties between godliness and sorcery seemed sometimes. Lady Susan had been on a visit to encourage the sick at the time.

His encounter with the old woman at "The Bell", last May, had been troubling him for some time. What had it meant? He had discussed it with no-one. Certainly not Master Beard, nor his uncles. Oliver moved nearer to the hearth where the fire blazed. March had not yet brought any warmth. He had deliberately extended his ride over because it was easier for him to discuss these matters first with Val. Easier at a trot than a gallop. But that had meant the cold invading his bones.

He had mulled over whether to bring the problems of Huntington to this learned gathering. He could use some wisdom in the current situation. William, his dear friend, was confident that all would be well with a new charter from the King. Oliver was not so sure. William was grieving the loss of little Mary still and his reasoning was not as sound as it normally would be. However, it soon became apparent that the gentlemen already had a full agenda and he became a ready listener. There was so much to be learnt about the intrigues of the court and of Parliament itself. The Montagues provided a valuable insight which Sir Francis was not privy to.

"Yes, I'm afraid we will have to leave, now. We're going to Hinchingbrooke for further talks with Sir Oliver. I can't say anymore just now as we're still discussing all the issues at the moment." Sir Sidney was soon striding out of the hall, followed by his brother.

Oliver desperately wanted to ask if Sir Sidney's business was to do with the sale of Hinchingbrooke but the gentlemen were out before he could gather his thoughts together. The remaining gentlemen relaxed and the conversation turned to local politics. They seated themselves and Sir Francis ordered the dinner to be served. Thomas Barrington seemed very morose and did not offer any opinion during dinner, but after a delicious dish of duck had been enjoyed, he seemed to be more amenable.

"Thomas, you are looking calmer today, How are you?" Oliver asked.

"Indeed the melancholia is lifting, cousin." Thomas was able to offer cheerfully.

This small exchange cheered Oliver's spirit. He had felt so guilty about Thomas' black mood the last time they had met.

"Do you think there is some undercurrent in the suggestion that Huntington should ask for a new charter, Sir Francis?" Val ventured.

Oliver was glad of the question and was interested to hear his uncle's answer.

"Without a doubt." Sir Francis was most emphatic. "Have you been stirring up enemies in Huntington, young Oliver. This sounds like a power play, eh?"

"Well," Oliver replied, "It's no secret that I disagree with Master Bernard's idea to enclose the common land. Where will the likes of John Lowry graze their sheep? He doesn't have a farm and so is reliant on the grass on Long Meadow to put his few ewes on."

"Yes, Oliver I understand your point. You seem to have a lot of sympathy for the ordinary man. That's a good thing." Sir Francis replied. "But diplomacy is also required."

Oliver nodded in acknowledgement that his tactlessness might leave something to be desired. Sir Francis continued,

"We have never held with disputes here in Hatfield, Oliver. We have always managed to discuss the matters in question like men of honour. You know Robert Rich, of course. He extends quite an influence on our company and he makes sure there is a suitable gentleman to represent our godly views. Here, we do not like petty squabbles, but not all counties are the same.

Local matters are important but with war currently on the continent there are more pressing issues for Parliament to consider. After all, Parliament must give the lead to the citizens. Too many men today are eager to look after their own interests before the good of the country. This war will not advance our cause in this country as some may think. There is no doubt, England will not accept Papist rule again."

Rosalie Weller

    The company continued to discuss matters of both local and national importance. The following day promised another opportunity to fly his hawk, Joan, and enjoy Val's company. With this Oliver was content.

Chapter 40. Joy

Elizabeth

'The Friars', Huntington 3 April 1621

Oliver is due to arrive home for dinner at twelve. I have managed to complete all the farming chores and am pleased with myself. Since last week when I talked with Mistress Cromwell and Margaret, I am more at ease. I am so excited to tell Oliver about the baby now my kinswomen have confirmed it for me. Yes, I hear the horse's hooves outside. I cannot wait. I run outside. I know my face shows to all that I am so happy. I cannot stop smiling.

"Well Elizabeth, what is it?" startled, Oliver jumps off his horse and takes me in his arms.

"I think I am with child, my love," I blurt out, unsure of him.

He lifts me wholly off my feet and swings me around. He is so exuberant and noisy, that I am quite embarrassed. Trenchard stops his work and scratches his head. As we go in, Mistress Cromwell stops her beating of the eggs and takes off her apron.

Oliver clasps her hands too, "Such wonderful news, mother," he says, "My news is not worth mentioning. Nothing surpasses this. A child. Elizabeth, this is so amazing. The Lord is blessing us."

"Oh what is your news, Oliver?" Mistress Cromwell asks.

"I am to stand as the county sheriff. Some of the gentlemen are not happy with Thomas Maples. Apparently he has been threatening some of the citizens to force them to vote for our candidate. Sir Thomas says he admires his enthusiasm but gentlemen do not act in such a fashion. Anyway I will be backed by the Essex councillors. Richard Rich will speak to Sir Oliver and then it could be a seat in parliament. Sir Francis has won his seat back in the house; the others in the counties are willing to listen."

Oliver looks at my puzzled face and comes over to reassure me.

"Elizabeth, you knew I would follow in my father's footsteps and his father before him. I must serve this county as a gentleman."

Indeed I did know but I had not expected this to happen for quite a while and with the little one on the way, I expected to have more of Oliver to myself for quite some time to come.

Mistress Cromwell is looking at me sternly. I do not want to have any further disagreements with her and I certainly don't want to disagree with my husband on such a joyous day, so I smile. Indeed, I do not wish to disagree with anyone, especially not today.

"Perhaps we can talk about it later, my dear," I say resignedly because I do not want the rest of the household to be part of this conversation. I want to talk to Oliver on my own.

"That was a good solution for the Barratts, Oliver," his mother fills him in with the details of the farm life which he has missed these four days he has been away and I set out the tankards and pewter on the table in preparation for our meal. Soon we are a jolly company again.

"Oliver, I can now read, just a little. Elizabeth says I am making fine progress," Anna announces.

"Oliver, were there any gentlemen for me to become acquainted with at the Barringtons?" Catherine asks.

"Catherine, I thought it was to be Roger Whitestone for you!" Oliver winks at his desperate sister.

All I want to talk about is our baby. We will need a crib. Will Margaret have clothes to lend us? I would love Lizzie to embroider on the clothes for us. I must go and tell Bridgett. I hope this will not darken her grief. No, I'm sure she will be happy for me.

"It must be a boy," Robina says, "We don't have enough boys in this family. It's not fair on little Valentine. He wants a cousin to play with. But it must be a boy!"

Robina is so assured in her comments that we all laugh. Everyone is so delighted at my news. I cannot bring up the subject which troubles me the most - the accounts! I must see them and know about the finances of this household. But for now, I am happy. I am going to have a child! Thank you Lord.

Chapter 41. A new charter

Oliver

William Kilbourne's house, Huntington 5 April 1621

"But we must begin to draw up our proposals, Oliver. We will not succeed in this opposition if we do not have an alternative plan. We cannot stop progress and we need a new charter from the King if we are to see our town take a share in the new wealth of the country." William's argument was forceful.

Oliver had strolled to William's house to discuss his ideas on the new charter for Huntington. He believed the charter must be carefully thought out otherwise the greedy merchants in the town would get their way and the town would be run by profiteers. He had seen the new money take a hold on relationships before. Good men could often be turned by money and the old traditions and customs were not honoured. Oliver felt he was stuck in the middle. By birth he belonged to the gentry so the burghers did not easily listen to him; there was much resentment and talk about the deference of favour and privilege. Times were certainly changing. People no longer respected their betters. The impeachment of Sir Francis Bacon had reached down even into small towns like Huntington. The words "corruption" and "injustice" were on everyone's lips even without their knowing the whole story.

Oliver hesitated as he reflected on the wisdom of what his friend was saying. He replied steadily,

"Yes, I accept that point but if we include the item about a permanent lecture here in Huntington in the petition, we can assure a pure faith in this area for years to come. Our trading rights must go alongside our beliefs to worship in the true way. This is a route to assure that Huntington goes in the same direction as Essex. After all we have secured the right to lecture against witchcraft already!"

The discussion continued in this vein as William put forward his fears of including trade and worship in the same petition. He was not sure that they would succeed if they did not make the two issues separate. William knew that there was considerable opposition from the other burghers who could sit with happy consciences regardless of who was in the pulpit.

Oliver did not feel the certainty of faith that Thomas Beard or Sir Frances had or even for that matter his own Elizabeth. How she had blossomed over this past year. He had watched a plain caterpillar emerge into a beautiful spirited butterfly. He loved that pious energy which she had acquired – always pressing him to take the right course. Alas, she didn't know him at all. Yes, he followed the outward duties in attending church and helping the poor but he knew that inside his heart was empty.

The shameful secret of his gambling debts had not been disclosed nor settled. Oliver had ignored all questions about finances. Each time the subject came up, there was a borough problem which needed his immediate attention. His creditors had been kept at bay by the good reputation the name of Cromwell held in the Huntingdon area. He had managed to feed the hungry creditors with dribs and drabs as he procured them from his father-in-law and his other relatives. He had decided to not think about what he could not change. So he blocked these problems from his mind and concentrated on the things he could do something about.

The news of a child had not surprised Oliver at all. He had noticed a certain tetchiness about Elizabeth of late and he was glad he could now lay a reason for it. Maybe now she would cease her gentle but persistent complaining about his mother and sisters. He knew they would have to part their ways with his family as theirs increased but he hoped to enjoy the advantages and comfort of remaining in his boyhood home for just a while longer.

Mistress Cromwell had been in touch with her family in Ely. Long overdue thought Oliver. He had been concerned about his mother's health. The worry of his father's sudden death and the mess the estate was in had taken its toll on his mother in these last years. Now though, her vibrancy had returned, especially with the news of another grandchild on the way. He trusted his kin to take care of his Elizabeth at this time. He was surprised that Lady Frances would not be involved but he knew Elizabeth's strongest affection was for Sir James. How could he ever live up to that character? In godliness never. In wealth hardly likely. In love, most definitely. If he dwelt on his responsibility he would become quite morose. He had seen that happen to Thomas Barrington and did not want to follow in that direction so he made up his mind to visit the physician, Dr. Simcotts, but for now he had some hope that he would be able to clear his gambling debts. His mother had announced a long overdue visit from her brother Thomas Steward in the coming months.

Oliver had not seen his maternal uncle for several years. He was happy his mother was refreshing this relationship. Uncle Thomas would bring news from the family in Ely. Oliver welcomed the opportunity to hear firsthand what was happening in the Fens. He had heard rumours that there was a movement to drain the land but it had received considerable opposition from the common people. Oliver wanted to know the true story.

Oliver also knew the reason his mother had invited her brother was that his uncle was childless and had no heir. This held some promise for Oliver's future financial situation.

Chapter 42. Uncle Thomas Steward

Elizabeth
'The Friars', Huntington 15 September 1621

I have never met good uncle Thomas, Mistress Cromwell's brother, but he is due to arrive tomorrow for a short stay. Why must he visit now? I cannot understand but my mother-in-law is insistent on this occasion. Mistress Cromwell has been very kind if somewhat distant to me during this pregnancy so I wish to oblige her. That is more than I can say for my own mother who will not be sharing my confinement. I am not disappointed as there will be more than enough companionship and encouragement from Oliver's sweet sisters, especially from Margaret. Oliver enters the room quietly and slowly and addresses me,

"Are you sure you are amenable to meeting Uncle Thomas? I know he is calling at a difficult time. I do not want you to be anxious before your confinement?" he says.

"It is fine, my love," I reply, "but who is this uncle and why does he want to visit now?"

"Mother has not really spoken about him but I understand that he didn't get on well with father. He is childless himself and I suppose he wants to acquaint himself with his sister's children. He lives in Ely where mother lived as a child. They were once close but the years have taken their toll. Thank you my darling for agreeing to this visit. It means so much to mother."

As we enter the hall, I see uncle Thomas and the first thing which strikes me is that this man is in ill health. My heart immediately warms to him and my mother-in-law. I wonder how it is that families lose touch with each other like these two have done? I suppose the daily activities of life just take up too much time. I know I have not seen my own sisters for so many months because I have been resting considerably and have been unable to ride out to Little Stambridge Hall. I do miss my sweet Alice but the others, I care for less.

We sit by the fire and are ready listeners as Mistress Cromwell and her brother discuss their family and Oliver's participation in the life of this town of Huntington. It has not been easy for Oliver since his father died. I am overwhelmed at the thought that this child continues not only the Cromwell line but also the Steward line. Oliver's uncle at Hinchingbrooke has never been nable to assist financially due to his own rising debts. They say he has been more than generous when the king has been on his procession but it hasn't helped the family at all. I think it may have been the ruin of him, but of course I haven't said this to Oliver or his family.

I think Oliver's father died so suddenly that he, Oliver, has been launched into manhood prematurely. Isn't it always difficult to step into your father's shoes? But I am happy with Oliver's advancement. Our life here is comfortable. Oliver is busy with the affairs of the town. The farmland is not generous but the income from the leaseholds is sufficient for now. As they talk, my mind begins to drift and I start to think about this confinement, as I often find myself doing lately. Will it be a girl or boy? A boy – I am sure! I am a little afraid. Margaret has explained the labour will be a trial but I have begun to recite the Psalms and that brings me comfort. I trust in God. My life and that of my child will be in His Hands.

"Mother, Elizabeth must rest now. It has been so edifying to meet you uncle Thomas, but please excuse us."

Oliver's voice overtakes my thoughts and I smile at uncle Thomas as we leave the hall to go to our chamber, hiding my surprise.

But I am shocked. Why did Oliver bring the conversation to such an abrupt end? Is it my near confinement or is it something else? I can't help feeling that there is something else which Oliver and Mistress Cromwell want to discuss that they don't want me to be privy to. I have hardly spoken to this fidgeting old man. And now I am whisked away so soon? We have heard a little about his town but his thoughts are so random, quickly switching from one topic to another. He leaves long gaps in his conversation, barely able to release his words sometimes. What is this about?

We ascend the stairs and enter the bedchamber. I am careful not to raise my voice as I challenge Oliver.

"What is this all about? Why did we leave so suddenly? There is something you and your mother are not telling me. What is it?"

"It is nothing to concern yourself with, Elizabeth. You just concentrate on our child. I don't want you to tire yourself." Oliver replies.

I am not satisfied. After discovering the brewhouse, I have begun to study the workings of our family. More and more I see it is Mistress Cromwell who rules here.

"No, Oliver," I say firmly, "Why has uncle Thomas visited now. This is not just about visiting his sister is it?

You know I am quite fed up. You and your mother have plans which no one else can know about. I am your wife and I will not be put aside. In fact, Oliver, it really is time we set up house on our own. Why are we still living in your mother's house? I need space to nurture your children!"

I feel I am near to tears but I will not weep. I will not. Oliver does not answer. He quietly closes the latch to the chamber behind him as he leaves the room. I hear the front door close and his footsteps on the gravel outside. Well that is not where the matter ends. We will finish this discussion after uncle Thomas has left and I will have an answer. And I will have it from Oliver.

Chapter 43. More secrets

Oliver
'The Friars' 16 September 1621

Thomas Steward had once been a discerning and astute man. It was clear to Oliver that he had lost that sharpness. He seemed confused and agitated, although it was not clear why. Maybe it was because he hadn't seen his sister for a number of years, or maybe it was the effect of living a solitary life. Oliver knew that his mother wished him only to meet her brother and then to take Elizabeth to retire. His mother would then guide her brother to the subject she wanted to discuss - his heirs. She would secure for her son an inheritance that her late husband had been unable to provide.

Oliver was glad to retire early. The conversation had come round to his yearly income and expenditure and neither his mother nor his wife knew the whole truth. It did not suit him to have them confer or deliberate on his finances. He knew they would never do so in private but either one of them might take the opportunity to do so in family company. He had hoped to settle his debts by now but there had been unexpected outgoings. After all, he was making his reputation as a gentleman interested in the affairs of the borough and that cost money.

Indeed he had made his mark in effecting the Poor Law in this area. True some of the burghers had complained at the rate of the levy but he had explained that it was the King's direction for the poor in every village, and in every town to be cared for. Each parish was responsible for those in their area, in particular the widows and orphaned children. This work gave him much satisfaction. He was able to talk to the people of the parish and although he had not formally studied the law he was able to direct some of them to make the most of what they had, or at least to prevent that downward spiral to total poverty.

Margaret had directed Elizabeth to consult the town midwife for her confinement but Oliver was not sure that this was wise. Surely his mother and Margaret could deliver the child by themselves. Although accusations had died down in the last decade, wise women and their potions seemed to be a bonfire that could be relit at any moment. His affection for his own family prevented him from inflicting his will on them but he was unsure about Mistress Cooper.

After Thomas Steward had departed, Mistress Cromwell drew Oliver to one side, saying there was an urgent matter to discuss. Once again Elizabeth noticed this with displeasure.

"Oliver, I think it may be necessary to get your uncle censored. He is getting old and confused. Your inheritance is assured today but what of tomorrow?" Mistress Cromwell said quietly to Oliver.

Oliver was shocked by the callousness his mother was exhibiting. There was no malice, of that Oliver was sure, but he was used to letting matters work themselves out in a natural way. He did not like the sound of what his mother was suggesting but on matters of family, he was easily persuaded by her.

"What! Is this really necessary mother?" he replied then bowed to the piercing glare. "Very well, if you think so, I will contact Oliver St John and see what can be done."

Oliver paused for a moment and then continued, "Mother, I am concerned about Elizabeth."

"Why? Is it the child?.....well she did ask again about the accounts," Mistress Cromwell said.

"Yes and she wanted to know why we invited Uncle Thomas now. I could not tell her that his physical deterioration made it a necessity." Oliver replied.

"Keep your own counsel. It is not necessary for her to know everything yet." Mistress Cromwell said.

"But Mother, Elizabeth is my wife. I don't like being at odds with her. She is even talking about us moving out and setting up on our own!" Oliver's alarm was clear. He knew he could not afford to move out of his mother's house.

"Talking is a long way from doing. Remember that, Oliver. Elizabeth will begin her confinement tomorrow. That will be time enough for you to do what must be done, without alarming her."

With that Mistress Cromwell made it clear that the conversation was closed. She sat down at the table and began to pray, softly and deliberately.

Shortly after, Oliver instructed Oliver St John to apply to the court to confine his uncle. His uncle, however, was able to recover his wits sufficiently to convince the court it was not necessary to restrict him. This caused some embarrassment to Oliver and his family but the expectation of the delivery of his first child sweetened the pill for him.

Part III. Mother

Chapter 44.

Elizabeth
'The Friars', Huntington 13 October 1621

Dark thick curtains shield the sunlight at the window. I do not feel rested. I feel gloomy!

"Margaret, I'm so tired of not being able to move properly. How much longer do you think?" I say.

"Well Elizabeth, you've only had a few niggles so far, but that is usual. Continue with the sewing, that'll keep your mind off it," she replies and sits down beside me to help me concentrate on my sewing.

"Very well," I reply, "I don't mean to complain but we have been in here for three weeks. I just want this child to be born, to see him, feel him, smell him and touch him."

"There you go again, Elizabeth, saying 'him' It could be a girl!"

I smile. I know it is a boy. Then quite suddenly a sharp pain. It does not last for long but it is unmistakeable. The pains so far have been what I have experienced during the course but this is different. Margaret glances up, sensing something, but I say nothing immediately. And then

"Margaret, shall I come through this?" I am able to contain myself no longer.

"Of course, Elizabeth, why should we doubt it?" she replies.

"And my child? Will he be sound?"

I am weeping but as I look up I see the pain on Margaret's face. How cruel I am. I had quite forgotten about Margaret's loss. Bridgett's Mary gone too.

"I'm sorry, Margaret, but suddenly I am so filled with anxiety!" She pats my arm gently.

"That's natural. Remember, Elizabeth, it is the Lord who gives and who takes away." I am taken off guard by her innocent piety. She rarely mentions the Lord.

"Margaret I think maybe it is time. I am getting sharp pains now. Do you think we should send for Mistress Cooper?"

"Yes dearest. When she arrives she will be able to tell if this will be an easy birth. She may leave after she examines you and come back later. That's what she usually does. But yes, let's send for her now. Robina can go and fetch her. It should only take her fifteen minutes."

Margaret's face is a strange mixture of anxiety and excitement. I put my cloth down. I think I will walk a little. As Margaret exits, a pain, much more severe than the others comes upon me and I am almost knocked off my feet. Am I in danger of death from the coming of this child? Is this what all women experience? I have so many questions but do not know how to ask them. I trust in the Lord. I pick up my bible, glance at Psalm 100 and start to read it aloud. It brings some comfort to me.

"Make a joyful noise unto the Lord, all ye lands. Serve the Lord with gladness: come before his presence with singing. Know ye that the Lord he is God: it is he that

hath made us, and not we ourselves: we are his people and the sheep of his pasture."

I like the comparison with sheep. I have watched the sheep grazing over the hills of Essex all my life. They nibble and feed very leisurely. They are confident in their shepherd. Yes, Lord, I am confident, you will ...ah ah ah oh."

The pain has become so very demanding. I do hope Mistress Cooper is here soon. All that I can do is make a noise – albeit not so joyful. Yes, another sound outside the door heralds a visitor and I hear the footsteps along the short hallway. While Robina has been collecting Mistress Cooper from the village, the birthing stool has been brought in.

As I look at it, I begin to thank God for the past months and my new life with Oliver. Reflection is a pious activity and I am glad that there is time between each extreme pain for me to do this. Indeed I feel that this is a most holy activity. Of late, Oliver and I have been growing together more as we discuss our hopes and fears for the future. We have decided to go to the New Lands, not just yet, maybe in a few years. Thoughts of what will be, help me to get through this present pain.

We have heard such exciting stories from some of the pilgrims who have gone before us. It was so sad to hear about the Martins. The whole family has perished. My heart aches for the two boys. But Master and Mistress Martin are still to be admired for their adventuring spirit. It has been a hard year for the colonists but the colony is growing despite illness, the natives, food shortages and all the other problems, which go with pioneering in a new land. Of course, there are joys. God is strengthening the communities in fellowship and freedom. No prayer book or persecution there.

Ah, oh, oh another severe pain. How will I ever endure this?

"Now let's have a look at you," Mistress Cooper says as she waddles into the room and she is a welcome sight indeed.

She helps me onto the bed. Her examination causes me some discomfort but she is a practical woman and I am pleased to be in her hands.

"You have a few more hours to go. Can I give you some 'erbs?" she asks.

For the first time in this new experience, I am not sure. God has decreed that women should have pain in childbirth. Is it right then that we should try to dull the pain?

"Of course, Mistress, have you mugwort?" Margaret answers for me and I am relieved the decision has been made.

Margaret helps me off the bed. Standing seems to help a little. We pace the room slowly. Mistress Cooper takes out the green leaves from her basket and pummels them with the pestle. The birthing stool is ready. Not yet! I endure another painful movement in my abdomen. How can we women endure such torturous agony? Mistress Cooper passes me the mugwort and indeed it is not long before it begins to dull my senses somewhat, although not nearly enough.

Further movement at the door signifies another visitor. Familiar dark brown eyes peer at me.

"Alice, can it really be you?" I cry.

"Oh Bessie you should have told me." She reprimands as she enters.

Her excitement is a reproof to me. Although I may righteously not include my proud mother, it has been very cruel of me not to include my sisters. How has this been made known to Alice though? Of course- Margaret. I look at her and know it was her. Her face betrays an uncertainty and does not hide her guilt.

"Oh Margaret, oh Alice!" I can only say their names. The pain has taken up my whole consciousness. This is more horrendous than I could ever have imagined.

"Just a little while longer," Mistress Cooper encourages me.

My thoughts return to Margaret and her suffering. It must have been so sorrowful for her to endure the death of her daughter. There was no reason that the doctor could find. It was not croup. It was not fever. It was not plague. One day she was there and in the morning she was gone – pale and lifeless.

"I must tend to my own family awhile. As you are here Alice, it is a good opportunity for me to go now." Margaret excuses herself.

Alice is dabbing my face with cool water and I am glad she is with me. I am suddenly aware that she has a thickening waist.

"Alice, can it be?" I ask and before I can finish my sentence, she is laughing and nodding.

"Oh my dearest, I am so happy for you. But I hope this experience does not make you afeared!"

"Dearest Bessie, you are enduring so well. I hope I can be as brave as you," she replies and I catch her hand as another strong wave hits me. No, I do not think I am enduring well at all. I am anxious and complaining, not a good example to anyone! I am feeling dazed now. Mugwort is definitely helpful.

I glance at the clock. The whole day has passed already. Six o'clock. Alice positions me above the birthing stool and stands beside me so I can grasp her arm. Mistress Cooper is standing by my other arm.

"How much longer, Mistress" I plead with Mistress Cooper

"Nearly there, Mistress. When I say 'push', you must draw down as if you must shit. Don't 'push' until I tell you. Is that clear?"

Yes, I think I know what she means. My head is swimming, my body aches. There's another tremendous pain and she says 'push'. Pain and respite, multiplied a hundred times. Then the moment arrives. Mistress Cooper catches the child as he emerges. Alice, Anna, Margaret all are here now. Delightful claps and gasps.

Before I know it, I am holding our son and Oliver is next to me, smiling and pleased as can be. I am exhausted but I have come through this.

"We'll name him for my father, Elizabeth. Is that alright with you?" Oliver says.

"Yes," I reply and look into Robert's cute, scrunched-up red face. Mistress Cooper hurries Oliver out of the confinement room but allows him to take Robert, now swaddled, to show everybody.

Chapter 45. Baby Robert

Oliver
'The Friars', Huntington 14 October 1621

"Mother he is such a perfect child!"

Oliver's delight in his son was obvious to everyone who met him. Gone was the melancholy which had blighted his former cheerful playfulness. Mistress Cromwell had been worried about him and had wondered about the gloom which had beset him. She was delighted that the child had been named for her husband. It was a fitting memory of him. Margaret's children were a great blessing but somehow this was different – her son's son. Margaret's son, Valentine, was a Walton. This boy was a Cromwell. He would be as proud as his father to carry this name forward.

For Mistress Cromwell it was an eerie sensation as she held her new grandson. She sensed a feeling of re-living the moment she first held Oliver - holding a special child. He wriggled in her arms, asserting his will, making his presence known in the world. Mistress Cromwell had not experienced this when she held Margaret's children. She loved each one very much and had been delighted to welcome them all into the world, but this one, just like Oliver, was different.

Oliver too was filled with a joy he could not explain. He had expected to feel the pleasure of the birth successfully accomplished but this new softness of heart, he could not explain. It was as if the whole world had been gifted to him by God; yes, children were certainly a gift from God. Oliver was thankful that Elizabeth had come through this birth safely and with a new glow. Her delight was easy to see although Oliver was not sure it had been wise of her to send away the wet nurse. Still he knew his mother and sisters had already arranged to complete Elizabeth's household duties and indeed were glad to do so. But now it was time for the womenfolk to celebrate and Oliver was glad to provide the means to do so.

Immediately following the birth after he had returned Robert to a tired Elizabeth, and made sure the women were able to celebrate as they well deserved, he had ran through the town to find William. He could not contain himself. His joy, as he had held his son, was far greater than anything he had ever felt and he just had to share it with someone.

But as he neared the "Fountain Inn", it was obvious something was amiss. The rector from St. Mary's came out of the doorway shaking his head and wringing his hands. The neighbours had gathered and were looking around, despair on their faces. Oliver entered with some reluctance and it was William who gave an explanation. Oliver was shaken to the core. He had rushed to his friend to share his joy but received only sorrow instead. How could he share this dreadful news with Elizabeth? He must wait.

Oliver, unable to return immediately, walked through the town. He walked as if the effort would shake off the shocking news he had received. The cold air only chilled his bones. He could do nothing; there was nothing to be done.

On his return to "The Friars", baby Robert was again being passed from hand to hand and delighting the whole company. Neighbours came in, too, to join in the sense of thankfulness that the whole family felt. Oliver could now imagine what it would be like to take his son along hunting, to introduce him to the hawks, to accompany him riding. He just hadn't been able to imagine what it would be like before, but once he held his child in his arms it all became real to him, and finally he could imagine how his son's whole life would be. Oliver was determined that this child should take his place as a gentleman in this little town. How could it be that at one end of the town the folk were rejoicing but at the other end they were mourning? What a world we live in, Oliver reflected.

"You seem so distant, Oliver, is something wrong?" Mistress Cromwell knew her son's moods so well.

"Later, mother, I have something to tell you but it must wait until my sisters are abed." Oliver replied.

The evening passed quickly. The sisters talked eagerly about the new baby. Who did he look like? What a thrill to have another boy in the family at last. Oliver, his mother and his sisters gathered around the fire as the night was cold. Baby Robert's cries in the upper chamber could be heard now and again. It was a new sound in the house, strangely comforting rather than disturbing.

"I knew it would be a boy!" Jane chatted excitedly.

"I said so too," Robina competed with her sister.

"Boy or girl doesn't matter," Lizzie drawled, "He is healthy .... What shall we embroider for him, mother?"

"We shall see what Elizabeth wants soon enough. After all the excitement it is time for you girls to be getting to bed." Mistress Cromwell kissed her daughters on their heads, an unusual display of affection. She folded Robina's cloth for her, knowing she was slow to go to bed.

Mistress Cromwell could sense her son's nervousness. She accompanied her daughters upstairs to the chamber to make sure they were settled. It was but ten minutes and she was by her son's side again.

"Now, Oliver, what is troubling you?" Mistress Cromwell wasted no time after her daughters had retired.

Tears just wetting his eyes, Oliver said,

"Mother, I cannot breathe. The news is so difficult to fathom. Bridgett ... and the children perished. I cannot find a way to soften the blow. Elizabeth must not be told, not yet."

His mother listened in silence, unable to make any comment. They sat together by that fire in the hall as they had done many evenings before. They did not speak but each drew comfort from the presence of the other.

After an hour, Oliver was ready to retire and see his wife. He endured endless details of the development of their new infant. Under other circumstances it would have been a joy but not tonight. Elizabeth was so talkative and attentive to her young son, that she did not notice her husband's distraction. Oliver knew he could not share this dreadful secret yet. It was just another dark burden he must carry for the time being.

Chapter 46. Churching

Elizabeth
St John's church, Huntington 18 November 1621

A musty dank odour greets me as I enter St John's church. A few congregants are returning to their seats after the holy communion. Bobbing caps turn round in curiosity and I see an extravagant feather I recognise. I know every eye is on me as I carry Robert in. How silly I am! Every eye is on my sweet new baby. We are all ready to rejoice. I am the one who is different. I am a mother. There is a mixture of pride and thankfulness welling inside me as I glance at my son. I survived. To many, childbirth is a natural feat but to me it is a miracle. Oliver is sitting beside his mother and the sisters in the family pew, third row from the front. They make a grand bunch indeed. Mistress Cooper rustles beside me - her best frock aired for the occasion; I am grateful to her for my safe delivery.

Reverend Beard is already at the altar, the golden cross gleaming as the sun streams through the crack in the side wall. We walk to the front and I sit on the small chair placed there for me. I pass baby Robert to Alice, seated on the front pew with the rest of my own family. My head is covered with a white lace veil - delicately crocheted by Lizzie. I know I don't have to wear it. Father says he does not know why we still have churching in this day and age. But I want to do what is expected of me in my new town. I am glad to do what the other mothers have done for centuries; I am grateful to have come through this ordeal. The pain I endured is already forgotten. It has been pushed out of my thoughts by my joy.

I am surprised to see my lady mother. She is not known in Huntington at all and now she wants to be noticed. Well she and father do indeed make a handsome couple.

"We thank you O God our Father that you have seen fit to preserve your servant Elizabeth through the trial of childbirth and we thank you for the gift of a son to Oliver. May you bless her and grant her the further fruitfulness of her womb to the glory of Jesus Christ your Son, Amen."

The blessing has been given. As we exit, I am surprised that I do not see Bridgett and William here. I had expected to see them. Margaret said they were not at Roberts' baptism either. Perhaps they have illness in the house? I can be welcomed back into civil company now, so yes, I shall visit them first. Even idle gossip will be welcome to me after the long weeks of confinement.

"Good day to you Elizabeth. What a beautiful son you have there. You must be very happy."

Mistress Walden greets me. She stands together with Mistress Altham, soon to be Mistress Robert Barnard. I do hope Mistress Altham is not too much influenced by her friend. She is a sweet young woman now.

I smile because I do not know how to answer Mistress Walden. But I need not be afeared. She is well able to continue the dialogue without my participation.

She continues, the feather in her hat wavering in the slight breeze.

"It was such a privilege to meet Master John Hampden again at Robert's baptism. Oliver chose wisely in inviting him as godparent."

Yes, that is probably the only truth you have uttered recently, I think but do not say so.

"Yes and so pleasant to meet your sister Alice. When is her child due?" Mistress Altham chirps in.

"Good Day to you Mistress Altham," I reply, "Alice said you were all so kind and attentive to her. Her child is due in the spring. Mother says she had no grandchildren and now she will have two.

Mistresses Altham and Walden laugh - their pretence sounding loud as a gong. Then they move on to greet my lady mother and father. I am glad. Yes Oliver did choose wisely regarding the godparents - John Lowry the chandler, John Hampden statesman and Alice my dear sister. I wonder why William and Bridgett were not asked. Sometimes Oliver does confound me! There has been no time to discuss these matters with him yet.

"Thank you so much Master Beard," I say as he greets me at the entrance, "That was a real blessing to me. I am overcome with the peace of the Lord."

"Yes, Elizabeth, sometimes these old customs can bring comfort to our souls," he replies.

The rest of the congregation gather around as I exit; to snatch a glimpse of the new member of the community. I look down at little Robert and I notice his skin is just slightly tinged blue. I don't want him to become chilled and I must nurse him soon.

"Oliver," I call, "I must take Robert back indoors. I don't want him to become chilled. Will you see my mother and father and tell them I am returning home?"

Oliver waves in acknowledgement and I am soon walking towards "The Friars" again. My shoes click on the cobblestones. The road is quiet as I am the first to return from church. I hug Robert into myself. A horse snorts in greeting as I pass the blacksmiths. The remaining autumn leaves flutter to the ground, as I enter the gatehouse.

I am quickly upstairs and prepare to nurse Robert. I wonder, was this such a good decision? Why did I object to Mistress Cooper's wet nurse? It seems absurdly silly now. It will prevent me from being in polite company. I haven't really seen Oliver this past month because he busies himself with the parish duties, and now I cannot accompany him. I love Oliver so very much but this new responsibility, my son, takes up so much of my time and my thoughts. What am I to do? I am torn between my two obligations.

Chapter 47. Debts

Oliver

Hinchingbrooke House, Huntington 19 November 1621

It was not entirely unexpected when Oliver received the summons the next day from his godfather to attend him at Hinchingbrooke House. He knew what the reason was. Oliver detoured from his usual route that morning and turned his horse toward Hinchingbrooke. It was a cold crisp morning which threatened snow. He kept the horse to a trot as the ground was hard and a little icy. Neither his mother nor Elizabeth would suspect he had paid a visit to Hinchingbrooke, as it was his custom to take a morning ride every day. It was just the venue which he had changed.

When he arrived, he was greeted by the pleasant visage of John Maples, the manservant, who showed him into his godfather's study, where to his dismay, he also saw the surly face of Robert Pepys, the bailiff. I'll receive no quarter from him, thought Oliver.

"Oliver, come in, no time for preliminaries I'm afraid," Sir Oliver plunged in.

"Good day, Sir," Oliver was uncharacteristically brief.

"I'm afraid Master Pepys here has acquainted me with the large sum you owe him - from the card table!"

Sir Oliver held his palm up to stop Pepys from embarking on the lambasting that Oliver knew he deserved. For this Oliver was relieved. He knew his debt. His shame was blazoned on his very soul. But he didn't know what he could do and the last thing he wanted was a reprimand from the likes of Robert Pepys.

Sir Oliver continued, "I don't see any easy solution. Oliver, you must sell your remaining fields. Unfortunately I cannot loan you anything from my estate. I have debts, too." Sir Oliver turned to the bailiff.

"Will that satisfy you, Pepys?"

The bailiff said no word, merely nodded. Pepys put his black felt hat back on his head and strode from the room, not glancing at Oliver.

"I am really sorry, uncle," Oliver began to apologise.

"No need, young man," his uncle replied. "Just bring the deeds. I know the house belongs to your mother. She must keep that but everything else must be disposed of to pay the debts. That way it won't go into the Magistrates' charge."

"Thank you, sir." Oliver was humbled but grateful a solution could be found. He had been desperate to find an answer but it was now clear his uncle's solution was the only one feasible. Much to his regret, Oliver would have to sell his land.

"You know Oliver, the gossip is all around Huntington. That bailiff could not keep his mouth shut, especially to his aunt, Paulina. She married Sir Sidney Montague, you know. It's bad luck, Oliver, that's all that can be said, but I don't think your Elizabeth would be very impressed. Quite a god-fearing woman that one, hmm. I suppose she is still occupied with your boy? Congratulations, by the way."

"Thank you, sir." Oliver repeated. "I would be grateful if you could keep this quiet, sir.. Elizabeth doesn't know."

Sir Oliver smiled and Maples' entry to offer refreshment prevented further discourse. Oliver declined the ale. He wanted to alleviate the tension of the conversation. His godfather did not seem embarrassed by the incident but Oliver was. He was in a hurry to get home but as he was about to leave, in came two men several years Oliver's senior.

"Father you didn't tell us you were expecting our cousin!" John said.

"Yes very remiss of me," Sir Oliver said not hinting of the finished business.

"So Oliver, will you come with us? We are off once more to fight Frederick and Elizabeth's cause in the Palatinate. We leave tomorrow." The older brother said.

"Not to Heidelberg?" Oliver was trying to recall what had happened to the Princess and her husband in the past year.

"No," said William, "They are in Prague now. Crowned last year but the Archduke is fighting back and it looks like a very bloody war will be on us. We're going to fight to keep the Papists at bay."

"Yes, and I think they could do with your strategic skills, John. I was impressed by you, when William and I were there for just that short while. Take care. Sadly, I cannot join you. I'm wed now, did you not know? My wife and I are thinking of going to the New World, taking our newborn with us ..... yes, a son, Robert."

"Yes, you leave the soldiering to us, Oliver. You're far too lean now." John joked.

Oliver smiled, "I must take my leave now."

Yes, under different circumstances it would have been good to join them in such a worthy cause - fighting against the papists in Europe. But Oliver's life had taken a different direction now. He would have to sell two of his fields to satisfy the debt. He had sowed peas and barley in those fields last season and it would be a meagre harvest next year with two fields less. He could not sell off the pasture lands because they were needed for the sheep. He had hoped to buy a new herd, both beef and dairy, but now that was just a distant dream. How had he let it come to this?

As he mounted Chestnut, helped by the groom, he could see Ferrer and Pepys standing at the side of the barn. Pepys was smirking and talking behind his hand.

"You'll not get the better of me!" Oliver mumbled under his breath, as he galloped past them. But he was soon slowed to a safer trot by the icy path.

Oliver assumed correctly. Neither his mother, nor his wife, were aware of his visit to Hinchingbrooke and the consequences. He did not know how long his secret could be kept. He could delay the sale for a while. But for now he wanted to relish in the joy of his newborn son.

Chapter 48. Disagreement

Elizabeth
'The Friars', Huntington 13 December 1621

Nearly two months have passed and I am adjusting to this new life as a mother. Baby Robert is a miracle as far as I am concerned. He is just so perfect and I feel the Lord has indeed blessed me. He is a chubby fellow and growing well and when I look at him I am filled with joy. Oliver told me he was so proud when he presented him for baptism at St John's. I felt just the same on the day of my churching.

Mistress Cromwell is a doting grandmother and is delighted to take Robert to comfort him if he cries. She is so overjoyed that we have named our first child for her husband and we were glad to do it. My decision not to employ a wet nurse has not caused as much consternation as I had originally feared.

Mistress Cromwell runs the household now. When I first came here I had thought that would be my work but we have settled into a convenient routine so I have a lot of time to nurse Robert. This is what I want to do, although I did have some doubts at first. The God-fearing authors recommend it, as it is natural. And there is nothing written in the bible to contradict this; the bible does not say it is good to give your child out for another to nurse. So that is what I will stick with. I think I have incurred Mistress Cooper's wrath as she had a woman lined up for me. But the town of Huntington sports a number of newborns. My unfashionable ways will soon be forgotten.

I do not quarrel with Mistress Cromwell. Who is in charge is no longer important to me. We are one family.

Margaret is delighted that Valentine has a cousin. Anna too wants to learn about the practicalities of motherhood and so is willing to help with Robert's care. I think she has a sweetheart but when will they marry? I do not know.

Now that I have been churched, I will be able to take part in the community again. We have been invited once more to Hinchingbrooke House but Oliver is reluctant to visit. I don't understand why. We haven't visited there since the fair before we were married. So once again Oliver and I are in disagreement.

"Why do you want to accept this invitation, Elizabeth? You do remember the fair, don't you?" Oliver reminds me sternly.

"Oliver," I reply, "Yes, of course I remember but that was not Sir Oliver's doing. I want your relatives to meet our firstborn son! He has so many aunts and uncles at Hinchingbrooke. He must begin to make their acquaintance."

"Yes I know but on this occasion I agree with my mother that Uncle Thomas is the relationship we need to nurture just now. He is a simple God-fearing man, not taken with ostentation and opulence." Oliver tries to dissuade me.

"But Oliver," I persist, "It is merely a dinner invitation. It is very near – not far for Robert."

I do not understand why Oliver is so reluctant. Can it be so bad? Why must we choose between these different relatives? Surely all of them must share in our joy.

"No, Elizabeth," Oliver replies gruffly, "There is more than our child to consider. It is not as simple as it seems. Sir Oliver is a close supporter of the King and it is rumoured he sponsored opposition against the Sabbath Day bill. Sir Francis is relying on my support and I cannot fraternise with Sir Oliver at the same time. Sir Francis has warned me that I must be careful whom I am seen to support."

"No, Oliver, it is not Sir Francis who is advising you. It is Ezekiel Rogers, Aunt Joan's chaplain! He is the one warning you of the company you must keep!"

Now I am cross. I am stunned that our child seems less important to Oliver than this silly squabble between the King and the gentry. I realise that I am out of touch with what has been happening in our country. I used to be so interested and discuss these matters with my dear father. But even so, I have heard about the King's Sports Bill and that the Parliament has met to discuss it. No it does not seem right for people to engage in sports on the Sabbath. But I can see the King's reasoning. Not all people are as devout as they should be. You cannot impose your own beliefs on other people. It must come from the heart. Godliness cannot be ordered!

Since Robert's birth I find I have lost interest in the current news. It used to be so important to me but now as I look into his soft brown eyes and his chubby face, I am overcome with love for him. Who would have thought that such a small creature could change me so? His every whimper is my concern. I check his breathing and warmth every hour. Quite simply, he commands all my time and I would have it no other way. At first it was frightening to bear the responsibility of another human life but gradually I have become accustomed to what he wants. The more I seem to sense his needs correctly, the more I want no one else to care for him. I am convinced now that I am the only one who can be committed enough to care for and nurture him.

"Elizabeth, my dear, I know Robert has become the centre of your world. I understand that, but on this matter, I will not be thwarted. We will not be visiting Hinchingbrooke in the near future." Oliver speaks decisively but I am only vaguely aware of what has been said. What alarms me is the vehemence in which this statement is made. Oliver steps out of the room and is gone!

I do not remember father speaking to my lady mother in such a gruff tone. What has got into Oliver? We seem to be growing apart more each day. I must visit Bridgett and discuss this matter with her. She always has some words of kindness and wisdom for me.

Chapter 49. Gentlemen

Oliver
Barrington Hall, Hatfield Broad Oak 14 December 1621

After Oliver's initial delight in his heir, he decided to return to more frequent discussions with Sir Francis and his father-in-law, Sir James Bourchier. The knowledge these two men had, impressed Oliver. Their understanding of King James was far superior to his own because the circles they moved in included a sweep of nobility and gentry which he could not hope to match. But more than that Sir James, being a merchant, had a wider perspective of the problems in the country than Oliver could ever hope to gain by himself.

Oliver had been a more frequent visitor at Hinchingbrooke of late and he realised this was a dangerous pattern which he had allowed himself to fall into. His argument with Elizabeth on the previous day had consolidated the thoughts and ambitions which he had been trying to think through. He had to make a choice. He could no longer be in both camps. If he wanted the support of the Essex gentlemen then he must show some loyalty. Hinchingbrooke had only brought him unhappiness.

He wondered why the presence of his other uncle, Sir Francis Barrington, made him feel so uneasy. Was it because he was such a pious man and a man like Oliver, heaped as he was in sin, could not but be suffocated by all the godliness surrounding him? Once he had acknowledged it, Oliver could, superficially at least, pretend to be more devout than he was. The odd thing was that piety made people trusting and so easily fooled.

As he arrived at Barrington Hall that December morning, Sir Francis and Sir James and several other gentlemen were already locked in a heated discussion. No one paused to glance at him, as he entered. He was a frequent visitor to the hall and his appearance no longer merited attention.

"But I cannot trade easily if the King continues to issue trade monopolies which cut me out from the market."

Sir James tried to remain calm in the face of opposition from many of the gentlemen in the room.

"Yes," rebutted Sir Francis "but the most important issue at the moment is the right of the gentlemen of the House to discuss these problems when they relate to the broader issues of what we may and may not discuss. It has always been our right to discuss such things. We will not be silenced. The royal marriage has a direct bearing on our country, especially in matters of our religion. We will not barter our religious freedom so that the King can get his hands on a handsome dowry. We know what that will mean! His wife can buy more jewels and fine clothes!"

Oliver was interested in the topics which the gentlemen present discussed but he knew he was not in a position to influence any of the agreements made. He was very aware that he knew another side to the arguments – one proffered by Sir Oliver - but he was disinclined to offer any insight from that quarter. That was part of his secret life. Besides, his most urgent need was a personal one. Since that day, nearly a month ago, when he had been summoned by Sir Oliver to sort out his debts, he had agreed to sell some land but he still clung to a slim hope that he could secure a loan or even a gift from either his father-in-law or this uncle. He just needed the right moment to test the waters.

The topic changed to the saints who had gone to the new world – a topic which did interest Oliver enormously.

"It was a sad affair to hear about the Martin family perishing. I am so glad we were able to meet them before they embarked." Sir James stated.

"Indeed yes," Sir Francis continued, "Such a brave undertaking. I understand that you were part of the Mercers financing that venture, Sir James?"

"Yes, and it looks like we will take a loss for quite some time. I had hoped to be trading in furs from the new world by now. I understand the beavers' fur there is quite exceptional. Probably something to do with the extreme cold. But we have been unable to get any deals finalised." Sir James replied.

On hearing about the poor prospects of the fur traders, Oliver's heart sank. It would be no good to ask his father-in-law for a loan again yet. His profits had not increased since the last time they had spoken.

Well, it was always good to hear John Pym's views. He was such an interesting fellow. Oliver turned to him.

"Master Pym, your work has recently taken you to the Midlands. Have you heard the new lecturer, John Cotton?" Oliver said.

"Indeed yes," Pym replied, "There is something grand happening there. Almighty God has seen fit to bless that ministry. John Cotton preaches a fine bible message and as a result, many people are coming to serve the Lord Jesus Christ. And I understand he is working with another godly person, a woman in fact, Anne Hutchinson. God is no 'respecter of persons'"

"Really, but I heard that a lot of the villagers from Scrooby will be travelling to the new world as soon as they can." Sir Francis interrupted. "That is where John Cotton has been lecturing,"

Sir James then took his opportunity to introduce John Pym to the new Earl of Warwick, Robert Rich, son of his old friend. It was rumoured that Warwick would himself be trading the new world. Sir James had an idea that the affairs of the mercers and traders could be aided by a keen financier like Pym. Besides Sir James, a shrewd merchant, was always keen to be in on a new deal.

Oliver, not content that John would be whisked away before he had a chance to probe that keen mind, interrupted,

"But Master Pym I hear you are soon to take a seat at Whitehall in time for a long overdue sitting of the house. Are you excited?"

"I certainly am, Oliver. It's such a grand opportunity. I have been waiting for this and was fortunate enough to gain a Somerset seat. I just hope the House manages to stay calm and grant the sovereign some of the subsidies he will ask for."

"It seems to be concern over the Palatinate that brings good king James to discussion, then."

Oliver was eager to gain more information.

"Yes I think so, but Parliament must concern itself with the business it needs to accomplish and not squabble with the sovereign. It has been such a long time since we had this opportunity. We must not waste it," said Pym

"I am hoping to represent Huntington but there is no influence to be had at the moment. If you get a chance to speak a word for me or get any inkling of a change there, perhaps you will let me know." Oliver requested.

"Of course, Oliver," Pym replied, "but you have a wife and a new son to take up your time at the moment. Congratulations by the way. There's plenty of time for you yet to make your mark, Oliver."

With that John Pym turned again to the Earl of Warwick. Oliver was satisfied. His turn would come.

Chapter 50. Bridgett

Elizabeth
'The Friars', Huntington 16 December 1621

Why has Oliver such a sombre look today? He has been so delighted with the progress of little Robert. I plan to start visiting again next month. The demands of nursing have curtailed my outings these last two months but I am sure I will be out again soon. This cold weather also makes me reluctant to step out but soon it will be Christmas. Robert's first. It shall be a time of rejoicing indeed.

"Elizabeth, do come and sit," Oliver gently guides me to the nursing chair but Robert is chuckling quite happily.

"Oliver, I was just going to come downstairs and help with the chores. And I must encourage Anna with her lessons again."

Oliver's face is dark. Is he cross with me again?

"No, Elizabeth, sit down." He commands and I can sense something is wrong.

"What is it?" I ask.

"My dear, I'm sorry I have no flowery way to dress up this bad news. Our friend Bridgett is drowned and her youngest two with her. William is beside himself with grief. He will take no comfort. I could not tell you before. It happened the day Robert was born."

I cannot take this in. How can my dear friend and her two children be drowned? Was there an accident? She would not have taken them to bathe when it is so cold! I try to picture what has happened. We have been down to the river so often in summer and yes, we have taken the children with us. They love to splash about. Once Robina and Jane came with us as did Margaret's two and we had such a jolly picnic. But that was in the summer. She would not have taken them to swim at this time of year. That doesn't make sense. My mind is whirling; I am feeling dazed.

"Elizabeth, Elizabeth," Oliver says.

I realise that I have not said a word. What response can I give? A terrible accident! How has this happened? I hear a gasp, a stifled cry and know it is coming from me. Tears begin to fall on my face. I can feel their wetness and still it does not touch my heart. I am frozen, unable to talk.

"Elizabeth, I will leave you for a while. Robert – I will carry him downstairs. Mother and Margaret will take him for a while."

Oliver hesitates, then picks up our son. I watch him but it is as if I am in a dream, a nightmare in fact. He continues,

"Elizabeth, you rest for a while."

I have to make sense of this. What did he say? Bridgett has drowned together with her two youngest. But she can swim. How can she drown if she can swim? The river is quite shallow by the old bridge. That is where we went in summer.

I catch my breath sharply, trying to get in more air. How can this be? Bridgett – always so cheery, delighted with her children and enjoying her work on the post with William. Her youngest two were girls with yellow curls, always laughing and giggling. This is too awful to contemplate. I just can't take it in. But Oliver didn't tell me how it happened. Can he mean it was not an accident? I must know more. Who found them? What part of the river was it? All these details matter. They will point us to the truth of what happened.

I get up. I must go down and question Oliver. I descend slowly, gathering my thoughts.

Mistress Cromwell sits with Robert on her lap. She sees me and says,

"Oliver has gone with the others to collect kindling for the fire. He said he would go to William's as well to take some for him. William still has the oldest two to care for - poor little motherless mites." She stumbles over those last few words. I can see it is hard for her too. Her eyes, though, betray no information.

I'm desperately trying to control my tears now. This has at last reached my heart but my mind needs also to be informed. I ask quietly,

"Mistress, do tell me how this happened? How can such an accident occur?"

"Elizabeth, I am afraid it may not have been an accident," she whispers.

"But who would want to murder such a wonderful wife and mother, mistress?" I still cannot comprehend it.

"Elizabeth, there is talk that Bridgett took her own life."

Mistress Cromwell can barely utter these words. As soon as they are out, she stops. I gasp. How can my sweet friend have committed so heinous a sin? Why would she do such a thing? It is not possible.

Robert seems to sense that something is wrong and he begins to cry so that once more I am reminded that I must nurse and care for my own child. I take him from Mistress Cromwell, uttering a barely audible thank you, and return to our bedchamber to nurse him. I am so shocked. I am numb. I am performing my tasks without thinking; just doing what I know I must. But inside I am unable to feel.

I sit with Robert and he begins to suckle. I look into his face urgent for solace and nourishment. How could a mother kill herself and her two children with her? I cannot take this in. I know Bridgett so well. She could not do such a thing. She would not. She had not spoken of any worries. There must be some mistake. Oliver said it was on the day Robert was born but that was over seven weeks ago. Bridgett must already be buried and I did not go to the funeral. They did not tell me. Oh Bridgett, Bridgett, what has happened?

Chapter 51. Reflection

Oliver
Huntington 16 December 1621

Oliver had been to deliver kindling wood to William, but the atmosphere was so heavy and oppressive there that he could not stay. There was no comfort that he could offer that could be acceptable to William. As he turned his feet homewards his thoughts drifted and he found himself taking a different path to the one he usually trod. His heart was heavy and he could not bear to walk in the vicinity of "The Fountain" today; That whole end of town was an open wound to him. But the direction towards Godmanchester held new promise. As he left the town and entered the forest, he felt more at peace.

He had not expected Elizabeth to take the news of Bridgett's death well. After all Bridgett was Elizabeth's one true friend in Huntington. How could anyone accept the death of a young woman without raging at the sky – without shaking a fist at God?

He had a lot to mull over since his recent visits to Hinchingbrooke House and Barrington Hall. How strange that his relatives were diametrically opposed on life's spectrum. Hinchingbrooke represented life's excitements and frivolities; Barrington Hall, piety and godliness. Recently Oliver had come to see that Barrington Hall stood for much more than a desire to seek godliness. It was about the life of gentlemen landowners wishing to make godly decisions which would encourage the whole nation.

Oliver thought too of William. His grief was destructive and debilitating. It was the unnatural method of Bridgett's death, as well as the many unanswered questions which she had left behind, which caused the darkness. William could think of no reason why his wife should take such an action. But she had. Bridgett's body had been discovered in the river still clasping the hands of her two small daughters. There could be no doubt that it was suicide. Could it have been her tormented grief over little Mary's death?

Of course, William's new venture was now in serious jeopardy. There had already been a downturn of business due to the lessening patronage of a weakening sovereign. This added rupture of the demise of the main administrator had sunk the business lower than was viable. If this postal system could not be relied on, the customers would quickly turn to other means.

As the first bridge came in view, Oliver spied the sheep being brought down. Their worth will only be counted at shearing time, he thought. Sheep would not help in his financial crisis. Besides the trade in wool had been declining of late as well. Where would it all end?

Around the next corner on the other side of the road sat a cunning woman. She was watching the travellers as they crossed the bridge. Oliver stopped. He did not want to be confronted by her. He knew her well as his business as Poor Law administrator had meant he had to talk to her about her behaviour in town. He had warned her not to loiter and so she was careful to go about her herb-gathering briskly and to keep to the forest rather than come into town.

Oliver was sure her acquiescence to his warnings was as much to do with the hangings of the 'Flowers' women as to his own authority. He had followed the case quite closely as he wanted to understand more about that prophesy which had been made over his own life, but he was no nearer to comprehending it. Oliver did not understand these women. He paused for a moment. This woman was different from Ol' Margrit, who was more of a soothsayer, more like the Flowers women. This woman was really just an old woman who gathered herbs to make a small living. He did not think he was in any danger from her, but he was not sure. His work connected to the Poor Law had not been onerous. Huntington did not have many idle poor to deal with. He turned around and began to retrace his steps back to Huntington. It did not suit him to confront this woman and he had walked far enough anyway.

After Elizabeth's outburst over the brewhouse, he and his mother agreed Old Mistress Cromwell would take back its control. Aaron was an able lad and was well fixed to help Mistress Cromwell with the daily management. At least that was one secret which no longer had to be kept. Oliver knew that Elizabeth did not accept the activity but she had stopped scolding about it. Yes, and now Elizabeth knew about Bridgett. That was two secrets exposed. Elizabeth was not handling these life-wounds very well. Yet she has a strong faith and that should sustain her, he thought.

"Yes, her faith in the Almighty is certainly stronger than mine!" he said aloud.

Still one secret remained. Oliver had been unable to secure a loan to pay his gambling debts. Sir Oliver had made it very clear that he agreed with Robert Pepys that Oliver must sell off his fields to pay his debts. Oliver could not risk that Elizabeth would find out about that at present, which was one of the reasons he had declined to dine at Hinchingbrooke. He realised that Sir Oliver had not pressed him aggressively about the sale of his lands because of the previous service he had rendered to the crown but that goodwill could not last much longer. He had spoken to Oliver St John about the sale but now the transfer would have to be made firm. He could delay no longer.

Matters had not gone Oliver's way this year. What really troubled him was Master Walden's insistence that Huntington needed a new charter. Oliver knew Walden was trying to sideline him and William. Lionel Walden had enjoyed power in Huntington for too long. But what sort of man jumps to press his case when his opponent is devastated with grief? The town's citizens were impressed by that smiling face and ready handshake; they did not know of his callousness. He held all the arrogance of the eldest son of one of the richest families in the town. It was rumoured that he was a papist as well but so far that had not been proven.

Going through these issues in his mind, Oliver knew he had neglected Elizabeth of late. True she had been occupied with Robert and had herself little time for discussion and companionship. That was natural after the birth of the first child. But Oliver missed the laughter and sparkle in his household. Life seemed to have been drained from all of them.

As he approached his house again, he admitted to himself that his walk had been refreshing and had enabled him to think through some of his problems. He had begun to feel hemmed in. He determined to make another visit to Doctor Simcott and get some mixture to lift his spirits. He also needed to buy some mithridite to ward off plague. Rumours were circulating that the land would once again be smitten by this terrible disease soon. He did not know whether that was the truth but he would take no chance.

Chapter 52. Grief

Elizabeth
'The Friars', Huntington 16 December 1621

I close my eyes and ask the Lord, my father in heaven, to help me. I confess my pride and selfishness and am enveloped by stillness. Slowly, I am filled with peace and the blackness of my soul is engulfed with light and joy so that I want to sing a psalm. I don't though.

Instead, I sing a lullaby quietly to my little one and know that I have another day to make amends. I slumber in fits and starts as I nurse. I cannot wean this child yet. I must finish what I have started but this boy will be the only one privileged to be nursed by his mother. In future I shall stick to convention and the wet nurse will be called in so that I can encourage and support my husband. I hope that Mistress Cromwell will inform me about what Oliver has been doing these past four months. I need her help to be the best wife I can be.

The sudden passing away of my good friend Bridgett is a devastating blow to my heart. I cannot function nor speak to anyone, except to nurture my boy. I have been able to examine my sentiments and have not been able to find a satisfactory explanation. I feel betrayed and let down by my poor tortured friend. For surely that must have been how it was for her - torture - to drown and take her babies with her. Her betrayal is in not speaking to me. I am her friend. I was her friend. How was it that she could not confide in me? Was it a weakness in me, or in her? I have searched and searched and gone over our conversations and have found nothing which could betray such a sadness. And now she is damned forever. I have not been able to visit William or indeed speak to Oliver about all this. I have spoken to no-one excepting our Lord. My prayers have been fervent — for all of us.

I must be strong. Oliver needs me. I have seen, of late, his worried frown. He is trying to make his way in this world. As much as Mistress Walden is petty and vain, she supports her husband in the business of the town. She has a young son, just as I have, but she is always visiting and conversing. It is so long since Oliver and I have really talked together. I realise now that I must concentrate on being a wife - not just a mother.

I put Robert in his crib and go to find Mistress Cromwell. When I find her sitting by the fire in the great hall she is alone. This is a good opportunity but I feel nervous suddenly and I slow my step, practising my words over and over again in my heart.

"Mistress Cromwell," I hesitate, "we have been distant recently. My time has been taken up with Robert. I do not know what Oliver has been concerned with ...I cannot continue like this."

I hear sobs and feel pressure mounting in my breasts. I tell her I have made mistakes. Oliver is angry with me and I do not know how to make it right. I beg her to help me.

"Elizabeth, hush now, your baby is beautiful. He is your first child. Of course, he takes up all of your time. Oliver knows that and he is not angry with you. But he does want you take an interest in his life as well. He has been attending the Parish Council Meetings and he has been made responsible for the collection of the Poor Rate. He also has to take charge of the repair and maintenance of the main street, organising the list and the labour. Sir

Francis is satisfied with his progress and will nominate him as the candidate for election when the next Parliament sits.

Mistress Cromwell's magnanimity overwhelms me. There is no trace of smugness or arrogance as she smiles at me reassuringly.

"But what shall I do?" I wail.

"Just talk to him. Explain as you have to me," Mistress Cromwell says,

"Where is he now?" I ask.

"He has just gone out to take the air, I believe."

I step outside. The air is cold and I have not donned my cloak. No matter, I will just look and perhaps I will see Oliver. Ah yes, here he comes. He has spotted me and hastens to reach me.

"Elizabeth, is something wrong?" he says, at once, concerned.

"Oh Oliver, I just wanted to say I am so sorry. I know I have been distant but this shock... this shock with my one true friend has ...." I catch my breath holding back the tears.

"Elizabeth, do not fret. I understand. You have nothing to reproach yourself for, my love. But look at you- you have no cloak. Come inside or you'll catch cold."

I am overwhelmed by his consideration as we go back inside. I cannot explain myself. I do not have the words but I am beginning to feel a much desired peace. I want to explain to him how much I love him and how I think I have failed him but Oliver will not hear a word. He draws me to the fire and the merry chatter of his sisters dissolves the moment of openness. Again we have not spoken our sentiments. Still, his manner encourages my heart even if his remoteness remains.

Chapter 53. Confession

Oliver
Huntington 17 Dec 1621

Elizabeth and Oliver had reached a steadied peace and Oliver felt strengthened by it. He now felt able to visit his bereaved friend. He felt more able to accept his responsibilities. As Oliver walked past the church, he looked at the statue of the dying Christ. He could feel the pain the Lord must have felt. Christ murdered, betrayed, lonely, cast out, without a friend. Yes, Oliver felt that pain. But he was not friendless. He could talk to William. He could explain how bad his financial affairs were. He could explain about his gambling debts. No, not explain. He would confess to William. He did not need a priest or even a minister. It seemed a scandalous idea. William would listen and help him find his path again. But could he put such a burden on William when he had such a weight to carry himself?

Oliver had already consulted the physician about the melancholy he felt. The doctor's remedy was brisk walks and plenty of fresh air. The doctor had also given him the mithridite, for his concerns about the plague. Many of his London friends had started taking it and he thought it was a sensible precaution considering he had begun to make regular visits to London to further those acquaintances he had made who could escalate his political ambitions. However, Dr Simcotts had warned about other effects of the drug like stomach pain. But surely that was not as bad as death by plague! Oliver smiled. These doctors had such a strange way of viewing the world, but then Doctor Simcotts did not know about the heavy weight Oliver carried. Oliver could not bear that any stranger would know. But William was not a stranger. He was dearer than any brother. Yes, he would confess to William.

As Oliver reached the door, his friend opened it with a pleasant greeting, which reassured him. He did not want to bring his problems into William's house yet he could see no other solution.

"Let's walk down to the meadow, William," he suggested.

William readily assented, glad for the air and the renewal of their friendship. The two friends strode boldly across the fields which lay behind the main street. Much to Oliver's relief, William straightway attacked the problem.

"Oliver, I have seen for many months now that you are troubled my friend. It cannot be my own troubles. What is it that ails you?"

For once Oliver was glad of his friend's forthrightness. He replied,

"William, my household is near to collapse. I cannot pay the butcher nor miller, nor furrier. I am in debt to them all."

His friend's face clouded with worry and suspecting an undeclared reason for this trouble, he enquired cautiously,

"My goodness, Oliver, I had no idea. How have you come to this?"

The silence was palpable. Oliver sat on a low hanging bough and began to weep, while his friend paced up and down, unable to utter any words of comfort for sheer surprise. At last William ventured,

"Oliver, you must tell me all. What has brought about this catastrophe? I know the price of ribbons and linen has risen. Wives and children must be adequately provisioned. But this just does not make sense."

Oliver knew he had to reveal all to William Kilbourne, his dearest closest friend, but he was ashamed. Ashamed of his behaviour, ashamed of his gambling, ashamed of his neglect to his duties. He was overcome with despair. William's tragedy was not of his own doing. His was! His words came out in short bursts amidst weeping and then a struggle to control himself.

"You know my father did not leave us well cared for. He had debts which we could not hope to repay. I was introduced to the table at Cambridge and won some considerable sums from my fellows. Of course, we kept it quiet, not wanting the more devout fellows amongst us to be aware of it. Later, when I was at Hinchingbrooke I came across another couple of fellows who invited me to their table. It was a jest at first – a casual remark thrown out while the horses were groomed. But I joined them – at first just occasionally but then it became a regular practice between us and I did not know how to withdraw. In any case, I could not. My losses were too great. Each time I seemed to pay off something, I became more indebted."

As Oliver paused to collect himself, he glanced at the stricken face of his friend and he became aware of how deep into sin he had sunk. He had not just committed an injury to his wife and his family but to Almighty God himself.

Rosalie Weller

Oliver continued to the real worry – the crux of his debauchery.

"William, I have injured the one who has meant most to me in my whole life – my dear Elizabeth. How can I ever tell her? I have gambled the very food out of little Robert's mouth. I am too far in this sin now. I am held. I am chained by it. I have tried to leave it alone but still it draws me back. I am going to have to sell my fields to pay. Yet still it holds me and wants to lure me back."

A long silence ensued then William drew a deep breath.

"There is no easy way out of this, my friend," William said, "You must break this chain which binds you. There is only one way you can do that. Yes, prayer is good, but more than that is needed. You must tell Elizabeth for surely she will stand by you. She is a pious and loving woman. She would not desert you. She knows how I have suffered since I lost my Bridgett. How alone I have been. She understands how a husband and wife must work together. To be together is everything - to have each other." At this Oliver groaned.

"Leave your mother's house and go and till tenanted land. Your sisters Catherine and Anna are settled on. Your mother could manage now with the younger girls. There are good tenancies to be had in St. Ives. Yes, you will be as a common yeoman but your debts can be halted. Remember it is only your toiling which puts you at that station. You were born a gentleman and whatever you do, you will remain so. You must make a fresh start."

Oliver did not want to do this but he could understand the wisdom of Williams's words and as his friend developed his idea further, he just nodded in recognition that no other solution was open to him. Yet, how could he tell Elizabeth?

Indeed, on the walk back to "The Friars" Oliver procrastinated about the decision he had made for the words were easier than the action. He knew that once the first step had been taken, there would be no easy return.

After that day, Oliver did not see William often. He had lost the desire to converse with one who knew his darkest secret. He became even more morose, frequently going back to read the family bible for comfort and solace about his situation. Gradually it dawned on him that there was no other way out. He must act on William's advice.

Oliver began to withdraw from those duties he had undertaken for the parish. But still he did not tell Elizabeth the truth. The longer he left his decision, the more paralysed he became. Elizabeth was glad that her husband was less involved with his civic duties and spent more time at home now, especially taking time to talk to Robert, and now another child was on the way. He was even taking an interest in the jam and herbs which she was producing, though there was still a strange moroseness which haunted him. Slowly Oliver had begun to rebuild his relationship with his wife. Despite this, his financial position had not altered.

Chapter 54. Resolutions

Elizabeth
Huntington 14 February 1622

Oliver has just greeted me with some roses and a kiss, to celebrate St Valentine, he says. This is not a date I am used to celebrating, but my heart softens to him because of his attentiveness. It is a new season for us all.

"Oliver," I say, " We still seem so far apart. I am so sorry. I never wanted it to be like this. We just seem to be making each other so miserable."

Tears well up in me. As I say the words, the pain of our estrangement deepens in my heart. I look at him to see some sign of encouragement. He turns slowly and his face has softened to me.

"Elizabeth, sweet girl," he says, "I feel the same. I never intended a distance to grow between us. But now we are here we must act and resolve never to grow apart again."

His eyes are sparkling with this new resolution.

"Robert will be weaned soon and I can accompany you in your visits to the townsfolk. Margaret says she thinks he is ready for porridge." I am excited at the prospect and continue, "Perhaps we can leave him here and I shall visit my mother, yes, and be reconciled with her too."

Oliver immediately warms to my plan. He says,

"I shall make the arrangements with mother straight away. We shall set off early next week. We can ride to Barrington Hall together and then I will stay there with Thomas while you ride on to Stambridge Hall."

He kisses me affectionately and then he is gone. I hear the animated conversation between Oliver and Mistress Cromwell as he makes the arrangements. It is not long before I hear him ascending to the chamber again.

"Oliver, I've been thinking. Perhaps as matters seem more settled for your sisters, we may consider going to the New Lands now. It would be a fresh start for us. Your mother could manage by herself."

I try to sound caring but I'm a little afraid it sounds as if I have had enough of living in his mother's house, so I'm surprised by Oliver's cheerfulness.

He says, "Yes, I think we could consider it. As you say my sisters are more settled – Anna now Mistress John Sewster, and already we have begun negotiations for Catherine. I think Lizzie knows she will never marry but Margaret will continue to include her in family gatherings and such like. Yes, we can think about that."

"I'll be sad to lose Lizzie's help with young Robert, but we must move on sometime." I say, glad that I have broached the topic. I remember something else I have been meaning to bring up.

"Oliver, our boy is growing fast. I need some more linen to sew him some bigger clothes. Can I not order from the draper yet?" I ask.

"Can't you get something from Margaret? Young Valentine has plenty of things which Margaret cannot re-use." He answers gruffly.

I'm disappointed as I really want to sew something new and get Lizzie to do some of her exquisite embroidery on it but I suppose Oliver is right. Margaret will be glad to give me some of Valentine's clothes. She has stored them so beautifully since he grew out of them.

"I suppose so," I answer.

I don't want to destroy this new understanding Oliver and I have come to. I still feel a great sadness for Bridgett. I haven't yet asked where she's been buried and I am afraid to open such a topic. It must have been outside of one of the churchyards under the circumstances. Oh, it's just too terrible to contemplate. My daily prayers include a prayer for her soul.

I take Robert downstairs to hear what Mistress Cromwell has to say about our proposed visits.

"Oliver says you will care for Robert if I visit my mother next week." I say.

"Yes it will be a delight for me, Elizabeth" she replies.

While we are alone and she's in such a mellow mood I decide to tackle her about another subject that has been bothering me for a while.

"Mistress Cromwell, I have not heard any talk of the ploughing yet. Surely it must be started soon, shouldn't it?" I ask.

Our household seems to have ground to a halt. Yuletide has been over for a month. It has been so different here to what I have been used to and I am not yet used to the customs and ways here.

"Well, I did ask Oliver about it yesterday, but got no sensible answer from him." Mistress Cromwell replies, as she returns to the larder. It is clear this is not a topic she wishes me to explore.

Farming is so different from the fur and leather trade. There is still so much I do not understand. I broach the other subject I want to discuss.

"Very well. Will there be any problems with the wet nurse?" I ask.

"No she is a clean and respectable woman. I saw her in town yesterday and she asked if she could be of any help until Robert was properly weaned?"

"Well maybe that would be a good idea. Although Oliver doesn't seem to be so involved in the Parish duties as he was. I don't want to give out money when it is not necessary, mistress." I answer.

Oliver, hears our conversation as he descends from the chamber and kisses the top of my head as he says,

"Yes, a frugal woman is a godly one indeed, Elizabeth."

"Oliver, I was just asking your mother about the winter ploughing to prepare for the spring sowing. Why are the fields lying fallow?" I ask.

"Don't you worry about that Elizabeth. You will soon have another little Cromwell to care for. That must be your main concern. You shouldn't be fretting over these household matters," Oliver replies and then goes out of the door without a satisfactory explanation.

Once again I do not understand why I cannot get a clear answer to my question. These uncertainties disappear as I feel the child inside me stirring and I no longer worry about the finances, nor the fallow fields. Those details do not matter anymore. A strange fluttering has developed into more insistent movements as an embryonic limb glides against the wall of my womb. I feel more

Rosalie Weller

confident this time around - birth is no longer a mystery, but it is still a wonder.

Chapter 55.

Oliver
'Barrington Hall' 21 February 1622

The following Tuesday Oliver woke Elizabeth early in the morning. He did not wish to delay as he knew she might change her mind about leaving Robert with his mother. They took the usual route to Barrington Hall through Godmanchester with a rest at Royston. Oliver was reluctant to stop at 'The Old Bull' but could give no logical reason to Elizabeth as to why they shouldn't so he was relieved to see Ol' Margrit was nowhere to be seen. They finally arrived at Barrington Hall in time for dinner.

Sir Francis and Lady Joan were delighted to see the couple ride in together, as they usually welcomed Oliver on his own. Lady Joan would not hear of Elizabeth riding further on that day.

"My dear," said Lady Joan, "It is out of the question. You must not tire yourself out. With that she whisked Elizabeth off to the chapel to say prayers before dinner.

Dinner was a leisurely meal. The Barringtons' table was always sumptuous and for once Oliver could enjoy his fill of meat without worrying about the cost. To his relief, Elizabeth retired early and he was able to enjoy further conversation with Sir Francis and Thomas.

"Yes, Oliver St John is arriving tomorrow so you can talk to him. I am sure he will join us to release the hawks and get some ducks in the pot" Thomas said.

"Good," Oliver replied, "I do have a matter I wish to discuss with him and the hunt will be a relaxed occasion to converse.

At last Lady Luck was smiling on him. Oliver could delay no longer on the sale of the fields; it had been three months since Sir

Oliver had summoned him. Oliver St John was discreet enough to handle such a sale without his mother and Elizabeth finding out about it. Maybe the future would present a way to recoup his fortune.

The next morning after a good rest, Oliver was able to see Elizabeth off on her forward journey to Stambridge Hall.

"Enjoy the ride and stay as long as you like my dear. Don't worry about Robert. He is in good hands." Oliver said reassuringly.

Oliver's spirits lifted as he heard the screech of the hawks, still hooded and reminding their handlers that they wanted respite from their captivity. Although they could not see they still responded by turning their heads towards familiar voices.

"Master Cromwell, good to see you again," John the groom said and continued listening to instructions from Thomas concerning the hawks.

The mews were intricately designed and built to suit the needs of the different species. Oliver was thrilled when Sir Francis had suggested many years ago that he kept Joan there. Huntington did not have the craftsmen required to build such a system and the Cromwells did not have the money for such a venture. The falconers took out the hawks as their masters watched. Oliver was eager to assist with Joan but his attention was caught by his cousin.

"Cousin, I am so glad to see you. I need some legal help.... with the sale of my fields." Oliver addressed Oliver St John.

"No problem, just bring the relevant documents and step by to Lincoln's Inn on your next visit to London. I see you still have Joan, such a magnificent bird, Oliver. "

"Thank you, cousin" Oliver replied.

"And congratulations on the child. A boy! You must be very pleased." Oliver St John said.

With that the party walked towards the lake on the far side of the estate, accompanied by the falconers who carried the hooded birds as their masters conversed. The dogs yapped at their heels, eager to retrieve the kill. As the birds were released one by one, they soared high in the sky, vigilant and searching. The dogs bounded towards the water's edge only too happy to disturb the family of ducks abiding there. And so it was. The natural order - hawks swooping on fleeing ducks.

Joan did not disappoint. She soared to the heights with the other hawks below her. Her eye fixed on the ducks. Her powerful wings flapped in the chase. When she swooped, the deadly talons engaged with its unsuspecting prey and death was instant. The duck was dropped. The dogs raced to retrieve it and the party were assured of a hearty meal later that week.

Oliver was always delighted with Joan's performance. Her magnificence far outstripped the other hawks, who performed only adequately. The gentlemen made their way back to the manor house. Midday and dinner was ready to be served on their arrival.

Chapter 56. Reconciliation

Elizabeth
'Little Stambridge Hall' 22 February 1622

"Sarah, why is it mother is in her bedchamber?"

I am panicking because I did not realise, did not even think, there could be something amiss with mother's health.

"Elizabeth, she has been lying in bed since the riding accident last week. The physician has examined her and recommended rest." Sarah replies.

"Riding accident!" I exclaim as I rush up the stairs to the chamber.

Sarah is rushing after me, Her dress swishing in her haste. and I can barely concentrate on what she is saying.

I unclasp the door catch and it rattles announcing my entry. Mother sits upright in alarm.

"Oh, oh," she gasps.

My compassion is roused.

"Mother why did you not send word?"

My mother starts to babble and I note she looks considerably frailer in her bed. I am ashamed I have not come sooner. I walk towards her and sit on the edge of the bed. The deep cover sinks under my weight. I hold her hand to my cheek, a gesture of comfort to which she responds with an embarrassed laugh.

"Elizabeth, my dear, you have your own family now... Sarah has been attending me. John Hamilton has allowed Alice to visit and she says she may even take her confinement here if my recovery is slow. Of course Frances is still here. I didn't want to distract you from your own duties. How are Oliver and his family?"

"They are all well mother. Mistress Cromwell is overseeing the wet-nurse for Robert. Oliver is at Barrington Hall. But mother, what about you? How has this happened?"

"Such a silly accident. No, I wasn't thrown. It was the new mare. As I was conversing with a guest at the Hattons, the silly animal trod on my foot, twice, as if once was not enough. The physician says there seem to be no bones broken but it is badly bruised and swollen. He says I must rest it for a while, which is what I am doing. Sarah, will you bring us ale, please."

Sarah goes to fetch mother's refreshment, giving me my opportunity to make amends.

"Mother, I did not call for you at my confinement. I was being rather difficult, I must confess. I see that now. I feel so guilty with you lying here with such weakness. I am so sorry. Can you forgive me?"

Mother smiles and puts her hand on my shoulder. She caresses my cheek oh so gently - something she has never done before, and she says,

"Elizabeth, you silly goose. I had to be strict with you; you were always so wilful but I have done my duty. And now Frances will be married soon - my last daughter. You will understand the worry when you have daughters of your own. Of course you are forgiven. I am sad not to see my grandson, though, on this visit."

"Yes, I will bring him next time. Mother. But there is another matter I would like to discuss with you. It concerns Sarah."

"Of course, what is it?"

"You will have heard of the death of my dear friend Bridgett….. I am so worried about her husband William. He is struggling to care for his two oldest and carry on with his business. Can Sarah come and help?"

Mother only hesitates for a moment and then replies,

"Yes, she can ride back with you and I will send for her sister Rachel to come here in her stead. She has been asking to come for a while. It will work out, don't fret now Elizabeth."

I am touched by this rare kindness from her; maybe I have misjudged her. She sinks back on her pillow and closes her eyes. Acknowledging that this is my signal to go downstairs, I get up.

As I descend I hear a familiar voice,

"Alice," I exclaim, "Why did you not send for me?"

"Bessie," she replies, "You were still grieving for your good friend Bridgett and I know you have lost your fondness for mother anyway. We are managing to keep her comfortable and the physician is visiting regularly."

"Well, Alice, I am thankful that I came. I decided it was time to make amends with mother. I have done that and I am glad. How long until your confinement?" I ask.

"It's only about a month. How is baby Robert? It was such a joy to be with you. It looks as if I may be here for my confinement. I can't think about leaving until mother is fully recovered and John is so understanding. He is busy with trading business in London so he is glad I have the security of Little Stambridge Hall while he is away."

"I can only stay for a few days myself this time as Robert is not used to the wet nurse yet. Oliver and I shall return to Huntington separately. He, too, is not sure how long he will stay at Barrington Hall this visit. You can never be sure whether Sir Francis or Thomas will be called away. So sister, is married life agreeable to you? I find it is so different to what I expected."

"Yes it is different." Alice replies, "It is the quiet solitude which I must get used to. After the raucous noise of Little Stambridge. Ah here comes Sarah with refreshment for us.

As Sarah puts down the pewter pots of ale, I notice she hesitates.

"Has my mother spoken to you about coming to Huntington?" I ask sensing that may be her enquiry.

"Yes, Mistress Elizabeth, and I am happy to come but it may take a couple of weeks for me to arrange for Rachael to come here. I don't want to leave your mother without assistance."

"Take that worried look off your face, Sarah," I reply kindly, "Master Kilbourne is indeed in need of help but our first priority is to my mother. Make your arrangements when you can."

I smile and then add cheekily,

"I may even get Rachael to come and help us when mother has recovered. Do you have any other sisters?"

At that Sarah laughs.

Chapter 57. Return to London

Oliver
Huntington 6 April 1623

True to her word, Lady Frances Bourchier sent her niece to Huntington to help William Kilbourne. Her recovery from her accident was slow which meant she was able to share her daughter Alice's confinement. After her churching and the infant's baptism, Alice was able to return to her own home. With Frances frequently staying at the house of her betrothed, Little Stambridge Hall became a haven with its more relaxed atmosphere. It was a house full of masculinity now – nine brothers vying for attention. With marriages settled on her three daughters Lady Frances was able to relax. It was her husband's responsibility to teach her sons the fur and leather trade.

Oliver's lands were sold promptly once he had signed the documents with St. John, who was surprised by the action but was not interested enough to enquiry why he was doing it. The new buyer was happy for Oliver's sheep to graze until he was ready to use the land he had purchased. The other field had already yielded the barley and peas which had been sown in that first year. In the second year it had lain fallow and as this was usual practice, no one had enquired about it until Elizabeth did. Oliver had been able to distract her curiosity. Indeed Oliver's fields were mercifully saved when others had lost theirs in the dreadful fire. Neither Mistress Cromwell nor Elizabeth noticed the change in their fortunes but in truth, the rent from the remaining tenant was not enough to live on so that the household debts soon began to mount again.

The only pleasure that Oliver could gain was on the days he managed to visit Thomas and fly Joan, the bird still being housed on the Barrington Estate. That was one area where Oliver was respected and sought out for his expertise - hawking. He had got to know quite a few of the gentlemen in Essex and shared odd days with them.

Thomas was not able to accompany Oliver as he used to, due to his father's weakening condition. So hawking with new friends made an enjoyable distraction for him.

Oliver was struggling to face Elizabeth and answer all those questions she seemed to be asking recently. Her questions had abated during the time of the birth of their second son, also named Oliver, but had now begun again with increasing fervour. All questions led to one point - their financial situation. His mother knew something was wrong but she did not scold. Oliver had noticed that she seemed to stare at him and go quiet, wondering.

It was quite a surprise when Uncle Thomas turned up and gave Oliver a gift - a good sum of money. Uncle Thomas said it was for baby Oliver, but he didn't mention it to either Elizabeth, nor to his mother. Oliver did feel guilty for a moment but it was necessary for it to be used in the maintenance of his household. It would last at least a year. So Oliver was able to put off his moment of truth with Elizabeth for a while longer.

It had been a mild winter and so it was that Oliver decided to visit London once again for two purposes. He wanted to nurture his relationship with Richard Fishbourne. This was not for selfish reasons but to secure the promised lectureship for his friend Thomas Beard. The second was to consult the famous physician Dr Theodore Mayerne, who had been recommended to him by Dr Simcotts, for the stomach pains he had been suffering. Dr Simcotts had been unable to advise a remedy, except this specialist consultation with a man more revered than himself.

Chestnut was soon saddled up and the journey began. Oliver planned his usual stop at Saffron Walden. He had long ceased to visit Hinchingbrooke so his journey was not delayed by other considerations. He had been striving to resist the temptation to gamble which had led him into so much trouble already. It was this dreadful vice that had meant he had to sell off some of his land, which could never be recovered. Although this had reduced his debt, it had also reduced his income, and led him into the sin of lying to both his wife and his mother. It was with this sobering thought in his mind that Oliver rode towards Saffron Walden.

When he reached "The Old Bell", it was still early enough to merely rest Chestnut for an hour and then he could resume his journey. He hoped to reach London in time to dine with Richard Fishbourne. He knew he was taking a chance that the old gentleman would be at his house, but he had heard that Fishbourne had been somewhat sickly recently which would have necessitated him remaining at home.

Oliver soon recognised the familiar townhouses on Tower Hill where James Bourchier had a house. It was only a step further and he was outside the residence of Richard Fishbourne. Much to his relief, when the door was opened the manservant informed him that Master Fishbourne was indeed inside. Oliver was led in to the parlour and found the ageing gentleman with foot elevated and reading a pamphlet.

"Good day to you, Master Cromwell," he addressed Oliver, "It is still too cold for me to venture outdoors today, but how glad I am to see you."

"Yes, good day. Is it the gout which is troubling you sir?" Oliver asked politely.

"Yes indeed but you surely haven't come here today to talk about my ailments. How fares Huntington?"

Oliver was again able to inform Richard Fishbourne about the latest events in Huntington. He also broached the subject of the new charter being pursued by Robert Barnard and Lionel Walden. He was delighted to hear that Master Fishbourne agreed that the issue was being driven by personal ambition on the part of Oliver's two adversaries. The two men continued their lively conversation over a tasteful dinner. Two hours later Oliver was ready to leave, having received reassurances about the finances for the lectureship in Huntington. Fishbourne approved of the choice of Thomas Beard to conduct the sermons but explained that in the terms of his legacy the final decision would have to be in the hands of the corporation, which Oliver was disappointed to hear.

But it was with renewed energy that he once again mounted Chestnut and rode in the direction of Theodore Mayerne's consulting room.

Chapter 58. Visiting

Elizabeth
Huntington 13 October 1623

As my little family trundle up the High Street on their regular route to the "Fountain Inn", I am grateful to see that Sarah has settled in. After her return to Huntington and her introduction to William, she agreed to take the position of housekeeper for him. She does not seek to replace Bridgett but completes her tasks suitably. I have taken it upon myself to teach Sarah all she needs to know in this regard. Poor Sarah has had her own grief to bear. Her fiancé quite suddenly took the pox, and died, after visiting his own village, just before she came here to live. At least the delay in leaving my mother, while they waited for Rachel to arrive had proved opportune as it gave her time to bury her fiancé and put his affairs in order. I think it is advantageous that she and I were acquainted before she took up this employment. It seems to have helped her to overcome her grief.

I smile at the transformation I have made from wife to mother this past two years because without it, I may still have been linked to the foolish and vain ambitions of women like Elizabeth Walden and Mistress Bernard. My household has increased as I was able to persuade my mother to part with Rachael as well as Sarah.

"Hold onto Rachael's hand."

I call as I encourage my Robert in his confident strides. He is indeed a big child for which I am grateful. It is his second birthday today and as a treat we are visiting Sarah. He is so like his father in physical build but so unlike him in temperament. His darling face betrays an innocence to which even I am not accustomed. His bright blue eyes convey such trust and naivety. I never want him to encounter the cruelties of this world. I want to protect him always.

Robert looks back at me and smiles. Obediently he grasps Rachael's hand. We have but a short distance to walk but I regret now that I did not take the carriage. The baby Oliver is a weight which I am struggling with. I wonder whether it is his liveliness which makes him so heavy. For indeed he is little like his sweet brother. Baby Oliver has already shown signs of an ill disposition. He is strong and determined to assert his will on all he encounters. I look at his brown curly hair as he wriggles in my arms.

"We are almost there," I soothe him, "Soon you can get down."

But alas he takes no comfort from my words and begins to wail loudly. As I walk through the entrance of the "Fountain Inn", I have become quite red-faced from the struggle with my youngest son and as I encounter Sarah, she is laughing.

"Come now, naughty Oliver," she addresses him as she takes him from me. "Come and play with Henry and Edward."

We are soon disrobed and Rachael discreetly steps into the kitchen to help the girl there make the refreshment for us. I am sure she wishes to converse with her sister but she is such a polite and cheerful girl, that she is content to wait until I have had a chance to speak to Sarah.

"I am so glad Rachael has come to us," I say. "She is so sweet when Oliver is naughty. Mother was indeed patient when I asked her for both of you to stay. Quite unlike her!"

We both laugh. Sarah knows our family so well she is not offended by these slights I make of my mother. I am glad that Sarah was, and now Rachael is, part of my new family. Sarah was never really a servant but more a companion.

I notice Sarah is pale and thin. It is several days since I have been to visit her and am alarmed by her worn appearance.

"Elizabeth, do not concern yourself. I am quite well, but as the coach service has increased, William has asked for my help with it. So I am delighted to see you. I can sit down and talk to you for an hour before I am needed to tend to the Inn's business."

So we sit down to talk, only interrupted by the appearance of the refreshment.

"Sarah, please advise me. Your mother is well renowned in our village, so you must have learnt some things from her, even though you are still a maid. I have had these two boys in so short a time. I wonder if there is anything to be done about delaying the arrival of the next one?" I implore.

"What a modern idea, Elizabeth! One that I have not closely attended but I have heard stories from many of the female travellers of how they have delayed the appearance of yet another baby. And you are right, Mistress Brockett has knowledge of these things."

I have soon gained the information I need but I am not sure how effective it will be. I am not sure it is the right thing to do either. Sarah has advised against it. She is sure it does not develop a comfortable relationship between husband and wife. For the moment I will take her advice. I still sense a strain in our relationship. Matters have not improved as much as I had hoped. This has been the situation since Robert was first born. Although we were briefly reconciled in February, Oliver still seems distant and I do not want to do anything to further this damage.

It is not long before Rachael joins us and it is a delight to be part of their sisterly conversation. After their sharing of news, Sarah turns to me and says,

"I understand that you do not visit Mistress Walden as you used to."

"No," I reply, "I will admit that Bridgett's death caused me to ponder and reflect about my intimates as I had never done before. To be honest, Sarah, I still do not understand it these two years later. What ailed Bridgett so that she should do such a thing?"

There is a stillness in the conversation and I realise I have put to voice something which has been hushed.

"Sarah, do tell, how you perceive it." I encourage her.

"Elizabeth, you are a conscientious mother. Your boys are a great credit to you. Little Robert is so polite in his speech. Even though baby Oliver is not yet a year old, you have said yourself, he is a difficult child - so different from his brother. But you adore them both, as mothers do. Bridgett may just have been exhausted from life's troubles. Little Mary had been so sickly. Her passing may have been too much to bear."

The tears are again coming to my eyes.

"But why, oh why did she not tell me?" I plead.

"Elizabeth, do not upset yourself. I have heard that in these cases, there is a blackness which comes over you, which you cannot make sense to. Be reassured, Elizabeth, Bridgett treasured you as a dear friend. Her mother who comes to visit the older two told me this. .. But here are the children again with their sweetmeats."

Sarah pauses as the door opens and the servant girl brings in Robert, Oliver and the two young Kilbournes. The room is now alive with childish delight as they continue in their play. But now it is time to return home. With a heavy heart, I make my way back to "The Friars" with Rachael and my two boys, arriving just in time for dinner.

Chapter 59. Cousins

Oliver
Huntington 5 June 1624

More than two years had passed since Oliver's confession to William. Oliver had only divulged a fraction of their true situation. Elizabeth was occupied with her continuing duties in the nursery. Mistress Cromwell was always very willing and capable of caring for the two boys, to free Elizabeth to spend more time with her husband and yet Oliver had noticed an increasing reluctance by Elizabeth to let this happen. It was as if she could not bear Robert and Oliver to delight in anyone else's company but her own. A wet nurse had been employed to nurse Oliver but still Elizabeth would not share her duties to her children. Mistress Cromwell had remarked on this strange phenomenon but Oliver had casually replied that it was understandable since Bridgett's death.

On one occasion, Oliver had almost confessed. Elizabeth had complained.

"We are getting meat and fowl from Hinchingbrooke. Your mother is providing the vegetables. But I am still not permitted to converse with the shopkeepers about my needs. There is never any money available! Where does it go? We must consider a pony for Robert soon. Chestnut and Arabella are far too frisky for a young child, Oliver. I ask you questions but I get no answers. Your mother does not seem to have answers from the accounting books. This is driving a division between us Oliver and you don't seem concerned about it."

Elizabeth had confronted him with unusual vehemence and he had been tempted to retaliate, but he held his tongue. He was furious with her. She had spelled out their true situation and he couldn't stand the truth of it. He whistled to his dog who needed no explanations for his behaviour and strode out to enjoy the warmth of the summer day.

After that, Oliver had tried desperately to talk to Elizabeth about his problems but her attention was always elsewhere. With reluctance, Oliver decided on another plan to help ease his burden. He would visit his cousin, John Hampden, in Buckinghamshire. He had always trusted John as a straight-talking, intelligent man. Only four years his senior, John had already taken a seat in the house, representing Cornwall. Oliver was still interested in the adventurers and their progress in the New World and wanted to discuss new possibilities for sailing, and to understand John's views on the matter.

Once again Elizabeth was with child. God be merciful, she would come through the confinement as easily as she had with the boys. Oliver knew he was not as good a father as he could be. When Margaret had her children, Oliver had delighted in teasing Valentine and Annie, and now Agnes. But it was not the same being a brother or uncle as being a father. The responsibility weighed heavier. With his own boys he held back, as if contact with their sinful father somehow sullied them. He hoped this next child would be a girl, with Elizabeth's dark curls and honest face.

Also Oliver decided it was time to act on Sir Theodore Mayerne's advice to take the waters at Wellingborough. He had not been able to obtain a full consultation with the great physician because he had not made an appointment, but a brief discussion had resulted in the waters as a possible solution.

On the way he would stop at 'The Old Bull', Royston and see if Old Margrit was at the inn. He didn't feel anxious at the prospect any more. His first encounter with her had been a shock but now he was intrigued to know what further insights and details she could add to her prophesy. Sometimes he was afraid that he was losing his mind and that maybe he had imagined what Margrit had said to him. But last year he had seen a vision of a cross rising above Huntington and it seemed to say to him. "By this sign conquer." At first he doubted his senses but it was imprinted, not only on his eyes, but on his heart as well. This had given him the courage to think about going back to try and confront Margrit, and find out more.

So it was that he set off early on his sturdy palfrey, Chestnut. He covered the twenty two miles quickly and made his stop at 'The Old Bull'. There was ol' Margrit sitting outside the inn again, but this time he was not intimidated. He was intrigued. Would she recognise him? As he approached her, she cackled.

"Good day, sir," she said.

"Hello, Margrit. Do you remember me?"

To his delight, she smiled.

"Yes, of course," she said, "You came a few years ago. I saw blood on your hands then. But you will be a great leader. Unafraid."

"I don't understand what you mean. Can you explain what you see?"

Margrit just laughed and Oliver could get no sense out of her. All she would say was,

"I see it. You must explain it!"

Oliver was not prepared to argue with her, he could see it would get him nowhere. He entered the inn to have his ale while his horse rested. The rest of the company in the inn could offer him no conversation of interest, so he was pleased to get on his way again.

He felt obliged to visit Barrington Hall before he went to see cousin John. Oliver wanted to see how the Barringtons were coping with the troubles that had assailed them over the past years. He had received news that Sir Francis was ill and he wanted to see if he could offer any solace. Thomas also was grieving the death of his wife, Frances although Oliver had heard a rumour that he was already arranging a second marriage to Judith Lytton..

When he arrived he found quite a heavy atmosphere. Thomas' steward John Kendall, opened the door to him, and he was surprised to hear that Sir Francis was in the main house rather than in "The Priory". He soon discovered that Sir Francis was a worried man, brought down by two events. He greeted Oliver warmly with only a hint of a reprimand.

"Oliver, it has been quite a time since you last visited."

"Yes, uncle," Oliver replied, "we have two lively boys now and Elizabeth is expecting our third. I'm sure you know how much time that occupies."

"These new baronetcies which good King James has introduced are just another way to raise money. I have refused to pay. The court tries to tell us what an honour it is; I just don't know what will come next!"

"It is certainly a worrying time, Sir Francis. And Thomas, tell me how is he coping after the death of Frances?"

Sir Francis just shook his head.

"His year of mourning will be completed in October. I have suggested he marries again straight away. Thomas is not well, you know" Sir Francis said.

Later, Oliver had seen for himself the symptoms of Thomas' health problems but did not wish to think about it. His own mood was black enough without someone else's misery intruding and so he was quick to depart. It was a short space to Great Hampden - thirty odd miles. Although Chestnut would not be happy to set off again so quickly, she was a strong mare, well able to cope. He should reach Hampden House before nightfall.

He received a fine welcome from John's parents, who were anxious to receive news about the Barringtons. Elizabeth Hampden had a close relationship with her sister, Joan, and being the younger, had always looked up to her god-fearing sibling.

"Tell me Oliver, how is Thomas faring after his bereavement? I know Sir Francis is keen for him to marry again soon and I suppose it is better than to leave the boys motherless." Elizabeth said.

The phrase 'motherless boys' evoked an image in Oliver's mind which he had not pictured before. He thought of Bridgett's oldest two. Then he thought of his own sons. And he thought of his own mother and how he would have fared if it had been her death and not his father's which he had to endure. It was unthinkable. The very thought of it aroused a strong physical pain in his stomach so that he felt quite weak.

John had not yet returned and after a light supper, Oliver was able to excuse himself and retire early to ease the exhaustion of fifty miles in the saddle. His mind was troubled still, but his hope was stirred at the prospect of a discussion about the New World the next day.

Chapter 60. Another confinement

Elizabeth
Huntington 6 June 1624

I have not been able to get outside until now. The weather has been unseasonably cold although dry, but today it is warmer. Oliver has gone to visit his cousins for a few days. I am glad. Perhaps he can find solace there. He has something on his mind which I am not able to penetrate. We are both trying so hard to bring comfort to each other but somehow we draw no closer. I know for my part there are things in my heart I just cannot bring myself to say. I am still grieving for my dear friend, although it has been almost two years since her passing. I do not think I will ever be able to accept it.

But the child stirs within me - just a gentle movement. So precious - life! New life always brings joy and hope. I wonder if this time I will have a girl with Oliver's grey-green eyes. If it is a girl, I shall name her for my dear friend - Bridgett.

"Elizabeth, why don't you take a walk into town this afternoon? It's such a pleasant day. I will mind the boys, and I am expecting Margaret with her young ones. Robert and Oliver can amuse themselves with their cousins." Mistress Cromwell says.

"Yes," I reply, " it's such a long time since I paid my compliments to Mistress Walden and I hear her good friend Mistress Altham is now married to Master Robert Bernard. It will be pleasant to converse with them again."

This is a small town. It does not bode well to hold grudges. I try be pleasant to the gentlewomen of the town because maybe Oliver will represent them in Parliament one day. I walk slowly, conscious of the weight of the unborn child inside my body, but it is warm today. I am soon at Walden House and I can hear lively conversation inside.

"Good day to you all," I greet all six ladies present.

I am soon in conversation with them. It is so wonderful to have a fuss made of me because of my near confinement. I am offered sweetmeats and ale. I feel quite special. Paulina Pepys, now Montague, is beside me. I hear her say to Elizabeth Hatton,

"Yes, it is imported from Italy."

Then she turns to me, "I was just talking about my new writing desk, Elizabeth."

She waves her gloved hand to indicate I must sit next to her and graciously flutters her fan. It bears the image of a mating peacock that seems to disappear and reappear as she waves away the warm air. It really is a beautiful item.

"I was very sorry to hear about the accident at the moat, Mistress Paulina." I say.

Mistress Pepys' son Henry had nearly drowned recently.

She nods courteously, for the near drowning of the two year old at Barnwell touched all of our hearts. For just a moment my mind returns to the drowning of Bridgett's two little girls. Two such incidents, yet it is surprisingly not such a common complaint. Like Little Stambridge Hall, Barnwell Manor is well guarded by a moat. It really is an ancient structure so unnecessary these days. I sometimes think such features should be made safer; then accidents like that could not happen. Poor little chap having such a shock at only two years old. It was only the quick action of a manservant passing by the very spot where he fell in, which saved the little mite. What on earth the nurse was doing at the time, I cannot imagine. I pause to collect myself. I realise she has addressed me but I cannot quite fathom what she means.

"Yes, my nephew Robert says his losses at the table have been quite considerable!"

What is she talking about? Losses? Card table? Is she talking about Oliver at Hinchingbrooke. I am lost for words. Can this be true? I do not know so I cannot refute it. Suddenly I feel faint, but I remain seated. I do not want to be governed by this snippet which Mistress Paulina Montague has dropped. My situation is saved by my hostess, who has become more sympathetic to others in recent years. She must have glimpsed the alarm on my face, because she rushes to me.

"Mistress Elizabeth, you have come over quite pale and you are shaking. Are you not well, my dear?" she asks.

"I am not as composed as I thought. I think I shall have to leave," I say.

"Can I order the carriage for you, my dear?" Mistress Walden thinks my distress is because of my condition.

"Yes," I reply quite feebly. They help me to the carriage and soon I am at home to reflect on what I have learnt.

I will say nothing to Mistress Cromwell or the sisters. I do not know whether this is true but I suspect it might be. I have been betrayed again. My heart is disturbed but I will not let the Cromwell family see that.

Robert Pepys is the bailiff on the Hinchingbrooke estate. If this were not true, why would he say such a thing to his aunt? If it were a lie he would be in serious trouble with Sir Oliver, wouldn't he? I must stay calm. My confinement will be soon. I cannot upset myself. My child is relying on me to stay calm. As I come through the door, the noise in the Hall becomes quite overwhelming as Robert and Oliver jump up to greet me.

"We playing wif Vally," says Robert. Oliver, his brother, babbles beside him.

Valentine, now aged six, has taken charge of his cousins. Annie, his sister, does not want to listen to her brother and would rather play with my baby Oliver; although eight months younger, he towers over his delicate cousin. Mistress Cromwell rocks baby George, still swaddled, back and forth. Margaret and I have not been so close this past year. We don't agree on so many matters concerning our children. Before I had Robert and Oliver, I was content to take her advice and listen to her. I no longer do that. Margaret hurries to greet me and enquire how I am.

"I just need to rest," I tell her.

I allow Margaret to help me to the bedchamber, confident that Mistress Cromwell will tend to Robert and Oliver. What did Paulina Pepys mean? I know Oliver played the card table at Cambridge but that was years ago. Did she mean Oliver, or was she talking about someone else? I must concentrate on this child I carry and put all the other worries aside. I will discuss this matter with Oliver on his return.

I have not heard from Oliver for a few weeks but I did not expect to. He is visiting John Hampden to find out about the next voyage to the New World. I focus on this idea and calm myself. There must be a simple explanation to this accusation by Paulina Pepys. Oliver will be able to clarify.

Chapter 61. Taking the waters

Oliver
'Hampden House', Buckinghamshire 6 June 1624

Oliver could hear lively chatter coming from the kitchen and he recognised the cheerful voice of his cousin. He was glad to get up and renew his acquaintance. Indeed John's wife Elizabeth was scolding her youngest while John, not helping, looked on smiling.

"Oliver, welcome. You know Elizabeth and our eldest, but I don't think you have met our youngest, John, still a baby but sturdy on his feet."

John Hampden picked up the toddler and hurled him in the air, causing the youngster to giggle irrepressibly. Then he turned to his wife and said,

"Elizabeth, excuse us while I talk with Oliver. He wants to hear about our enquiries to join a sailing to the New World."

Elizabeth Hampden ushered her little charges into the garden as the air was warm - a definite start to summer. John led the way into the great hall and sat down in one of the huge armchairs beside the fireplace.

"John, I am keen to know if you have started talking to others about financing a new company. I must admit I have been suffering from severe melancholy of late and need some firm direction in my life. I am resolved that the New World could offer that."

John replied, "I am sorry to hear about such a condition. Have you consulted Simcotts?"

"Yes, I have," said Oliver, "And after him, Theodore Mayerne."

"Ah, the eminent Sir Theodore. I understand he is a quirky chap, but he is the Royal Physician. I suppose you're allowed a few foibles when you get to his position. Is it true he is so large he has to stay in his house and if you want to confer you must go there?" John asked good-naturedly.

"Quite so." Oliver replied.

"But what did he recommend?" John enquired.

"Well I didn't have a full discussion with him. No appointment, but he did say to take the waters at Wellingborough. So as it has warmed up I decided to do so before Elizabeth goes into her confinement. This will be our third."

"Splendid suggestion and so you must. Now, to the New World. Is your Elizabeth willing to give it a go? It is difficult for the godly in England at this time. New taxes all the time. Pay for baronetcy, pay for knighthood. I even hear Good King James is thinking up another strange tax! I have learnt so much in my sessions in the house. It isn't quite how you would think it should be Oliver. We just get going and then another adjournment is called and there is nothing we can do about it. How about you? When will you take a seat in Parliament?"

His cousin's innocent question caused Oliver to hesitate in his answer.

"There have been some difficulties for me in Huntington. But the New World, cousin? You said a while ago about a new company of adventurers. Has it got off the ground yet? I am eager to get information."

"Patience, Oliver," John Hampden laughed at his cousin's single-mindedness. Oliver merely smiled in response.

"The first sailing on the "Mayflower" left us a lot to learn about survival in these new lands. You know yourself, Christopher Martin, whom we all met, was one of those who perished. Indeed I believe almost half of those people did not survive. It is important Oliver, not just to get there but to have a reasonable chance of survival. It is June, already far too late by the time something could be arranged; winter would be upon you and you are dead. Sailing must take place about March or April. But remember you have to get a patent from King James and he has been so sick just of late, no one can talk to him.

John Winthrop is thinking of a mass migration but he still must get his company formed. That takes money - a lot of it. He is thinking of Massachusetts, where they have a good chance of success. The Dutch have some further sailings scheduled but nothing has been confirmed. Master Pym and Oliver St John are among those interested. We must proceed slowly. Sound preparation is needed.

You can't just decide one day and go the next. Oliver, I know you are interested and I will mention your name next time there is a meeting, but for now we must all be a little patient. Now tell me all the news of Huntington."

The Hampden household was a joyful place and Oliver enjoyed the company of his cousin for the rest of the day. As fifty miles to Wellingborough was too much to accomplish before nightfall, Oliver was to stay overnight with his friend before setting out the next day. There was much to discuss. Oliver was eager to hear of John's experience of Westminster and it confirmed much the same as he had heard from Sir Francis Barrington. It seemed that to get to the New World was going to be far more difficult and lengthy than he expected. He must be content with his lot in England for the present.

The next morning, Oliver arose early and set off on his way to Wellingborough. This was his first visit to the medicinal waters and he was eager to see if it could do him any good, if it would raise his spirits. He stopped at "The Hind" to reserve a room as he had been told that often the inns in the town were full because of the Red Well and he was glad to partake of a hearty dinner there while he listened to the advice for taking the waters from the proprietor.

He was recommended to walk the half a mile to the well to drink the first pint of pure water and then after that to take another walk before drinking another pint. Unlike Bath and Tunbridge there were no facilities for bathing but nevertheless the waters were said to be of the highest quality. The physician had told him that he had to adhere to this routine for at least six weeks and Oliver was willing to give the remedy a try, but he soon became weary of the routine and after a week he decided he would ride home.

The thirty miles were soon accomplished and he thought maybe if he found the treatment to have been effective, he could go again to the waters for a few days at a time; they lived near enough after all. Tunbridge, another source of healthy mineral water, was too far to ride. Perhaps he could invite William to accompany him next time. It was the want of company which had made this trip not as pleasant as it might have been.

So it was that Oliver returned home with a heavy heart. There seemed to be no real opportunity to go to the New Lands and he was still suffering from severe melancholy. Soon the money from Uncle Thomas Steward would run out. There seemed to be no new opportunities for him to recover his fortune. What could he do?

As he entered his house in Huntington the atmosphere was sombre. The sun had set and the house was quiet.

Chapter 62. Confrontation

Elizabeth
'The Friars' 7 June 1624

I rise as the sun is beginning to appear. I enjoy its warmth as I descend to the kitchen. The door lies open beckoning me outside. Rachael is outside gathering the eggs. As I step out, the herb garden waves to me, lavender fluttering in the gentle breeze. The chives and basil are beginning to grow and will season our food in the weeks to come.

I have left my husband asleep in our chamber. I did not hear him ride in last night, but my upset during the day had caused an early sleep. It is so good that he is home. He has arrived sooner than I expected but not a moment too late. It will be a grand opportunity to sort out these misunderstandings with the town people. I pick some lavender. The scent is always so welcoming in the house.

As I re-enter the house, Rachael is already giving Robert his breakfast – a freshly gathered egg with some bread.

"What a glorious day it is Rachael," I remark, "Master Oliver has returned. It must have been late last night for I did not hear his horse. Let him sleep. That is, if baby Oliver allows. I have left him upstairs."

"Indeed, Mistress, are you feeling better today? Mistress Cromwell said you were quite frail yesterday on your return from town. You should try to rest. It can't be more than a month until the new one arrives."

"No, Sarah, I think I still have two months to go, about August, I think. But now Oliver is back, I will not fret. Why don't you take Robert to visit Sarah today?"

Cromwell & Elizabeth - The Beginning

Just as a plan was agreed, Mistress Cromwell, accompanied by Robina and Jane, opened the front door, carrying a parcel from the draper.

"Ah Elizabeth you have arisen, look here, some new cloth for the new child, what will you make?"

I am astounded. I have been asking for new cloth for a couple of months but was told by both my husband and his mother that I must wait. Now suddenly new cloth arrives. But before I can question her, she whisks Robina and Jane outside to tend to the hens. I open the parcel to find a good length of the lightest cloth, the new draperies, which must have arrived from Holland.

I hear baby Oliver stirring upstairs.

"It's alright Rachael. I'll tend to Oliver, if you wouldn't mind helping Robert with his clothes."

As I enter the bedchamber, Oliver is sitting in the bed with his son by his side. What a picture! The two of them are so alike it looks so funny.

"Are there you are Elizabeth, this young man is growing by the hour, I do declare." He says.

"You are home sooner than I expected but I am so glad to see you."

"Why Elizabeth, you have gone quite pale. What is it? I will take Oliver downstairs. Robina can tend him for a while."

With that he hurries down the stairs and I am left to compose myself. I suppose it just the thought of a confrontation which has alarmed me. It is only a matter of minutes before he reappears.

"Now, Elizabeth, you confinement is near. Do not alarm yourself so. Tell me what is the matter."

"Oliver, I was at the house of Mistress Walden yesterday and I overheard a conversation of Mistress Pepys. She claims you are in debt to her nephew Robert who is employed at Hinchingbrooke. Can this be true?"

I am shaking but I keep my voice calm. I want an answer. I will not allow my imminent confinement to be an excuse for no answer. Oliver does not give an answer. I wait.

"Oliver, I have asked you. Is it true that you are indebted to Robert Pepys because of the card table?"

Oliver turns towards me and smiles.

"The card table? My love, you are quite mistaken," he said, "It is Robert Ferrer, the estate manager who is indebted to Pepys. There has been a misunderstanding. Yes I too was shocked when I heard it. My uncle has warned the two of them; he will not tolerate a card table at the back of the stables. For that is what they have been spending their time on."

So there has been a mistake. Oliver has been a frequent visitor to Hinchingbrooke. That must be how the error has occurred.

Oliver continues, "Their work has been neglected for their gambling. Come now my love, you must stay calm and think on our new arrival. I'm sure it will be a daughter this time, what say you?"

The prospect of a daughter has so enlivened Oliver's heart that I am caught up in his merriment. We do not know if it will be a daughter but we wait in hope.

"Besides, my dear, I have warned you about listening to Paulina Pepys. There is another motive why she is so interested in the affairs of Hinchingbrooke. Do you not know that Sir Oliver recently received a ridiculously low offer to buy the house? Do you know who from? Sir Sidney Montague – husband of the gossip.

"Come Elizabeth, let us go down. I have some more sad news to recount about the New World. It was a good opportunity to talk to cousin John and we discussed all sorts of possibilities but let's go down so I can share the news with the rest of the family too."

We descend to the hall and there we find Mistress Cromwell, Robina and Jane, waiting to hear about Oliver's visit to John Hampden As Oliver tells us of his visit to cousin John's family and of taking the waters at Wellingborough, we are all a little sad. It seems that a voyage to the New World soon, is out of the question.

Chapter 63. Settlement

Oliver
6 September 1624

After that day in June, when Oliver had lied to Elizabeth, he became more secretive. He paid another visit to Hinchingbrooke to secure Robert Pepys' silence with the promise of payment within the month.

His last money from the gift from Uncle Thomas went on the new cloth for the baby and to pay off Robert Pepys. He was glad his mother had agreed to go out straightaway and purchase the new cloth as Elizabeth's suspicions were allayed. By now, his mother knew there was something amiss and Oliver was forced to tell her he had sold off their fields, although they were still using them. Mistress Cromwell agreed to keep quiet about their financial situation for a while, there being some comfort for her in knowing the truth before her daughter-in-law, even if she did not fully comprehend what had brought about this sad state of affairs.

A subsequent visit to Richard Fishbourne had borne fruit and enabled him to secure Thomas Beard as the lecturer for the parish. Richard Fishbourne had become so enraptured by Oliver's tales of Huntington that the ailing merchant gave him something for his trouble as well, which ensured their victuals for the coming winter.

In August another child had been safely delivered – this time the awaited daughter. Oliver was absolutely captivated. Although only a month old, Bridgett's brown curls reminded everyone of Elizabeth. Old Mistress Cromwell was in familiar territory with another female in the household and her joy was apparent. The usual weeks were observed for the child's baptism and the mother's churching. The accompanying fuss and rituals hastened the Yuletide celebrations so once again, Oliver was able to keep the truth of his situation hidden. The trades people he owed money to were too polite to press their cause.

So it was on that Autumn morning he took a brisk walk to visit Thomas Beard. He had delayed this meeting for too long but he now wanted to share the good news of the proposed lectureship with his old schoolmaster. He had done something worthwhile for someone else. It had lifted his spirits and made him feel good about himself.

As he approached the schoolhouse he heard the familiar prayer tone of Reverend Beard and he chuckled. Every morning of tutoring had started with what seemed like hours of prayer but was in actuality just one hour. How he had squirmed and fidgeted then. Even now Oliver did not like to be confined to one room.

He entered and the same damp smell hung heavy in the air. The sun's warmth had not yet soothed it although it was bright enough for lessons. Four boys sat obediently on the benches, heads bowed over their Latin grammars. They barely raised their eyes to acknowledge the interloper.

"Good morning, reverend, I thought to drop by on a matter of encouragement for you." Oliver began.

"Ah, Oliver, do come in. Carry on chanting the verb conjugations, boys."

"Good news. Master Fishbourne will finance the lectureship for you in Huntington. It is now only a question of the committee's agreement, which Richard thinks will go through without opposition. Good news, eh?"

Oliver was cheered by Reverend Beard's enthusiasm. Beard grasped Oliver's arm and pulled him out of earshot of his young charges.

"Oliver," he said, "Such wonderful news for the town. And for me. But there is also one matter I must press on you. There is talk in the town. Pepys, Lady Paulina's nephew is implicating you in gambling debts. Your good name is being sullied by this scoundrel's bad behaviour."

Thomas Beard paused.

"Oliver, a gentleman cannot be insulted like this. What action will you take?"

Reverend Beard did not think for one moment that his former student was guilty. How little he knew the man Oliver Cromwell had become.

Oliver replied decisively, "Reverend Beard, is not the message of Christ one of forgiveness and reconciliation? Robert Pepys is a surly bad fellow. He is pushing his own guilt on his betters. Be assured, my godfather Sir Oliver, is dealing with him!"

Oliver's authoritative tone was enough to confirm Reverend Beard's conviction of Oliver's innocence and he nodded.

With that brusque response, Oliver turned and left the schoolroom. He walked thoughtfully along the High Street. So Pepys continued to blacken his name despite the part payment he had made.

He had once more convinced someone else of his innocence of something which he was quite guilty. He became aware of his own oratory power. It was not the words which he used to convince but it was the authority with which he spoke. He could persuade men. Yet there was something about that which weighed on his heart. He knew he was wrong. Yes, he had tried to convince himself that his behaviour was excusable but he knew it was not. His face to face meeting with a godly man, Thomas Beard, shone a light on his own darkness. Indeed Oliver Cromwell did begin to fear for his eternal soul.

Chapter 64. The great leveller

Elizabeth
'The Friars' 27 March 1625

The peal of the bells resounds around the house. It brings a heaviness which I cannot explain. I desperately want to gather my three children to my breast but they are still sleeping. Robert my eldest, now four and a half, sleeps on a low bed with his two year old brother, Oliver. Their slow breathing is a comfort to me as their chests seem to rise and fall in rhythm with each other. I am surprised the bells have not woken them. I glance at Bridget in her cradle next to the bed. She is such a delight to me. Not yet weaned but she is full of gurgles and laughter. Will these bells bring changes to our lives?

Oliver, as has become his habit, has already risen and is out walking in the woods of Huntington. He says it is the only place he can find peace. He is still so troubled. It seems as if the days of blackness far outweigh those sunny days we used to have. I have spoken to William, his dearest friend, and he agrees; Oliver should see the physician again and take some remedy for what ails him. But what is it that troubles him so?

I suppose that he still feels the weight of the alehouse on him. And to think, it was by chance that I stumbled on it on the day of the fire. Oh, then I felt such anger and betrayal as I have never felt before. It was not the indignity of the running of a public brewing house, hidden from me yet known by the whole of Huntington and Godmanchester alike. It was the betrayal of a secret hid from me, his wife, that hurt me the most. It brought home to me that Oliver is not my Oliver, but the son of his mother. It is to her that he pledges his loyalty. But this disagreement will be overcome as sure as God is my witness in heaven. I will bear this secrecy no longer. It is time for Oliver to grow to be the man he surely is. But still the bells ring. I rise leaving my children in their slumber.

The mixture Oliver is taking is causing such severe stomach pains. Some days he will not rise from the bed. He says he must take it because his visits to London carry the risk of catching plague and indeed we have heard rumours that there has been another yet outbreak. The waters at Wellingborough did not help with his melancholy as we had hoped they would.

"What announcement are those bells making?" I ask Rachael as she builds up the fire to greet this still chilly March morning.

"Don't you know Mistress Elizabeth? King James is dead. He died during the night at Theobalds. He was supposed to hunt today but he just passed away. God rest his soul. He's gone."

"No, I did not know." I hesitate, "What change will this bring to our lives, I wonder....And when do we expect Mistress Cromwell and the sisters back from Ely?"

"Not until tomorrow, Mistress," Rachael replies.

I am surprised by the news, though not shocked. King James has been a sickly king for years, especially after the death of Prince Henry and the Queen. Another age is dawning. Will it be good or ill? I don't know yet. I cannot shake off this sudden chill.

Suddenly the door is kicked open and my husband stands, face creased with agony. He drops to his knees as if pleading. The sudden crash of the door has woken Bridget and her screams flood into our world. Rachael rises from attending the fire to fetch her and the sudden rush of her gown past me, awakens me to the intensity of our situation. I can only stare at this ghost of my husband and wonder what is amiss!

"Elizabeth," he whispers, "I have failed. We are undone." He pauses for breath.

I cannot understand what has brought this sudden ague on.

"Husband," I ask him, "What is it?"

"King James is dead." He says and I nod as he continues, "This death has made me realise how short our lives can be. Yes, he was sickly but strove to rule wisely. I was walking in the woods when the bells began to ring. I was near to Hinchingbrooke so I called in there. Sir Oliver told me the news. But it wasn't the news itself. It was the shock. The realisation. This world is changing. One day King James, the next day King Charles. None of us can escape it – death! Now that buffoon of a son will rule this land."

Oliver crawls towards me and I step back, a little afraid, unable to fully comprehend the scene before me. Still the bells ring.

"Yes, husband, we must all die sometime, but you are a godly man...." Oliver holds up his hand to silence me.

"No, my sweet Elizabeth, no, I am not a godly man" he begins to weep and I am quite disturbed.

Cromwell & Elizabeth - The Beginning

Robert has come down the stairs and is staring wide-eyed at his father, struck dumb by the terror of this sight - a broken, weeping man.

"I say again, Elizabeth, no, I am not a godly man. I must confess to you. For two years I have tried to tell you this. It has weighed so heavily on my mind and on my heart. I cannot go on like this. I have gambled away what little we had. I have drowned my sorrows in drinking too much. No, I am not a godly man. I have ruined us."

So it is true, what Paulina Pepys has said. I hesitate to ask him to explain further but he continues unprompted.

"I have had to sell off the fields. My debts are so high, we cannot purchase any of the goods we need from Huntington. We have been living on mother's thrifty goodness. I had hoped I would get the seat to Westminster but now that too is lost. The new charter has finished me. This new king will not favour us."

"Is this.... Is this... why I have not seen the accounts? Is this why I am not charged to get purchases?" I ask. Oliver and his mother's collusion now begins to make sense.

"So," I falter, "So, it is gambling debts too, Paulina was correct in her information from her nephew."

This time I will have the whole truth, every last ungodly act will be revealed. Oliver nods his head slowly in response. I am betrayed again. But I am not angry. I only feel pity for my husband; a sadness for his foolishness. It must also be said Mistress Cromwell most certainly knew of this, yet did not tell me. I am resolved. Oliver and I will take the children from her house and start up on our own. I can only stare at my husband, as does our son Robert. We are frozen and unable to comfort our protector, stunned by the severity of this news. Our ruin I can endure. But to see my husband, a broken man is just too much for me. Tears stream down my face. I walk towards him, only just able to hear his whisper,

"Forgive me, Elizabeth, forgive me."

Forgive him? Forgive, what else can I do? In this moment, I feel a closeness to my husband that I have not felt in a long time. At last I know what has caused his melancholy and the tension between us for all these years. At last I see my husband as he truly is. But I am not outraged. I feel no anger. All I feel is love for him and an overwhelming sadness. I move towards him, put my arms around him and cradle his head on my stomach, as he sobs.

"Yes, Oliver, I forgive you. We will make a new start." I reply, "Long live King Charles!"

Cromwell & Elizabeth - The Beginning

Major Historical Characters

Elizabeth Bourchier (1598-1665)

Little is known about Elizabeth in history. She was the daughter of Lady Frances and Sir James Bourchier. She married Oliver Cromwell on August 22 1620. It is known that she had a dowry of £1500 and a parsonage house in Hartford was her jointure. It is recorded that she had 2 sisters and 9 brothers.

Parents of Elizabeth Bourchier

Father: Sir James Bourchier was a fur and leather merchant. He owned three properties: Little Stambridge Hall in Rochford, a house in Felsted and a town house in Tower Hill, London. He was granted a coat of arms (three leopards passant in pale) in 1610.

Mother: Lady Frances Bourchier (nee Crane) was from a family in Newton Tony, Wiltshire.

Oliver Cromwell (1599-1658)

Much has been written about Oliver Cromwell, Lord Protector of England, Scotland and Ireland from 1653-1658, but very little about his early life. It is known that he was educated at Huntingdon Grammar School where Thomas Beard was the schoolmaster. From there he attended Sidney Sussex College, Cambridge until the death of his father in 1617. In 1628 he became MP for Huntingdon. He lived in

Huntingdon until 1631 when he moved to St Ives and then to Ely in 1636. He and Elizabeth had 9 children.

Oliver's great grandfather was Morgan **Williams**, a Welshman who settled in Putney. Morgan married Katherine sister of Thomas Cromwell. Morgan's son Richard changed the family name to Cromwell in gratitude to Thomas Cromwell after he received sizeable properties from the dissolution of the monasteries. Hence Oliver was also known as Oliver Williams.

Parents of Oliver Cromwell
Father: Robert Cromwell (1567-1617) was the second son of Sir Henry Cromwell.

Mother: Elizabeth Cromwell (nee Steward). She was a widow when she married Robert Cromwell. First husband was William Lynne Esquire of Bassingbourne, Cambridgeshire. He and a child died in 1589. Elizabeth had two sons who died before Oliver, and seven daughters (Joan, Elizabeth, Catherine, Margaret, Anna, Jane, Robina).

Sir Oliver Cromwell (1563-1655)
He was the uncle and godfather of Oliver Cromwell. He owned Hinchingbrooke House. He was the first son and heir of Sir Henry Cromwell. It is known that in March 1617 as part of the Royal Progress, King James 1 visited Hinchingbrooke and was lavishly entertained.

Hinchingbrooke was sold to Sir Sidney Montague in June 1627.

Sir Oliver became attorney to Queen Anne of Denmark, wife of James I, and a gentleman of the Privvy Chamber.

James I (1566 - 1625)
James became king of Scotland in 1567 and in1603, he became the first Stuart king of England as well, creating the kingdom of Great Britain. He was born on 19 June 1566 in Edinburgh Castle. His mother was Mary, Queen of Scots and his father her second husband, Lord Darnley.

In 1589, James married Anne of Denmark. Three of their seven children survived into adulthood.

One of James's great contributions to England was the Authorised King James's Version of the bible (1611) which was to become the standard text for more than 250 years. But he disappointed the Puritans who hoped he would introduce some of the more radical religious ideas of the Scottish church, and the Catholics, who anticipated more lenient treatment. In 1605, a Catholic plot to blow up king and parliament was uncovered. James's firm belief in the divine right of kings, and constant need for money, also brought him into conflict repeatedly with parliament.

Princess Elizabeth (1574-1619)
Elizabeth was the daughter of James I of England and Anne of Denmark. She married Frederick V, Count Palatine of the Rhine on 14 February 1613 and moved to Heidelberg. She briefly became the Queen of Bohemia in 1619. She was known as the Winter Queen because she only reigned for one year. after a take-over by Ferdinand when the couple were forced into exile.

Henry, Prince of Wales
Eldest son of James I and Anne of Denmark. Rather than leaving him to be educated in Scotland when they moved to England in 1603, he received an advanced classical education and was intelligent, brave, athletic and very highly regarded. Henry was created Prince of Wales and Earl of Chester aged 16; thereafter he established his own household and continued his passion for tournaments and for theatre and art.

Tragically Henry's health was never robust and, to great shock and national mourning, he died aged 18, probably from typhoid fever.

Charles I
Charles I was born in Fife on 19 November 1600, the second son of James I and Anne of Denmark. He became heir to the throne on the death of his brother, Prince Henry, in 1612. He succeeded, as the second Stuart King of Great Britain, in 1625.

Secondary Historical Characters in Alphabetical Order

Sir Francis Barrington (1560-1628)

First son of Sir Thomas Barrington. He was involved in the committee of repair and bridges in Essex (1614-22). He married Joan Cromwell **(Lady Joan Barrington)**, sister of Robert. Their eldest son Thomas inherited "The Priory" at Hatfield Broad Oak.

Sir Francis was elected MP for Essex in 1601. He was knighted in 1603. He was re-elected MP in 1604. He was called to the bar (Gray's Inn) in 1605/6. He was made a baronet in 1611. He was elected MP for Essex again in 1621.

Sir Francis Bacon

Francis Bacon was born on 22 January 1561 in London. He was the son of Sir Nicholas Bacon, keeper of the great seal for Elizabeth I. Bacon studied at Cambridge University and at Gray's Inn and became a member of parliament in 1584. However, he was unpopular with Elizabeth, and it was only on the accession of James I in 1603 that Bacon's career began to prosper. Knighted that year, he was appointed to a succession of posts culminating, like his father, with keeper of the great seal.

Bacon's political ascent also continued. In 1618 he was appointed lord chancellor, the most powerful position in England, and in 1621 he was created viscount St Albans. Shortly afterwards, he was charged by parliament with accepting bribes, which he admitted. He was fined and imprisoned and then banished from court. Although the king later pardoned him, this was the end of Bacon's public life. He died in London on 9 April 1626.

Rev Thomas Beard
An English clergyman and theologian. He was the schoolmaster of Oliver Cromwell.

Robert Bernard (1601-1666)
Lawyer and politician. He was also Recorder in Huntingdon.

Sir Edward Coke (1552-1641)
English judge, barrister and politician. He restricted the definition of treason and declared a royal letter illegal leading to his dismissal from the bench on 14 November 1616.

After the death of his first wife in 1598, he married Elizabeth Hatton. Coke had two children with his second wife, both daughters: Elizabeth and Frances Coke, Viscountess Purbeck. Elizabeth married Sir Maurice Berkeley. Frances married John Villiers, 1st Viscount Purbeck, but left him soon afterwards for her lover Sir Robert Howard, with whom she lived for many years, to the great scandal of the court.

Henry Downhall
He was a Cambridge friend of Oliver Cromwell. A letter addressed to him from Oliver Cromwell survives. He was a

fellow at St John's College when Oliver was at Sidney Sussex. He became a clergyman at Tofts in Cambridgeshire.

Robert Ferrer
Master of the Horse at Hinchingbrooke House

Richard Fishbourne
A London mercer who was born in Huntingdon. When he died he left a legacy of £2000 to be used for the benefit of the citizens of Huntingdon.

John Hampden (1595-1643)
He was the son of William Hampden of Buckingshire and Elizabeth Cromwell, daughter of Henry Cromwell. He was first cousin to Oliver. He opposed the ship money tax levied by Charles I because the tax was implemented without the consent of Parliament. He married Elizabeth Symeon.

William Laud (1573 – 1645)
Born into modest surroundings in Reading, William Laud became a leading hate figure for Puritans during the 1630s and 1640s. His determination to promote and enforce a 'high church' style of worship created many enemies.

Although he had served James VI/I as chaplain on his visit to Scotland, Laud's career took off following Charles' ascension in 1625. Laud saw the Anglican Church as part of the Universal church and preferred forms of worship which emphasised the priest's special intermediary role, a view which brought him into conflict with those who believed in a priesthood of all believers and rejected anything which lacked biblical justification.

Dr Theodore Mayerne
Mayerne was an expatriate Swiss Huguenot, who became court doctor to James I and Charles I of England. Mayerne's role in court life included high-level diplomacy and subterfuge. As a fashionable court physician, Mayerne's private practice was always busy, and he amassed a large fortune. When James I became ill and died, Mayerne managed to maintain his status but he was less popular with Charles I.

Paulina Pepys (1581-1641)
Sister of Samuel Pepys, well-known diarist, she married Sydney Montague in 1618.

John Pym (1584-1643)
He was the leader of the Long Parliament (1649-1660). He was born of minor nobility in Somerset. In 1614 he married Anne Hooke a strong Puritan. After the dissolution of Parliament in 1621 he was placed under house arrest in January 1622.

Robert Rich (1587-1658)
Robert Rich, 2nd Earl of Warwick was an English colonial administrator, admiral, and Puritan.

Rich was the eldest son of Robert Rich, 1st Earl of Warwick and his wife Penelope Devereux, Lady Rich, and succeeded to his father's title (Earl of Warwick) in 1619 (a younger brother was Henry Rich, 1st Earl of Holland).

Warwick's Puritan connections and sympathies gradually estranged him from the court but promoted his association with the New England colonies. In 1628 he indirectly procured the patent for the Massachusetts Bay Colony, and in 1631 he granted the "Saybrook" patent in Connecticut.

Ezekiel Rogers (1590-1660)
Puritan clergyman who was the personal chaplain to Lady Joan Barrington.

Oliver St John (1598-1673)
A cousin of Oliver Cromwell. He matriculated from Queen's College, Cambridge in 1616. He was at Lincoln's Inn in 1619 and was called to the bar in 1626. His sister emigrated to Massachusetts in 1636. He married three times. First to Johanna Altham in 1629, secondly to Elizabeth daughter of Henry Cromwell in 1638 and to Elizabeth Oxenbridge in 1645.

Thomas Steward
Uncle of Oliver Cromwell on his mother's side. In 1636 Cromwell's childless and widowed uncle, Sir Thomas Steward died, leaving him a substantial inheritance, including a house next to St Mary's Church in Ely and the position of collector of tithes in the two Ely parishes of St Mary's and Holy Trinity.

Lionel Walden (1620-1698)
The eldest son of Lionel Walden by Elizabeth daughter of Morrice Bowden of Somersby. His father was the first mayor of Huntingdon.

Valentine Walton (1594-1661)
Valentine Walton married Margaret, sister of Oliver Cromwell, in 1617.

Sources

Hill, Christopher, "God's Englishman", Pelican Books 1972

Fraser, Antonia, "Cromwell Our Chief of Men", Orion Books Ltd, 2002.

Hunt, Tristram, "The English Civil War At First Hand", Penguin Books Ltd. 2011.

Sim, Alison, "The Tudor Housewife", Sutton Publishing 2005.

Borman, Tracy, "Witches James I and the English Witch-Hunts, Vintage Books, 2014.

Tomalin, Claire, "Samuel Pepys The Unequalled Self, Penguin Books, 2003.

Purkiss, Diane, "The English Civil War", Harper Perennial, 2007.

Worden, Blair, "The English Civil Wars", Orion Books, 2009.

Fitzgibbons, Jonathan, "Cromwell's Head, National Archives, 2008.

Ashley Maurice, "England in the Seventeenth Century", Penguin Books Ltd. 1968.

Ackroyd, Peter, "Civil War", Macmillan, 2014.

The Cromwell Association, www.olivercromwell.org

Historical Notes

The spelling of Huntingdon

The Saxon chronicles talk about the town of Huntandene and in the Domesday book Huntingdon is called Huntendone. However I have chosen the spelling used by Speed in 1610 on his famous map. I hope this does not irritate my reader too much.

The marriage relationship

Oliver Cromwell and Elizabeth Bourchier are historical characters. The date of their marriage was 22 August 1620. It is not known where or when they first met and there are no details available about their courtship or their early married life together.

It is well documented that the couple had a very happy and long marriage. However it is often the case that the early years of marriage bring troubles of its own. This book should be viewed as part one of a trilogy.

From the few facts available and what is known about them in their later life, I have woven their story. It is a love story but one grounded in the godly beliefs and social conventions of the 17th century.

The question which has driven the series is, how could a Christian woman remain married to a man who once loved and admired, became so hated by the country which he tried to deliver.

Financial management and gambling

The strand of Oliver's financial mismanagement do not have a firm body of evidence. However Christopher Hill (see sources) does mention 'extravagance and mismanagment' on page 43 of his book.

Brewing activity is mentioned by Antonia Fraser in her excellent book on page 17.

Again the gambling thread is not based on sound evidence but rather a mention by Antonia Fraser on page 28 where she recounts "the first years of his manhood were spent in a dissolute course of life in good fellowship and gaming."

These elements have been woven into a story which can then explain the couple's downturn of fortune and the move to St Ives.

Many other historical characters appear in the book and I have tried to maintain the historical relationships which are recorded but it is first and foremost a story. The historical relationships are important and form the basis for the continuing stories in the trilogy

About the Author

Before becoming a writer, Rosalie worked as a secretary both in London and Hanover. Later training as a teacher, she studied English Literature and History and included these subjects in a teaching career.

In 1982 she travelled to South Africa with her husband and five children to embark upon a new life. There she witnessed a country transformed by a post-apartheid government. Further study in theology resulted in her ordination as a minister with the Uniting Presbyterian Church of Southern Africa. In 2000 she returned to England as a missionary to pastor two churches in Gloucestershire.

She returned to work in education in 2004 taking up the post of faculty head of the Ethics department of a state school until she retired in 2011, when more time became available for writing.

Besides writing fiction, Rosalie writes bible studies as Reverend Rosalie Weller, available on Amazon. The Christian faith is an important part of Rosalie's life but she also spends time on her allotment as well as being an enthusiastic amateur photographer and traveller.

Rosalie is a keen member of a local writer's group who encourage and support one another. The group can be found at www.northantswritersink.net/.

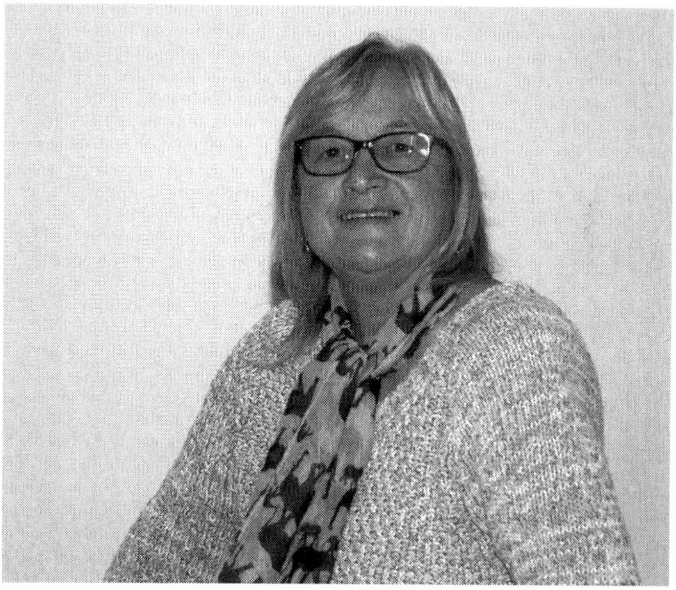

Printed in Poland
by Amazon Fulfillment
Poland Sp. z o.o., Wrocław